Also by Jack Petree

I0667181

Dangerous Game

Advertising Your Financial Services

The Shintaffer Road (with Mark Shintaffer)

Bellingham Cold Storage: 50 Years

Coming Soon

Fiction

Short Story Collections:

Accent On Murder And Other Mysteries

Selling Snake Oil And Other Oddities

The Mandate Of Heaven Murders

The Son Of Heaven Murders

The Mistakenly Sent Letter (a translation)

Non-Fiction

You're Next: The Assault On Traditional Rural Lifestyles

The Devil's Dictionary Two

THE MYSTERY OF THE SHAMAN'S SECRET

THE MYSTERY OF THE SHAMAN'S SECRET

JACK PETREE AND ED KAPLAN

NICETIGER

All rights reserved, under International and Pan-American Copyright Conventions, including the right to reproduce this book, or portions thereof in any form whatsoever without permission in writing from the publisher, except for brief passages in connection with a review.

Copyright © 2014 by Jack Petree

NiceTiger
5190 Neil Road, Suite 430
Reno NV 89502
publisher@nicetiger.com
www.nicetiger.com

ISBN: 978-1-937777-05-0

Please do not participate in or encourage piracy of copyrighted materials in violation of the author's rights.

Library of Congress Cataloging-in-Publication Data available.

This is a work of fiction. Names, characters, places and incidents either are a product of the author's imagination or are used fictitiously, and any resemblance to actual persons living or dead, events, or locales is entirely coincidental.

To friend and mentor Ed Kaplan and to the girls he used to call, respectively, "She who must be obeyed," Sal and Sue.

(Ed's use of the phrase was a jocular reference to the title character in the H. Ryder Haggard novel, "She." Read the book and you will not only get the joke, you will have enjoyed an afternoon with a terrific writer.)

Historical Note

The Mystery Of The Shaman's Secret was originally written as an educational tool. Ed and I had the idea that Chinese students trying to learn English would enjoy learning the new language a bit more if the teaching tool happened to be a fun read based on the long and interesting history of their own nation (albeit, fantasized a bit). I hope that is the case.

Read the following brief discussion of the Han Dynasty as provided by Ed. It will give you a bit of historical perspective and, hopefully, add to any pleasure you might receive from our story.

As is conventional in honest historical fiction, all of the main characters and main events in this story are true: Emperor Wu, Empress Wei and the other consorts, the Heir Apparent, his cousin Hwo Gwang, Jiang Choong, and even the shaman. The witchcraft conspiracy actually took place, and it is reasonable to speculate that the prosecutor was behind most of it. It is possible, though by no means established, that the Heir Apparent was also in some way involved. There is no question that many people engaged in or sponsored such practices as wugu in those days, and it would be anachronistic to label them as superstitious for having done so, unless one wishes to also so label the equally common tendency of contemporary statesmen to lavish attention on political scientists and pollsters (which may, come to think of it, be appropriate).

Soong Li, Chiang Bao, the Korean concubine, merchant Gao and his establishment, and the Han family of salt manufacturers are all wholly fictional. There really was, however, an Old Stone Hill iron mine run by an avaricious family surnamed Deng. The description of how brine wells were dug and brine boiled down by burning natural gas emitted from the brine wells is vouched for by contemporary sources. The wind-box, really a double acting piston bellows working much like a steam engine in reverse, also actually existed, and indeed is still employed for various uses, including the infamous "back yard" blast furnaces of the Cultural Revolution days of the 1960s. Its application to pumping air into mines and natural gas into containers is fictional. The reason given as to why such innovations were not welcomed—that it was not in the interest either of officials or holders of monopoly licenses of uncertain duration in such trades—is alas all too true, for our own time as for then.

It is also necessary to beg the reader's indulgence for our inevitable falsification of the minutiae of social and cultural life in first century B.C. China. We have all but totally lost our ability to understand such things for our own eighteenth century, so it should not be surprising that our knowledge of them for this much earlier period of a culture unrelated to our own is all but nonexistent. Hence the necessity to depict our characters as following minor social and cultural rituals much like our own, so as to make their actions understandable to readers of the late twentieth century. To a lesser degree, such necessary falsification also distorts conventional narrative histories.

Main Characters

Emperor Wu - *Lord of all that was Civilized Under Heaven and literal representative of Heaven on earth (historical)*

Empress Wei Dsefoo - *Chief consort to the Emperor and mother of the Heir Apparent (historical)*

Liu Jyu - *Son of Empress Wei and Heir Apparent (historical)*

Jyang Choong - *Chief prosecutor for Emperor Wu (historical)*

Shaman - *A mysterious person from an area called Shu (historical)*

Kim Soo - *Korean Harem Slave and known favorite of Emperor Wu (fictional)*

Kim Daijoo - *Eunuch inner court servant and brother of Kim Soo (fictional)*

Lord Hwo Gwang - *nephew of Empress Wei and Chief Investigator for Emperor Wu (historical)*

Soong Li - *Investigator for Hwo Gwang, trained in medicine and military arts (fictional)*

Chiang Bao - *Young intellectual, cousin and roommate of Soong Li (fictional)*

CHAPTER ONE

Crime And Punishment

Jyang Choong sat quietly watching the scene below. From time to time his eyes focused on the shaman but mostly Jyang studied the face of Emperor Wu.

The temple had been especially constructed for this occasion. Looking more barbarian than Chinese, it was shaped like a shallow drinking bowl. The floor of the bowl was bare save for a slightly raised platform in the middle. This platform was small, less than a pace across.

A man stood on the platform. At his feet lay two objects: a small oil lamp and a misshapen lump that had apparently once been molded into the shape of a human being and then buried.

The man stood as erectly and proudly as his wrecked body allowed. The effects of three days at the hands of the prosecutor's staff of torturers were obvious. The man would never walk properly again even should he survive the ordeal before him and horrible scars would mark him for life; but for now these were the least of the man's considerations. He stood silently, but gazed at his sovereign with a look of sorrow.

"Are you certain of the charges?" Emperor Wu asked as he watched the shaman perform the chants.

"There can be no doubt, my Emperor," Jyang Choong answered.

"He was one of my oldest and most trusted advisors," the Emperor mused. "I find it difficult to believe that he would practice wugu. Why would he be attracted to the evil magic?"

"There can be no doubt," Jyang repeated.

The Emperor's throne was located at the north rim of the bowl. Various functionaries of the court were seated at different points around the depression. All looked down intently at the man below.

The shaman continued his chants for a time and then suddenly stopped. He walked to a point in front of the Emperor, then prostrated himself. "The man has not practiced wugu," the shaman proclaimed.

The Emperor glared at Jyang.

"You find no fault with the man?" Jyang called out.

"There is an emanation of evil," the shaman answered, "but my efforts fail to detect what the man has done."

"What of chu-tsu shang?" Jyang asked.

A muffled gasp from the crowd followed the question; Chu-tsu shang, cursing the Emperor, calling down spirits to do harm to the exalted body, was as heinous a crime as a man could commit.

"NO!" The shout echoed through the temple. "My Lord Ruler knows of my faithful service. Do not dishonor my life and my death by such a charge." These were the first words the proud man on the platform had spoken in three days.

The Emperor turned to Jyang.

"You go too far," the Emperor hissed, fire flashing in his eyes. "He has been my faithful servant since his birth. I cannot believe that of him."

"Let the shaman test him then," Jyang Choong answered, loudly enough for all to hear. "If he passes the test, there is no dishonor, for he will have been proven loyal. The dishonor will then be mine and I will take his place on the platform and his place in death."

"You are so sure?" the Emperor asked.

"I am," Jyang answered.

"Let it be done." The Emperor nodded to the shaman who quickly resumed his place in front of the prisoner. The chants began.

The Emperor turned back to Jyang. "You risk everything?" he asked.

"I risk nothing," Jyang replied. "I exist to serve the Emperor. If I serve well, I live. If not, I die." The Emperor, inured to empty flattery, gazed quizzically at Jyang, but said nothing. Both men turned to watch the scene below.

The shaman was from north of the Great Wall, in the eyes of most of the Emperor's retinue, a foreigner. His clothing was dirty, barbaric in cut, and covered with strange designs. He whirled and twirled, here and there, mouthing strange words never before heard in the capital city of the Han. No one noticed him motion to a serving boy stationed at the top of the stairway leading from the bottom of the bowl shaped temple to the top. The serving boy signaled back, then nodded to his master below. The shaman embarked on a particularly vigorous series of moves, then froze in place, a wild, keening cry coming from his lips. His hands pointed to the prisoner in the center of the cleared space. All eyes focused on the shaman and on the object of his cry.

The shaman's keening wail seemed to go on forever. The watchers wondered to themselves how a man could utter such a noise and keep doing it for so long. Soon, all in the audience found themselves almost involuntarily leaning forward, hypnotized by the awful sound. Suddenly, when it appeared that the cry could go on no longer without something snapping in the old man's throat, there came a loud "WOOMP" and the entire floor of the temple seemed to have ignited in an explosive rush of heat and fire.

Instinctively the crowd drew back. Then, as individuals within it gathered their wits, the crowd surged forward towards what appeared to be a magical flame remaining after the initial explosion.

The Emperor was among the startled onlookers straining towards the platform. Only Jyang Choong remained seated, a slight smile playing on his lips. After a short time the prisoner ceased to scream.

CHAPTER TWO

An Emperor Under Threat

The braver members of the crowd edged forward but then quickly fell back from the charred corpse, covering dainty noses with kerchiefs, sleeves or whatever was close at hand. A peculiar, bitter-sour smell could be detected in the air. It mixed with the disconcertingly pleasant roast pork- like odor of burning human flesh. The shaman and the prosecutor exchanged glances as the latter at last rose from his seat and moved forward to the Emperor's side.

"So," the Emperor muttered, "he was indeed guilty. The conspirators multiply as I grow older." The Emperor Wu, Lord of all that was Civilized Under Heaven, the literal representative of Heaven on earth, seemed to age as he spoke these bitter words. His cheeks sank inward and his skin paled beneath the sheen of sweat evoked by the mysterious holy fire.

The chief prosecutor took this in. Jyang was a large, fleshy man, still in the vigor of middle age. Taking care to mask from his voice the contempt of the still young for the ineffectually old, the chief prosecutor sought to soothe his sovereign.

"Such is the price of success, Your Majesty," he said. "Always there are those who would plot the fall of the One who sustains us. But happily there are weapons against those men of evil. Your Majesty's enemies will continue to be confounded, for I have found a means of detecting the black magic men of darkness would use against the royal person. So long as I stand by the side of the Emperor, no man may practice such evil against him."

"Most impressive," Emperor Wu replied, regaining his emotional balance and directing a sharp glance at his chief prosecutor. The demands of power had long since taught the Emperor to mistrust even those closest to him. The just concluded lesson had only reinforced this mistrust. The chief prosecutor's methods were indeed powerful but such power brought with it threats to the Emperor.

"You and your agents have done well. I suppose you are right. This sort of thing is inevitable. That damnable Chen woman tried the wugu magic on me when I was little more than a boy. That was nearly forty years ago, but my stomach still crawls when I consider how close she came to implanting those damned magical vermin within my viscera!" A shiver shook the Emperor's frame.

Jyang suppressed a smile. "All fear the magical gu," he pontificated, stating what everyone already knew. "Without proper methods of detection they can be cursed into your body without your ever knowing they're there. Before you realize what's happened your bowels are rotting away and spilling onto the ground." The prosecutor stopped abruptly when he noticed the Emperor was losing color again.

"But, of course, what does that matter to us now?" Jyang resumed, hastening to reassure his sovereign. "This shaman I've brought in from the recently taken lands to the north seems to have the power we've sought for so long: the power to detect the presence of the evil emanations from one who would use the power of witchcraft."

"You say he's from the north?" the Emperor asked.

"Indeed he is," Jyang replied.

"Can he be trusted?"

"I will watch him closely," Jyang answered. "I, like you, distrust the foreigner in our land, but in this case we would seem to have no choice. Did you not see the power of the man? Who in this land possesses such power to detect evil?"

"Perhaps, perhaps," the Emperor bristled. "Use the man then, but watch him. I mistrust the machinations of foreigners, even if used to the advantage of the kingdom. Watch his every move."

"It will be done, Majesty," Jyang said. He began to withdraw, but then stopped as though a sudden thought had just come to mind.

"Yes?" the Emperor prompted.

Jyang paused for effect then spoke. "The man just punished," he began, "Wouldn't he have had accomplices?"

"Root them out," the Emperor commanded, speaking quietly but distinctly.

"I shall begin at once," Jyang replied, his face betraying no emotion. Not until he was well clear of the Emperor's view did he allow himself a self satisfied smirk.

CHAPTER THREE

Murder?

Seen through the low lying dawn fog, the little Korean cottage seemed suspended in isolation—almost as though it had been built of and in the clouds. Gradually the fog changed in color from gray to white and then thinned, revealing the dull stone walls of the inner palace looming behind the cottage.

A wispy swirl of fog separated itself from a wall of the cottage then resolved itself into a small figure. The figure approached an as yet invisible door in the wall of the cottage, paused for a moment then disappeared inside.

Only a few ticks of time later the door of the cottage suddenly crashed open again, breaking the quiet spell of the morning. A figure burst through the opening, staggered raggedly for a few steps, recovered, then, leaving the door askew, set out for the wall of the palace at a dead run, the skirts of a long loose robe billowing out behind him.

To any observer of the scene it would have been obvious that the figure was dressed in the robes of a eunuch attendant in the harem of the Emperor's Inner Court.

The figure reached the palace wall, fumbled for a moment, then threw open a door and disappeared inside.

By then the fog had lifted completely. The little cottage, which had earlier seemed an island of serenity, now looked completely out of place. Its Korean design clashed with that of the palace and the other nearby buildings, each of which had been carefully contrived to mesh with the traditional design of the palace.

The dichotomy between the appearance of the palace complex and the cottage was the result of an experiment by the Emperor. On commanding the structure be built, His Majesty had explained the cottage was to be the first of a series of dwellings characteristic of the various peoples whose lands had come under the dynasty's sway, especially during his own reign. These dwellings would enable both the Emperor and his officials, as true disciples of Confucius, to empathize with the ways of the many different peoples of the empire. Such at least was the Emperor's explanation.

Even the most humble peddler of noodles in the great city that lay beyond the walls of the Outer Court know the real reason for the cottage's construction, though few of them had ever seen the structure. This real reason went by the name of Kim Soo.

Kim Soo had been raised as a slave within the harem after having been brought back to the capital as a small child during the dynasty's second and successful campaign of conquest against the Korean state of Choson nearly two decades earlier.

Straddling the Yalu River, Choson's native Korean founders had been displaced just over a century earlier by Chinese refugee soldiers, losers in the civil war culminating in the reestablishment of the current dynasty. Emperor Wu had in his youth, conquered the area from the descendants of the refugee soldiers so, in a sense this small cottage was a visible reminder of the success of the dynasty under Emperor Wu. The structure's service as the residence of the Emperor's latest paramour only served to strengthen the symbolism.

Suddenly the morning quiet was shattered again. Other figures—also eunuchs judging from their dress—began to rush from the palace toward the small cottage. Several of them entered the structure. In a few minutes one of them came out again and sprinted away from the Inner Palace toward the buildings of the Outer Court.

By the time the sun had risen above the parapets of the Imperial City, the eunuch who had run away reappeared at the head of a substantial party of civilian and military officials. Jyang Choong strode along at the head of the group.

Accompanying Jyang and speaking earnestly with him was a tall, thin, pale-skinned but luxuriously bewhiskered man with dark eyes shielded beneath heavy brows. The bright intelligence which normally sparkled within these eyes was now veiled, black and cold as coal, betraying no emotion as the man spoke with Jyang.

"You cannot imagine how relieved I was, Lord Hwo, to find you had remained in your office overnight," Jyang commented as the two hastened along. The worried look on Jyang's face deepened as the two men approached the cottage. "Of course," he continued, "I will remain in charge over-all."

"Really?" Hwo Gwang's voice had an edge to it. "Why would the prosecutor have any interest in the death of a simple member of the harem?"

Jyang smiled. Lord Hwo was famous for his self control. Showing even a bit of emotion was out of the norm for the man. "There is almost certainly a threat to His Majesty's security here," Jyang replied. "He was to visit the Korean last night, or so he told me. The safety of the Emperor is paramount. I will be in charge."

"You have reason to suspect foul play?"

"None, at least not so far," Jyang replied, "But where the Emperor is concerned, there cannot be too much concern. When a member of the household dies, I assume the worst until I can prove otherwise; especially given recent events."

Hwo Gwang's voice returned to its normal tone, a deep yet surprisingly soft bass. "If the Emperor was expected there last night and foul play proves to have occurred, you are of course correct to take charge of the investigation." And, Hwo thought, aren't you the lucky one, having me, the nephew of the imperial consort and the cousin of the Heir Apparent, available, indeed obligated, to stick with the actual work of the investigation.

Hwo knew, as did all at Court, that every woman in the harem despised the Korean slave girl, the Empress no less than the rest. If the girl had indeed died under suspicious circumstances, the whole harem would be suspect. If charges had to be brought against one of them, it would be more prudent for the Empress's own nephew to bring them rather than for the prosecutor to have to take the risk himself, particularly as the prosecutor was not the most beloved man at Court.

On the other hand, Hwo realized, the investigation also provided the prosecutor an opportunity to enhance his own prestige at the expense of Hwo, the Empress, and perhaps even the Heir Apparent himself. If grounds for suspecting the imperial women could be discovered, and Hwo made no arrests, the prosecutor would undoubtedly go to the Emperor for sanction to move against both Hwo and the Empress Wei, which would automatically throw the succession into doubt. Jyang knew all too well the stakes involved.

The party reached the cottage. Jyang stood aside, a mocking smile on his lips, and allowed Hwo to precede him inside. The remainder of the party remained outside save for one slim young man who followed Jyang and then moved unobtrusively to Hwo Gwang's side.

Hwo sniffed the air. "This room has an odd smell," he observed.

"These Korean houses are like that in cold weather," Jyang said. "They heat them too much."

"I've heard they use an odd sort of heating system," said the young man. Jyang turned and glared at him.

"Who is this upstart?" he asked.

"His name is Soong Li," Hwo explained. "His family was, it is said, of the royal house of Soong. After the division of Soong's territory back in Warring Kingdoms days his branch of the family came on evil times and settled in my hometown, Jao, where my father and his grandfather became good friends."

"And now that you are in a position to take care of your relatives and friends through your relationship with the Lady Wei, you've made a sinecure for him," Jyang interrupted rudely, making his comment sound like the prologue to an article of impeachment.

"Hardly a sinecure," Hwo shot back, not in the least cowed. "Not on what I'm paying him. I think you'll find him highly competent. He's trained in medicine as well as the military arts, and he's a fine scholar besides." Jyang looked away from the young man, whose demeanor through this whole conversation had suggested respect for but not fear of the prosecutor.

"Let's get on with the investigation," Jyang said. "Where is the woman's body?"

"The heating system, sir," Young Li continued, "We were discussing the heating system in the houses of the Koreans."

"In effect," Li went on, politely ignoring Jyang's renewed glare, "the whole floor of one of these houses is like a stove top heated by hollow passages just beneath it leading from the stove to an outlet running up and through one of the walls."

"I see there are few windows," the prosecutor interrupted, "and you can see how these barbarians keep them tightly shuttered as soon as the weather turns cold. No wonder a stench pervades the place. Now, where is the body?"

The body proved to be behind a screen in one corner of the room. The screen masked a wide, low bed. The woman was half in the bed, half out. Her head and arms rested on the floor, her lower body stretched across the bed.

"Look at her lips," Li whispered.

"I see nothing unusual," Jyang said.

"Nor do I," echoed Hwo, puzzled. Li walked to one of the small windows and threw open the shutters.

"Her lips," Li repeated. "I've never seen a color like that before." Hwo bent over to gaze at the woman.

"A remarkable shade of blue," he agreed. "I too have never seen the like."

"Probably a barbarian's idea of beauty," said Jyang with distaste. "They color their lips and pretend they are ladies. The whore would become a lady." The sneering tone of this last made it an obvious allusion to the Empress, Hwo's aunt, who had first attracted the Emperor's attention as a female entertainer when he passed through Jao. Hwo did not let his face betray any of the emotions boiling within.

"I think not," Li declared, rather more loudly than necessary. He stepped forward and rubbed a finger across the dead woman's lips. He held the finger up for all to see. It was unstained. He next took a corner of his sleeve and dipped it into a small bowl of water that sat nearby. He rubbed the dampened cloth across the woman's lips. Again, there was no transfer of color.

The tension broken by Li's actions, the two antagonists stepped forward. Li raised a hand to stop them. "See here," he said, pointing to the floor.

Jyang shrugged. "A simple box of face powder," he said.

"Killed in a struggle?" Hwo suggested.

"There's no other sign of struggle," Jyang said, looking around the room.

"The woman spilled the powder," Li broke in. The other two looked puzzled.

"She has inscribed something with her fingertip," Li explained. "See here, it's faint but unmistakable." He crouched down and pointed to the place. Jyang and Hwo crowded in next to him, pushing him nearer the girl. Li swallowed hard as he looked into the black eyes staring sightlessly into his own. He forced himself to examine her more closely, noticing for the first time that the blue tinge of the lips extended more faintly across all the flesh of her face. A network of fine red lines was visible in the whites of her eyes.

"Not dead. Killed." These words, read aloud haltingly by Hwo , jerked Li's attention from the girl back to the powder spilled on the floor.

"What?" Jyang's face was white. "Can this be true?"

"Indeed it is, My Lord Prosecutor," Li said. "That is why I contended the lady spilled the powder herself. She realized her death was imminent and made sure we would know it was an unnatural end to her life."

"So, how did the woman die?" Jyang asked. Hwo looked to Li.

"Examine her," Hwo said. He took Jyang by the arm and led him around to the other side of the screen. After a few moments Li joined them, his face showing the strain induced by his observations.

"Well?" Jyang demanded. Li, though, reported to Hwo, his superior.

"There is nothing to indicate foul play," he began. "Save for the message in the powder, I would have said the death was natural."

"How do you explain the blue cast to the woman's flesh?" Hwo asked.

"I cannot," Li admitted. "I have seen old men with such a color, but never one so young."

"I must see," Jyang exclaimed. He strode around the screen and yanked back the sheet Li had replaced over the body. With rough motions he examined the body and then stood back, revulsion in his face.

"Witchcraft," he said, his teeth clenched.

"Or poison," Li added. Jyang glared at him for a moment, then summoned a guard.

"Search the grounds," he ordered. "Seek out places where the earth may have been disturbed, but do nothing should you find such, on pain of death. Call me when you've finished or if you find something."

"Why do you suspect witchcraft," Hwo asked. "I'd have thought your recent cleansing of the city would have put a stop to all that." Jyang turned to Hwo, his eyes seeming to bulge from their sockets.

"The putrid practice grows in the empire like some evil fungus," he hissed. "None are safe. Not even the Emperor. And I intend to make it my life's work to wipe out this abomination."

"And enhance your own prestige," Hwo thought, but prudently avoided saying the words. This Jyang was a dangerous man, with growing influence over the Emperor. He would have to be watched. Hwo was preparing a careful response to Jyang's tirade when, to his relief, Li saved him the trouble.

CHAPTER FOUR

Questions But Few Answers

"Sir," Li said, "should we not speak to the man who found the body while we await the results of the search?"

"Indeed," Hwo quickly answered. "Who actually found the body?"

"I believe it was the brother of the dead woman," Li answered.

"Too bad," Hwo said. "He certainly wouldn't be a suspect. Those Koreans stick together."

"Where the life of the Emperor is involved," Jyang said, death in his voice, "all are suspect."

"Well," Hwo said, "bring the man in." Soong Li went to the door of the cottage and called out. In a moment a man was led before the three investigators. He was a slightly built eunuch of middling years. His face was composed but retained signs of his recent grief. Aside from the eyes, the man didn't much resemble his dead sister.

"This is Kim Daijoo, sir," Li said, presenting the man.

"What were you doing out here so early in the morning?" Jyang barked at the man.

"I was…"

"Pardon sir," Hwo said. "Is this not my investigation? Should I not question the man?"

Jyang looked up, surprised at the intrusion. Hwo went on. "After all, I am in charge." Jyang hesitated, then stepped aside with a slightly exaggerated bow.

"Now, then," Hwo began briskly, confronting the man. "What were you doing here at such an hour?"

"I was visiting my sister," came the reply.

"At this hour?" Hwo asked. "Isn't that a bit unusual?"

"Not at all, sir," the eunuch replied. "I normally visit my sister at this hour. It is the least busy time of the day for me. The Inner Court grows busy by full dawn, once the first audience of the day is complete. The two of us—my sister and I—have always been close. When she lived in the Inner Palace we always managed to spend a great deal of the time together. After our kidnapping we..."

"You were captured in a war brought about because of your countrymen's refusal to accept the legitimate demands of the Emperor of all the civilized world," Jyang broke in harshly. "That is hardly a kidnapping."

The eunuch smiled fleetingly at this, then continued. It was all Hwo could do to keep a straight face.

"After our capture," the young eunuch resumed, his emphasis of the new word underlining his contempt, "we were brought here and my sister was placed in the Inner Palace. I gave up my manhood to stay near her. I brought her up virtually by myself. I was as much her father as her brother. When it became necessary that she move to this cottage, we missed our former intimacy. I eventually arranged my schedule so that I could be certain to see her each day."

"Even if," Jyang interrupted with a sneer in his voice, "His Majesty should have happened to favor her that night, he would have to have had left her bed an hour before you would arrive so as to be on time for the first audience at dawn."

"As you say," the eunuch replied.

"And, of course, you informed her last evening that His Majesty would not be coming last night." The sneer in the prosecutor's voice was almost palpable.

"No," the Korean replied, his voice unnaturally calm given the stress the man had to be under. "I did not do that. It would have been against the regulations to inform anyone outside of the palace guard where His Majesty was going to be at some future time, so of course I did not do so."

"And of course your loyalty to those who 'kidnapped' you and your sister is so great that you would never do anything that might lead those 'kidnappers' into harm's way?" Jyang was almost shouting now. The Korean remained unflustered.

Li glanced covertly at his master, Hwo, and was surprised to see the elder with a slight smile on his face.

"The situation my sister and I found ourselves in was without remedy," he said quietly. "My sister became a favorite of the Emperor. That is no secret in any part of the land. It was in our interest to be loyal. As loyal subjects we followed the rules of the Court. It was my sister's duty to by fully prepared at any time for a visit from the Emperor, and no man, aristocrat or commoner, can say that she ever failed in her duty."

For the first time since he'd been brought into the cottage, a flash of intense feeling showed on the eunuch's face.

"And no one would dream of saying she had, or ever would," said Hwo, reinserting himself into the interrogation. He stepped between the prosecutor and the eunuch, acknowledging with a faint smile the eunuch's nod of thanks.

"So far as you know," Hwo asked, keeping his voice low and unthreatening in deliberate contrast to the prosecutor's technique, "was anyone else from the Inner Palace—perhaps another of the inner officials like yourself with whom your sister was friendly—likely to be visiting her last night?"

"No sir," came the answer. "My sister and I have always kept apart from the rest of the Inner Court. Most of them wanted nothing to do with us, and that suited us well."

"And them," sneered Jyang.

"Indeed," returned the Korean.

"After all," Jyang continued. "A barbarian is a barbarian."

"My sister could read and write as well as yourself," replied the eunuch with some heat. Hwo didn't interrupt. This antagonism between the prosecutor and the servant from the Inner Court was interesting and potentially useful.

"As you well know," Kim resumed, "our former state of Choson had been ruled by men from China for nearly a hundred years before His Majesty decided to bring us fully within the realm of Heaven's lands. Reading and writing were, therefore, quite common among those of our nobility who had elected to associate themselves with men from China."

"So now you proclaim nobility," Jyang said with a leer. "Too bad you no longer possess the physical equipment to perpetuate your line." Jyang moved closer to the man, as though tempting him to take some rash action. Like his master, Soong Li watched this exchange with interest.

If the Korean was tempted, no one would ever know, for Hwo now once again hastily interjected himself back into the conversation. "Please resume your testimony," he prompted, his voice low and courteous. The Korean visibly relaxed then continued his story.

"My sister had no more to do with the other female servants than her rather limited duties required." The man had turned away from Jyang and was clearly addressing himself to Hwo and Li. Hwo defused the insult by moving round to a point near the prosecutor. There had been enough fireworks for today.

"I flatter myself that the company of servants far less well educated than herself would not have attracted my sister."

"And after she had found favor with His Majesty?" Hwo prompted.

"Why then, sir, she would have had even less reason to be gossiping with the servants of either sex. Under the circumstances, the ladies of the Inner Palace would continue to have no reason to have anything to do with her."

"Though for different reasons than when she was merely a servant," said Hwo, allowing himself to show a faint bit of amusement and thus completing the thought the Korean had left hanging. The Korean smiled too.

Jyang looked as though he'd just eaten something sour.

"Could your sister have had a lover from outside the court?" Hwo asked, as gently as he could.

"No! Never!" came the reply from an agitated Kim. "My sister would never insult the Emperor in such a manner."

"Would she tell you of the matter if she had?" Hwo asked.

"Without doubt," Kim snapped.

"Then there can be but two alternatives," Hwo mused. "The woman was killed by someone in the Inner Court who was jealous of her hold over the Emperor, or…"

Hwo didn't continue. The second thought was so horrid as to be unthinkable.

"Or, someone was out to kill the Emperor," Jyang completed. "In either case, the investigation leads into the palace and to the family of the Empress." The prosecutor stared at Hwo, steel in his eyes.

"The family of the Empress is but one faction within the palace," Hwo retorted, not flinching before the prosecutor's gaze.

"Indeed," replied the prosecutor. "Should you wish it, I can arrange for another investigator. Were your family to be involved, it could become embarrassing for you. If you wish…"

"I will conduct the investigation," Hwo broke in. "Should…"

CHAPTER FIVE

Foul Magic

A guard rushed through the door of the cottage, saving Hwo from the angry retort he was about to make. The guard's eyes were bugging out and his face shone with fear-induced sweat.

"Sir," the guard spat out, "out back... the ground seems to have been dug up recently... It's just like the ones in the park... You must come now to see the place. Everyone's afraid."

"Come. Follow," Jyang barked. This was his territory. None could nor desired to give the prosecutor the lead. Li and Hwo fell in behind Jyang as the man hurried through the door hard on the heels of the guard.

The light of the bright, clear autumn day hit their eyes almost as if with a blow as the three emerged from the dim light of the cottage and followed the guard around to the rear of the building. Once there they needed no guide. A ring of guards, assistants and bystanders clearly marked out the location of the disturbed earth that had just been discovered. A quick glance at the cottage showed Hwo the site was just opposite the bed on which the Korean girl had died. Jyang pushed his way through the circle of onlookers. Hwo and Li followed after hawking and spitting to clear their throats of evil spirits that might surround the place and snare even an innocent person. Hwo noticed Jyang had made no such effort.

On reaching the disturbed area Jyang stopped and unsheathed his sword. He circled the site twice, examining it from every direction, then marched up to it and began carefully removing the freshly dug dirt with the point of a sword he'd seized from the guard who'd led the little group to the disturbed ground.

After a few moments of poking about Jyang paused, looked into the hole he'd dug, then motioned for Li and Hwo to come forward. Li approached rather more rapidly than did Hwo, a look of eager interest on his face. Hwo could not conceal from himself the knot of fear he felt in his stomach. He had to force himself to move toward the hole.

A grotesquely misshapen figure—a kind of a doll—lay face down at the bottom of the shallow depression. On seeing it, Hwo quickly made the sign to ward off evil. Seeing this, the crowd fell back.

"Look here," Jyang said, poking at the blackened fetish with the tip of his sword. "Can you doubt any longer?" Hwo said nothing, but Li moved even closer to the thing, examining the grotesque intently. Jyang pried at the object and it flew out of the hole, seeming for a moment, to almost have a life of its own.

On seeing the object seeming to fly towards it the crowd turned as one man and bolted. Most didn't stop. A few overwhelmingly curious souls turned and carefully made their way back, though remaining well clear of the horrid object that now lay on the surface exposed to the light of day.

It was the twisted face of the thing that first drew attention. Only after a few moments of rapt examination of that did some begin to notice the pervasive stench filling the air.

"That odor!" Soong Li was the first to break the silence. "I've never actually encountered it myself, but the medical texts describe it quite explicitly."

"Yes," agreed Jyang, a tight smile on his lips. "I'm afraid there can be no doubt. The doll alone is enough, but the stench makes it certain. There can be no other explanation."

"Shaman poison—woojoo," muttered Hwo.

"Without doubt," Jyang answered. "Nor is there any doubt that it is aimed at the resident of the cottage.

"There can be no doubt," Hwo answered mechanically.

"And, as the girl can mean nothing to anyone, we must assume that this witchcraft was aimed at the Emperor." Hwo merely nodded, too stunned to do more.

"The investigation will begin at once," Jyang said. He began to give orders to the guards. Hwo walked slowly away.

"Damn," he muttered hollowly. "Damn, damn, damn!" He knew that sooner or later the prosecutor's search for suspects would narrow down to the family of the heir apparent. Hwo had been expecting such an attack for years, but he'd never been sure what form it would take. "Damn, damn, damn......"

Soong Li stood next to the doll, examining it intently.

CHAPTER SIX

The Investigation

Hwo Gwang was speaking slowly and carefully to the young Soong Li. Both men looked grim; Soong Li because of the responsibility being placed upon him, Hwo Gwang because he was being forced to count on a young, subordinate whose ability and loyalty were both still untested. Both men knew that the future of Hwo Gwang's family and perhaps even of the empire itself might be decided by the events of the next few weeks. Hwo's mind was still almost as paralyzed as it was when he left the scene of the crime. He forced himself not to slump back into his cushion.

"The perpetrator of the deed must be found out!"

Hwo might be shocked but that did not assuage his anger.

"This horrid person has cast suspicion on the Heir Apparent, on the Royal Consort—the Lady Wei Dsefoo—and on all in our family. This could lead to the end of this family, and that certainly would completely suit that accursed fellow Jyang." Hwo was well on his way to regaining his composure. "We must discover who put the Emperor's whore to death before Jyang."

"Could it in fact have been a member of your family?" Li asked, shrinking inwardly from the grim look on Hwo's face. "Someone, perhaps, who felt that the Korean girl represented a threat to the orderly succession of the Heir Apparent?"

Hwo Gwang bit back the sharp reply he'd been about to make. Young Li was correct. This possibility had better be faced.

"If so," Hwo said, "we must do all we can to find the man, and then I will personally behead him. If it was a member of my family, it is all the more essential that we bring him to justice, and we had better do it quickly lest Jyang Choong forestall us and bring us all down in the process."

"How do you suggest we begin?" Soong Li asked. Hwo's shoulders slumped. "I don't know," he replied. "How does one go about finding a witch?"

"By finding the one who is directing the witch," Li said quietly. He rose and poured two cups of stillbeer from an earthenware jug. Hwo Gwang watched his young assistant, a quizzical look in his eyes. Young Li gave one cup to his employer, then took his to a cushion at the far end of the large masonry stove occupying a third of the room and on which Hwo was already reclining and sat down himself. "It seems to me," Li said, "that it may be a mistake to take all we've seen at face value."

"What do you mean?" Hwo asked as his assistant sipped his drink.

"There are many who would usurp the place of those related to the Lady Wei," he said. "The Heir Apparent has many enemies."

Hwo nodded.

"Who really had a motive to kill the Korean?" Li asked. Hwo thought for a moment.

"There are two main possibilities," he said, finally. "It could be, as you suggested, a member of my aunt, Lady Wei's family, trying to protect the position of the family, or it could be someone outside the family making an attempt to discredit us and replace us as the new power in the empire."

"A third possibility exists," Li said quietly.

Hwo gazed intently at his assistant.

"Some third party could be involved. One who would gain much by the fall of the Empress's family. One who could not supply a new heir to the empire, but could nevertheless gain influence over both His Majesty and whoever does supply a new heir."

"Is that likely?" Hwo asked, carefully, though he knew how likely that could be and knew exactly who Li had in mind.

"It must be considered," Li replied. "There are those who would like nothing more than to see a struggle for power among the families of the court. For those the reward would be power."

"Have you any evidence for this?"

"Nothing firm," Li admitted. "I only point out the possibility lest we miss something important." Hwo was disappointed. For a moment he'd thought the young man might have noticed something that would solve their problem directly.

"Well," he said with a gesture of resignation. "All we can really do is keep our eyes and ears open. As this is a case of witchcraft, we are pretty much subject to the whim of the prosecutor."

"For now," Li said. Hwo darted another searching look at his young assistant.

"How so?"

"I cannot say just yet, sir. I have a feeling that all is not as it seems. I know I am new and still untried in your service, but I beg your indulgence. I promise you my loyalty and ask for leave to go out and see what I may see for a day or two. It may be that I can find something of use to you."

Hwo Gwang was a man long inured to the intrigues of the court. Trust came hard to him. Nevertheless something about the young fellow had evoked such trust from the beginning of his service. "See what you can do," he said. He left unspoken the thought that he had few other choices.

CHAPTER SEVEN

Li Goes To Work

As Li left the courtyard fronting the headquarters maintained by Hwo Gwang he looked about as though seeing the Outer Court, the headquarters of the bureaucracy, for the first time. Narrow lanes between the walled courtyards were already thick with civil servants and their servants bustling back and forth on the business of the world's most elaborately governed empire. He reflected that the humble courtyard he'd just left was, in terms of the power wielded within, one of the most important in the city. While most in the bureaucracy struggled over who might be most ostentatious, and thus most noticed by the court, Hwo Gwang deliberately kept the headquarters of his faction—the brain trust of the Heir Apparent's party—as inconspicuous as possible during the delicate period that all recognized—but none admitted openly—as the final years of the long reign of the Emperor.

At about the same time Li shrugged and started off through the lanes of the Outer Court, a messenger hurried into the offices of Hwo Gwang. "Sir," the servant said on being admitted to the presence of Hwo, "a special audience has just been announced and you are especially summoned to attend."

Hwo's face remained impassive, but his mind raced ahead.

"It may not be significant," he thought. "There have been many such audiences lately. His Majesty has been especially worried." As Hwo rose to prepare for the audience, he slipped a small but very sharp knife into the folds of his robe. Jyang was capable of anything. Hwo was determined not to die the death so many had endured in recent times. He hoped the precaution would prove unnecessary.

The dwelling Soong Li made his way toward was against the outer wall of the court in one of the least desirable parts of the small city within a city constituting the abode of the ruling class within the capital city. Li made his way through a tiny courtyard and into the only room of the dwelling.

The room had been blocked off from what had originally been a much larger dwelling. Near its front was a large masonry platform, the top surface of a north Chinese stove, part of which extended past the wall which had been erected upon it into some other residence.

The stove occupied nearly half the room. On its surface mats and bedding were spread about in disarray. Most of the perimeter of the room, except for the half occupied by the stove, was filled with chests of books. The books were scattered about in almost as great a state of disarray as the bedding. The tops of the chests were, for the most part, open, and the rolls of bamboo slats, the pages of the books tied together with cords top and bottom, stuck out of many of these chests at a variety of angles. The two low desks which occupied much of the remainder of the floor area were also covered with book-rolls, some still in their silk covers, others uncovered and opened. Writing brushes and two large ink-grinding blocks, both rather crusty with dried ink, completed the litter on the desks.

Clearly this room was neither bedroom nor clerks' office but rather the den of a pair of young intellectuals, newly away from home and content with only minimal attempts at housekeeping.

The one exception to the general disorder of the room was the elegantly dressed young man seated at the far desk, absorbed in the book that lay unrolled before him. Though seeming to be, based on appearance, a year or two younger than Soong Li, the young man was somewhat bulkier in build. The bulk did not mask the slight family resemblance in the face that Chiang Bao bore to his maternal cousin.

"What are you reading?" Li asked, using the familiar greeting used by earnest young intellectuals at all times and places.

"Nothing much," Bao replied. "Just the last chapter of old Doong's thing on the Lu Annals."

"Aha," Li replied. "Then you now must have it all figured out. What are we, then? Is our nature good or bad?"

"Well," replied Bao exaggerating the sing-song whine of the

classical Confucian scholar, "it seems that human nature is both bad and good!"

"Both bad and good?" Li's whine echoed that of his roommate. "But how can that be?"

"Very simple," Bao replied, trying to stay in character. "It depends on whose human nature we're talking about. If it be someone opposed to us, why then it is obvious we are dealing with a human nature that is in all ways bad. If, on the other hand, we are considering the nature of someone who agrees with us, then old Doong Joong-shu assures us that there is no question but that we are dealing with all that is bright and good in human nature."

Bao paused for effect. "And that's not bad," he added, and then joined his roommate's roar of laughter.

The two young intellectuals, now suitably impressed with each other's cleverness, turned to other things. Soong Li began to rummage through one of the more disordered of the book chests.

"What are you looking for?" Bao asked.

"The Internal Medicine Classic," Li replied, deliberately keeping his voice casual in tone. "I seem to remember something in it that may match the symptoms of the corpse I saw this morning."

"The Korean girl?"

"How did you know about that?" Li was genuinely surprised.

"It's all over the court," Bao assured him. "Already they are laying bets as to how long it will be until Prosecutor Jyang has the head of Hwo Gwang."

"I hope you put your few strings of cash on Lord Hwo's side," said Li as he kept rummaging through the chest.

"Why's that?" asked Bao.

"If Hwo Gwang loses his head, as his employee I will surely lose mine and as my friend and roommate you will part company from yours too."

"Here," Bao said, grinning broadly as he levered himself up from behind the desk, "better let me help find that book."

Two hours later Soong Li tossed aside the last of the scrolls and uttered a sigh of exasperation. "Find anything yet?" he called to Bao, who seemed to be all but buried under a pile of bamboo slats.

"Nothing," Bao snapped. "Are you sure you saw that symptom in the Internal Classic?"

"I think so, but now I wonder."

"Well, I think you'd…," Bao was cut off by a pounding at the door. Both rose to see who was there. It was a servant from Hwo Gwang's office, summoning Li back to headquarters. Li motioned to Bao to follow and the two hastened back to the room Soong Li had left just a few hours earlier. Hwo had returned from court.

"Have you had any luck tracing that symptom?" Hwo asked.

"No luck yet, sir," Li answered, "but I'm sure I've seen something on it somewhere. It's bound to turn up."

"Well, it may not matter much longer," Hwo said.

"How so?"

"There have been portents," Hwo said. "Something is going on and Jyang is doing his best to exploit it."

"Portents?"

"Lights have been seen in the sky to the south. In the far north it is said that fire hangs on the horizon, and there is even a report of a unicorn being sighted in the forests to the west."

"But these may be auspicious signs," Li suggested.

"Perhaps so, but they can also foreshadow tragedy," Hwo reminded them. "Remember that a unicorn appeared just before Confucius's death just as one did before his birth. The Emperor is… well…"

There was no need for Hwo to actually state the enormous impropriety he had led up to. All three looked grim. The Emperor's declining vigor was the great unspoken fact of life at court in recent months.

"Perhaps…" Hwo gestured toward Bao. The latter whispered nervously into Li's ear and glanced nervously at Hwo.

"My cousin asks leave to withdraw so as to continue our search for that symptom."

"Granted." Bao quickly left the room. The two men watched him go.

"I'm sure your servant is loyal…" Hwo began.

"I would trust him with my life," Li assured his superior, somewhat disconcerted at labeling Bao as a servant, though on reflection that was really his function.

"You may well be trusting him with your life," Hwo added.

"I understand, sir." Both men knew that their fates were now inextricably intertwined. There was no sense to maintaining a false discretion.

"The Emperor realizes, no matter what he says, that his end time is near," Hwo resumed. "These portents may foreshadow that end, but Jyang has planted the seed of another, curiously more hopeful thought, in His Majesty's mind."

Hwo paused, wondering anew how far he dared trust this young fellow, for all his aura of virtue that rendered plausible the Soong family legends of direct descent from the great Chi, the virtuous survivor of the royal line of ancient Shang almost a thousand years before. No matter. Hwo knew he had no choice but to trust this young man, if only because it was even riskier to not do so and as a result, not act at all.

"Jyang has convinced the Emperor these portents could be a warning from Heaven itself that attempts are being made against his life. I need not tell you what that could mean to us. Is there nothing else to be done except consult your medical texts?"

"There may be something, sir." Li spoke hesitantly. "But you should not be directly involved. Could you issue me a pass as your deputy investigator allowing me to move freely within the Inner Palace? It might be best if you did not know exactly what I would be doing with that authority."

"I appear to have anticipated you in this matter." Hwo smiled faintly and withdrew a bamboo tally from his sleeve. Li accepted it with both hands, met his superior's eyes and withdrew from his presence without saying anything further.

By the time he reached home and rushed through the door he was full of plans. "Come Bao, we have work to do. We must be off."

"You have work to do," Bao said sullenly.

"Come on. You can't sit around here getting splinters in your index finger crunching through the books."

"What can I do? If I have to leave the room every time his holiness feels like muttering some indiscretion, how am I ever to know what I may or may not do. How can I…?"

"Oh, come off it. Hwo Gwang's aunt is Empress, mother of the Heir Apparent. He has to be careful. I'm sure he hates having even to trust me, but the palace is full of spies and spies on spies, so he has no choice but to use me, just as I have no choice but to use you. All three of our families go back some distance together. With luck we'll go forward together some way too."

"To an early grave, more likely than not," Bao muttered, not quite ready to be mollified.

"Could be," Li replied with a laugh and a thrown hand cloth aimed at his cousin's head. "But it could be we can both climb the ladder of merit a long way because of this, and anyway it will be a grand adventure and a curious puzzle to solve."

"Some adventure. We may get to feel the edge of the executioner's blade, and the only puzzle to solve being whether the man was competent enough to hone his blade properly. Even if he turns out to have been remiss, how are you going to tell anyone about it?"

Li laughed. "Are you with me or not? I wouldn't blame you if you left for home this afternoon. That would be the prudent thing to do."

"Oh ho! First I am found unworthy of the trust of the great Soong Li. Now I have become a coward! What on earth will you accuse me of next? What…?" Bao stopped to catch a well-thrown seating cushion.

"So," he resumed, once he stopped laughing. "What next?"

"We are going to perform some surgery," Li answered.

"Surgery! A few months as apprentice to the village healer hardly qualifies you to perform surgery."

"The patient won't mind. I promise. She won't feel a thing."

"Now how do you propose to guarantee that short of killing the patient first?"

"No problem there. The patient's already dead."

Bao stopped smiling.

CHAPTER EIGHT

Unwelcome Autopsy

Y ou want to what?"

The Korean eunuch, Kim Daijoo, was almost screaming at Li. "How can you ask such a thing? First my sister is killed in this cursed land so far from home, and now you ask permission to mutilate her body. Have you no decency? Because she is the victim of witchcraft, I cannot even bury her properly, but must see her burned like some western barbarian. Now you ask this of me?" The desolate man buried his head in his hands and sobbed aloud.

"I'm sorry," Soong Li said, placing his hand on the Korean's shoulder to comfort him. Kim Daijoo shook him off. Soong Li kept on talking, as softly as before.

"I do not believe your sister was killed by witchcraft. I believe she was murdered, no more no less. An examination of her body might help prove that and make sure the murderer pays for his deed."

Kim Daijoo looked up, tears streaking his face. "Are you telling the truth?" Li nodded.

"How will this help you bring my sister's murderer to justice? What difference does it make how she was killed?"

"Murder by witchcraft is the business of the prosecutor alone. I cannot investigate such a murder, but if I can show that no witchcraft was involved, I can stay on the case and perhaps discover who the murderer actually was."

"Won't the prosecutor do that much?"

"The prosecutor cares nothing about the murder of your sister. He will merely use her death to solidify his hold on the Emperor. It would crimp his style if the murderer is discovered too soon. I promise you, the man who killed your sister will not be punished so long as the prosecutor remains in control of this case."

The Korean said nothing for a moment. Finally he stood. "I will do as you ask."

The temple where the body of the Korean girl lay was less than imposing, particularly as the girl had been the Emperor's favorite. Guards were at the door.

"Halt!" one of the guards demanded as the three men approached. Soong Li held up his hand. Bao and Kim stopped behind him.

"No one may enter," the guard said after Li explained they'd come to visit the body of the girl.

"Why not?" Li asked.

"Witchcraft," the guard replied. "Someone tried to kill the Emperor with witchcraft and this girl got in the way."

"Then why can't we see the body?" Bao asked.

"I have my orders."

Li pointed at Kim. "This is the woman's brother. Surely he can visit the body of his sister and do what he must to help her spirit set off for the Yellow Springs."

"I have my orders," the soldier said sullenly. "No one may enter the temple."

"Who gave these orders?" Li asked.

"The prosecutor, Jyang Choong."

"Oh," said Li brightly. "There's no problem then. I am investigating this murder for the prosecutor and must have access to the body to do so." At that the guard began to look uncomfortable, but still the man seemed prepared to stand his ground.

"No one may enter," he repeated.

"What?" Li shouted. "You dare impede an agent of the prosecutor in the completion of his duty?" He turned to Bao. "Take this man's name to the prosecutor. He is interfering with the performance of my duty. I want that made quite clear in your report. Better his head than mine." Li turned and began to stride off, but not so quickly as to discourage second thoughts on the part of the guard.

"Sir!" the guard called. Li had taken only a few steps. He turned and looked balefully at the man, but said nothing. The guard blushed, looked around for support from his colleagues, but their attention seemed to turn elsewhere. The guard cleared his throat.

"Perhaps it would be alright for you to enter the temple. Seeing as how you do represent the prosecutor and all, I'm sure it would be alright." Li appeared to be pondering the matter.

"Normally," he finally said, "I'd wait for the prosecutor himself to come and straighten this whole thing out, but I'm in a hurry and need to get on with the investigation, so I'll forgive your impertinence… this time, at least."

It was all Li and Bao could do to keep straight faces as they strode imperiously into the temple.

"I thought we'd had it," Li said with a smile once he had made sure they were alone in the temple. "Can you imagine how old Jyang would have reacted if he'd heard us claim we were from his office?"

"No thanks," Bao said, dryly. "I'd just as soon live to see another day." The Korean had moved ahead of them up to the bier on which his sister lay. He stopped, stared, then sank to his knees beside it, tears glistening in his eyes. Li and Bao moved to his side and Li gently touched his shoulder. "New guards may come at any time," he said. "We'd better get to work." The eunuch looked up, nodded, and then stood.

"I cannot watch this. I'll stay by the entrance and warn you if anyone comes."

"Good," Li replied. He knelt by the body and extracted a long, very sharp knife from a scabbard hidden inside the bosom of his robe. Looking away from the instrument, Kim hastened to his vantage point. Bao looked nervous, but stayed by his side. Li gently pulled the burial shroud back from the girl's abdomen. He placed the knife against the flesh and drew it across the body. A clear fluid welled up as he cut.

"Well," Bao said, hiding his nervousness behind a veneer of sarcasm. "I guess she got the point." Li did not look up. He continued the incision, cutting ever more deeply into the flesh.

"See here," he said finally. He'd cut well into the abdominal cavity. Bao came and stood over his shoulder, his face taking on a peculiar shade of green. Li pointed with his knife.

"This woman wasn't killed by witchcraft. There are none of the usual signs. She looks perfectly healthy. Wugu attacks from within by means of poisoned insects. There is no sign of that here." He paused. "In fact there is no sign of anything which could have caused her death."

"Someone comes!" The sudden hiss of the Korean's warning caused the two young men to jump up. Li quickly pulled the burial garment back to cover his incision and replaced the knife in its original position inside his robe. He motioned to the Korean to come and kneel by the bier. Just as the eunuch took up that position the door burst open. Jyang Choong stood framed in the doorway.

"What's going on here?" he shouted. Soong Li hurried forward and bowed low.

"We came to help prepare the body of the Korean girl for burial."

"He told me he was a member of your staff investigating the girl's murder." The guard Li had bullied stared malevolently at Li. The other guards seemed happy at an awkward situation they were clear of responsibility for.

"I am on the staff of Hwo Gwang," Li said quickly to forestall the roar of rage clearly ready to burst from the prosecutor's lips. "Doesn't my master serve your will? And if so, don't I as well?" Jyang glared at Li, began to say something, then seemed to think better of it.

"Get out of here," Jyang snapped, then turned and stalked off to where the guards stood. "From now on," he hissed to them, "no one is to enter this temple. No one at all. The prosecutor turned on his heels and marched off, his back stiff with anger.

Li, Bao, and the Korean followed, the guards shuffling out the door after them. As the three walked off a hunched figure detached itself from the shadows next to the temple, stood for a moment, muttering strange sounding words, then with a soft shake of a rattle directed at the retreating backs of the three men, turned and melted once again into the shadows.

CHAPTER NINE

A Warning

The two young men and the Korean eunuch had not yet gone far when they heard the booming voice of the prosecutor behind them.

"Hold up over there!" the prosecutor shouted, having turned from giving fresh instructions to the guards. Bao glanced nervously at Li.

"Some more excitement, huh?" muttered Bao. "I told you it'd be the executioner's blade for us."

"Not yet, old friend," Li grinned, sounding less worried than he felt. Jyang Choong strode up to where they had halted.

"You have interfered in a matter affecting the safety of the Emperor. You lied to my guards. Why should I not have you taken to the torture chambers and then killed?"

Li met the prosecutor's enraged stare. He'd never realized, until now, just how large a man the prosecutor was. "I must rely on your good judgment sir," he replied finally. "I thought I was serving my master Hwo Gwang, and through him, you, when I went into the temple."

Li was careful to balance these politely defiant words by looking humbly down at the ground immediately after saying them.

"Nonsense. Hwo Gwang is nothing more than an official of the court. In a case of wugu against the Emperor, I am the one responsible for any investigation."

"Again, I must ask pardon. I am but recently arrived from the outer provinces, but it seemed to me that all must guard the safety of the one who gives us life. I simply had some thoughts about the death of the young lady and wished to see her face once again. Her brother here wanted to send the spirit of his sister to its eternal place of residence in a proper manner. I saw no harm in…"

"Yes, yes," the prosecutor interrupted impatiently. "I'm sure you had only my best interests at heart, and the fact that you work for Hwo Gwang, whose family may well be involved in this affair, has nothing to do with the fact that you sneaked over here without my knowledge to see what could be found out about the case."

"But sir," Li said, taking care to keep his voice calm. "My master had no knowledge of…"

"Silence!" Jyang roared. He lowered his voice and continued. "Tell your master to beware. Some things are best left alone."

The prosecutor turned abruptly and walked away.

It was a moment before the three appreciated that they'd escaped arrest. Bao spoke first. "Let's get out of here before he changes his mind and takes us in after all." The three men turned and walked quickly off, too distracted to notice the small knot of men stalking along behind them.

"Aiiiii," Bao exclaimed after they'd turned a corner. "I thought we'd wind up spitted over a fire like so many fat geese. I was already begging forgiveness from my ancestors for being the last of my line."

"There was never anything to worry about," said Li, assuming a tone of aloof superiority. "I can handle the prosecutor. He was like putty in my hands."

"So I noticed, oh honored one of the silver tongue," rejoined Bao.

CHAPTER TEN

Attack, Death And Escape

My sister?"
The Korean broke in so abruptly that it was a moment before Li understood that he was being asked a question.

"My sister," the Korean repeated. "How did her end come?" He looked expectantly at Li.

"Not by witchcraft," Li answered, all the humor and bluff washed from his voice. "She was murdered, but not by witchcraft."

The Korean smiled for the first time since the two had met him. "I thank you with all my heart," he said. "In our land it is considered a great disgrace to die in such a way. One who dies from witchcraft is doomed to wander the void forever. Had my sister died from such causes I would have considered myself remiss for not having noticed the signs and so helping her to her death."

"But now," Li said, "we must begin the task of identifying the true murderer, for it is no less likely that the Emperor was his target, even if he did not employ witchcraft."

"That may not be so," Kim Daijoo said. "There is one person who hated and feared my sister. He approached her one day in the garden of the Inner Court and asked her and the maid who served her to…"

A sudden grunt interrupted the Korean's speech. He stopped and turned, a look of amazement on his face as his eyes contemplated the shaft of the arrow that had suddenly protruded from his throat. Li caught him as he slumped forward. Bao, unarmed, leaped between the back of his friend and the direction from which the arrow had come, grabbed Li with one hand and the Korean with the other and dragged the two of them to a recess in the wall fronting the street. Li helped halfheartedly, kneeling as they lowered the Korean to the ground. Li was trying to listen to the voice of the Korean as the man died. Finally there was a gasping shudder and the Korean's body shook, then sagged.

The man was dead.

Li made sure there was nothing more he could do, then stood.

"Do you see anything?" he asked Bao. The latter peered around the corner, then shook his head. "Nothing," he said. He looked down at the Korean. "Is he dead?"

"Very," Li said grimly.

"You were listening as he died. Did he manage to say anything?"

"Something strange," Li answered. "I really didn't understand. Something about the 'shaman master.'"

"Shaman master?" Bao exclaimed. "What in the world could the man have meant?"

Li shrugged. "I don't know," he replied. "but if we don't do something about getting out of here, it won't matter very much. Whoever killed the Korean is just as likely to try for us."

"I don't see anything," Bao reported, again sticking his head carefully out to look around the corner of the niche in the wall. "Maybe they're gone."

"Don't count on it."

"Well, we'd better find out. That arrow came from the roof over there. If they haven't given up, they'll be maneuvering to get a clean shot at us, and this doorway will only be safe for a few more seconds."

"So what do we do?" Li asked. Bao's reply was to dart out into the lane. He whirled and faced the direction from which the arrow had come, then just as quickly, dropped to the ground and rolled into a doorway across from that Li still occupied. As he rolled, an arrow passed through the space he'd filled only a moment before.

"I think they're still there," he called to Li.

"I believe you may be correct," Li called back in a hoarse whisper. "What do we do now?"

"Well," whispered Bao with a wry grin. "We can stay here and enjoy the excitement of it all, or we can run like hell."

"I say we run," Li said, "Excitedly."

"I'm with you. Follow me."

With that Bao darted into the lane. Li was on his heels. The two ran towards their attackers' position. There was a shout and a hail of arrows. Bao stopped suddenly, wheeled and slipped into another niche in the wall. Li tried to stop but slipped, then scrambled into the alcove with his friend.

"Why in Heaven did you run in this direction?" Li panted.

"They expected us to run away from them. If we had, they'd have had us for sure, but the surprise slowed them down a bit and by the time they'd retargeted, here we were."

"And now?"

"Well, I didn't say I had everything planned out perfectly," Bao grinned. His face turned sober again as an arrow chunked into the wall near his head.

"They're working their way around again to get a clear shot at us," he said. "We've got to do something quickly." He poked his head round the corner for a quick look, then drew it hastily back as two more arrows clattered off the wall.

"I think you're right. We'd better move," Li said.

"Then get ready to follow me," Bao hissed. He stepped into the street, stood for a moment, then ducked back. A fresh fusillade of arrows greeted the move. As the arrows whizzed by, Bao pulled at Li's robe and shouted out, "Let's go!" He leaped into the lane and began running again.

The next turn in the lane was Bao's evident goal. Once the two reached that goal they'd be immune from the arrows of their pursuers.

It seemed to Li as though the twenty yards to the corner took an eternity to cross, but it was really only a matter of seconds until he saw Bao's sturdy back disappear.

Li was already congratulating himself on their narrow escape when a searing pain racked through his body. He went down with a cry, rolling up against a wall. He looked down and saw the shaft of an arrow protruding from his leg. He was still staring dumbly when Bao reached his side, snatched up an end of his robe and dragged him round the corner amid another hail of arrows.

Once out of range of the attackers Bao allowed Li's inert body to scoot to a halt, then went back to the turn and looked round it. Men were visible on the rooftops, moving quickly.

"Is it bad?" he called to Li.

Li forced himself to examine the wound. The arrow had passed through the fleshy part of his thigh. The missile had nearly penetrated all the way through but tip was still inside the leg. From the angle, the arrow must have bounced off the wall of a house before entering his flesh.

"Hurt's but not fatal."

"Can you run?"

"Not with the arrow still in there."

"Take it out, then. They're coming after us."

"I don't know if I can," Li said.

"Let me see." Bao quickly walked back and bent down to examine the wound. "Forgive me, old friend, but we're dead men if we don't get out of here." With that he snapped off the fletched end of the arrow, then shoved the point through the rest of the leg.

Li sucked in his breath as an eruption of blood heralded the exit of the arrow's tip. Bao kept pulling until the entire shaft had passed through the wound. It hurt, but not as much as Li had thought it would. Bao pulled Li roughly to his feet. "Let's go," he said, pulling Li along. The latter hobbled after him with surprising speed.

At first the pain was not too bad, but all too soon Li began to feel as though a hot poker had been shoved through the leg and was being twisted by some sadistic torturer. He began to slow despite Bao's urgings. A shout from behind told them that they were still being pursued.

Now the two were in a part of town broken up into a labyrinth of alleyways and narrow lanes. Few people were abroad and those that were looked nervously away from the two young men who were obviously fleeing some trouble. Finally, when he thought he could not take another step without falling down in agony, Li felt himself pulled into a doorway.

"Have we lost them?" he asked Bao. In answer Bao pointed down and away at the ground. A trail of blood marked their passage.

"Not for long," Bao replied. He reached down and tore a piece of cloth from the hem of his own robe and used it to bind up Li's wound. Next Bao ripped a large piece of blood soaked cloth from Li's robe.

"Wait here."

Bao ran into the street, twisting the bloody cloth as he went, leaving a trail of blood drops behind. Li saw his cousin disappear into a side street just as he heard a shout.

"This way!"

The attackers were close behind. Li pushed his way behind a large urn that stood in the doorway then peeked out to see four men running down the street, following the trail of blood Bao had created.

There was a moment's pause as the men reached the corner around which Bao had gone. Li saw one of them point. Then they disappeared down the alley.

The next thing Li knew, Bao was shaking his shoulder. It took a moment for awareness of the dull ache in his leg to rise again.

"Sorry old friend," Bao was saying. "I led them astray, but they'll soon be back when they've realize they've been tricked. We'd better be gone when they get here." Pulling Li to his feet, Bao helped his cousin limp off. The two talked as they hurried along, as much to take Li's mind off the pain as for anything to say.

"Why were they after us?" Bao asked.

"I think perhaps someone doesn't want us to even attempt to track the murderer of the Emperor's consort."

"Why?"

"When we know the answer to that question we'll know who killed the woman," Li said. He winced in pain as he stumbled on a stone in the road.

"Enough of that," Bao said. He lifted his cousin onto his shoulders and carried him the rest of the way home.

CHAPTER ELEVEN

A Second Attempt

The shadows were lengthening as Bao finished binding up Li's wound following Li's advice.

"I'm not a bad surgeon," he said, stepping back and admiring his handiwork. "Perhaps I should go into that field."

"A surgeon is supposed to alleviate his patient's ills," Li observed drily. "Finishing the work of the archer by shoving an arrow through the victim's leg hardly qualifies as medicine. I'd say your methods were rather more painful than those of the ordinary physician."

"But quicker," Bao retorted. "You have to give me that. My method is certainly quicker."

"True enough," Li said, ruefully rubbing the bandage. He had to admit the pain was less than he'd thought it would be but, he knew he would feel the wound the next day.

"Now," Bao said as he went to get a couple of cups and a jug of fermented fruit juices. "What is all this about? What did the Korean tell you as he died and what makes you so certain that his sister was killed by something other than witchcraft?"

"I can't be absolutely sure the woman didn't die of witchcraft," Li told his cousin, "but the indications seem to me to point to plain, old-fashioned murder rather than to anything supernatural."

"What indications?"

"For one, the woman's internal organs were all normal. There was no trace of worm poison, and a good thing there wasn't. You know how infectious that kind of thing is. The Emperor could still be in mortal danger if the woman had been killed by the gu."

"Surely he takes precautions."

"No doubt he does, but still, it's good to know he's safe from that quarter.

"What if you'd been wrong and the poison gu insects had been present in the woman? We'd all have died as soon as you'd cut her open and released them."

"There wasn't much chance she had gu. All the external signs were against it, but even if she had, I took precautions." Li held up a bag.

"What's in that thing?"

Li opened the bag and shook a small amount of a grey powder out of it onto the palm of his hand. "Thunderstone," he replied.

"Thunderstone! Where did you manage to get that? Only the really rich can afford thunderstone and you're not rich."

"Old Wu, the man who gave me my start in the medical arts, gave this to me when he died."

"I see why you weren't worried about the gu," Bao said, respect in his voice.

Thunderstones were formed, but only rarely, beneath the ground where lightning had struck, and even the rich could seldom boast of their possession. "What if it had been some other kind of witchcraft, though, a hungry spirit or some other such apparition?"

"A hungry spirit couldn't even get near the palace grounds," Li replied, a hint of disdain for his cousin's country bumpkin ignorance creeping into his voice. "Sacrifices are made every day to ward them off, along with most of the other sorts of spirits. Besides, I've never heard of any victim of that sort of possession showing symptoms like the Korean's."

Li paused and sipped thoughtfully at his drink. "No," he said, at last. "There's no witchcraft going on here. I'm positive of that. Someone is trying to make it look like witchcraft to take advantage of the Emperor's well-known fear of the insect poison." He paused and looked earnestly at his cousin. "The problem is going to be in proving me right before we're killed. Perhaps it would be best if you left for home and…"

"Quite right," Bao broke in. "It would be best if I armed myself from now on. One never knows when a good throwing knife might come in handy."

Li began to protest, then thought better of it and contented himself with clasping his cousin's shoulder in appreciation. There was a knock at the door. Li answered. A servant appeared.

"The Lord Hwo Gwang would speak with you," he said.

"Good," Li replied. "Give us a moment to prepare and we'll be right along."

"I'll wait," the servant said, stepping outside. Li and Bao were about to follow him out the door when Li noticed the open jug which he turned aside to put away as Bao opened the door. A soft but sharp hiss jerked Li's attention to his cousin, who was holding the door open, but no more than a crack.

"What's wrong?"

"Bao beckoned him with a nod. Li came over and looked outside. The servant who had brought the message was speaking to a thin, roguish looking man and pointing back toward the door.

"Who's that?" Li asked.

"I don't know," Bao replied. "All I know for sure is that he's one of the fellows who chased us through the streets today. In fact he's the one who gave you that little present in the leg."

"What now?"

"Let's get out of here," Bao whispered urgently.

"But how?"

"Cousin," Bao said, "for someone who's so intelligent, you sure aren't very smart." He pointed to the narrow window at the back of the residence. It opened onto a small courtyard. In a very few moments the two had slipped out and were hastening towards the offices of Hwo Gwang.

Nearly two hours later the two had finished telling Hwo Gwang of the day's events. Li was sitting with his damaged leg elevated. Hwo had called in an expert who had, indeed, complimented the two young men on the patch up job they'd done. The leg still hurt every time Li moved it, but Li was determined not to let it interfere with his life.

"The Korean had been robbed," Hwo Gwang was saying. "The soldiers said it seemed to be nothing more than a simple murder and theft."

"Those weren't bandits," Li insisted grimly.

"How do you know?" Hwo Gwang asked.

"Bandits don't chase their victims through the streets," Bao interjected. "They hit and run. Those men were sent to silence us."

"Besides," Li continued. "Bandits wouldn't have tracked us down again and tried to entice us into yet another trap. A real bandit would simply have found another victim."

"You're correct, of course," Hwo Gwang sighed. "I almost wish you weren't, but I know—in fact I've known all along—that you are right." He stood and began to pace back and forth.

"The question now," Hwo resumed, "is who is behind all this, and what is his actual goal." He broke off again as a servant entered and whispered something in his ear.

"I am summoned to appear before His Majesty," he said. "It is my desire that you come with me." In a moment the three were on their way to the palace. This time there would be no problem with bandits. A squad of guards trooped along before and after the three men.

CHAPTER TWELVE

The Palace

The audience was being held in the Northern Palace. Hwo Gwang seemed lost in his own thoughts as he and young Soong Li, followed by Chiang Bao, strode briskly toward the front gate of the palace allowing their guards to set the pace.

Li hardly blamed his master for being in a distracted state. Here was a man who had deliberately spent his life in the shadows for the sake of his family's advancement.

The task of advancing family interests had not been an easy one in the always convoluted atmosphere of the court where everyone vied for influence and the smallest slip could bring disaster.

Hwo's presence at court in the first place had come as the result of an affair between Hwo's father and the sister of the current Empress Wei Dsefoo, an affair consummated before Hwo himself had birthed. The result of the affair had been a half-brother for Hwo. On becoming the Empress Wei, Hwo's half-brother had been invited to court and, in turn, Hwo was included due to his brother's admiration for the young man's sharp intelligence.

From the first day Hwo had begun to repay his brother's confidence with a diligent campaign aimed at enhancing the family's standing at court, always operating unobtrusively with great patience, giving a little push here and a little shove there as he played the stylized chess game that was life in the court.

The stakes were high. One day the Son of Heaven would pass on and, should nothing change, his place would be taken by the Heir Apparent, cousin to Hwo's half-brother, and son of the Lady Wei.

Now, Li knew, an impending crisis loomed, a crisis made more complicated by the recent events both inside and outside the palace walls.

Prosecutor Jyang Choong, hated the Wei family and was hated by them in return. The man had worked against the Wei family interests for years without success, but now a new opportunity had seemingly, and, perhaps a bit to conveniently, presented itself. The queen was getting old, and the Emperor had taken a new lover. Now that lover was dead and the Prosecutor had already hinted at possible links between her death and the Wei family. Hwo Gwang did, indeed, have much to worry about.

If Hwo Gwang was distracted, neither Li nor Bao were. They gaped openly at the sights of the palace, this being their first imperial audience, not knowing whether to be more impressed by the intricate lacquer work used to embellish the massive wooden beams of the structure, or by the spectacular vistas as courtyard opened upon courtyard so as to awe those who came to the palace with the vast power of the Son of Heaven.

Suddenly, as the three men walked toward the entrance of the palace, Bao gave so audible a gasp as to even awake Hwo Gwang from his reverie.

"What's wrong?" Li asked.

Bao pointed to a shadowed corridor leading to some sort of side court. Though the corridor was dark, the courtyard was brightly illuminated. Li followed his cousin's gaze and he too gave a quick gasp.

"What's the matter?" Hwo Gwang asked.

"Look," Bao said, pointing with his eyes. "The man on the left. He's the man who tried to kill us today."

"You're sure?" Hwo Gwang returned.

The tone of Hwo's voice caused both of the young men to look at him oddly.

"Of course we're sure," Bao said, rather more brusquely than was proper to a man of Hwo's standing. "Who is he?"

"That, my young friend, is Ju Anshih."

"Ju Anshih?" Li's voice rose questioningly. "The bandit?" The man in question was tall, almost as tall as the Prosecutor. Even at this distance a faint scar could be seen running down his cheek.

"Who's that with him?" Bao asked.

"Don't you recognize His Majesty, the Heir Apparent?" Hwo drawled sardonically.

"The Heir Apparent! And he's talking to Ju Anshih? Why that means the family of the…"

"It means nothing of the sort," Hwo rasped out. "The man is often in these quarters. He's performed deeds of one sort or another for half the families in the court. His being with the Heir Apparent means nothing." Hwo quickened his pace, leaving the two young men behind.

At this moment the man Ju looked up and saw Li and Bao watching him. A slow smile spread across his saturnine features. He winked, then turned back to his business with the next Emperor of All Under Heaven. Bao fingered the dagger he'd hidden inside the folds of his garment. He and Li hurried to catch up with Hwo Gwang.

"I'm sorry sir," Li said. "I meant nothing by my remarks. It's just that I was surprised to see so renowned a gangster as Ju Anshih speaking with the man who one day will be the Son of Heaven. You can be sure that neither I nor my cousin will say anything about this."

Hwo's face brightened visibly. "Save your oaths, my boy. If you or I don't mention him when we report to His Majesty, you can be sure old Jyang will. In fact if we mention it, no one will give it a second thought, as Ju has been hired by nearly everyone in the palace for some nefarious deed or another. If, on the other hand, we neglect to mention it, you can be sure someone else will, and that fat snake Jyang will hear of it and use it to make one more attack on my family. So when I call on you, be sure to tell the whole story. The truth may be our strongest weapon as it is a weapon seldom dusted off and used in palace politics."

"As you wish, sir." Li and Bao exchanged glances.

Hwo Gwang laughed out loud when he noted the look. "So you're shocked at our little court," he said. "So was I when I first arrived, but I soon learned better. You can be sure that nothing is as it seems here, and the sooner you learn that, the better off you'll be."

"That means we should trust no one," Bao said. Hwo looked hard at him. "Your cousin learns quickly," he told Li. "Listen to him." Then turning to Bao he told the boy in a low voice, "Trust no one but me. Trust me because you have no other choice."

Hwo abruptly turned and began to climb the steps of the palace.

CHAPTER THIRTEEN

Report To The Emperor

Hwo, Li and Bao were nearly the last to arrive in the throne room.

Jyang Choong was already in his accustomed place at the foot of the steps leading up to the throne. He would be on the Emperor's left. "For someone who hates the highborn, he certainly seems to enjoy keeping to a high position," Li muttered to his cousin. A piercing glance from the prosecutor made Li swallow hard. Could the man could read his thoughts.

The crowd gasped as the old general, Goongsun Heh, came into the room and took up a position at the Emperor's right hand. Once that had been the general's legal position, but recently he had stepped aside in favor of his son. Now the son was in the palace prison, accused of stealing some nineteen million cash that had been earmarked for provisioning the Northern Army for the upcoming year's campaign against the Huns.

Hwo Gwang grimaced as he saw the old general enter. Here was another weapon in Jyang's hands. Jyang had brought the charge against young Goongsun, and had quickly proven his case. The son's quick fall was all the more shocking in light of the father's status. Goongsun Heh had long since demonstrated his absolute loyalty to the Emperor, and to the Emperor's father before him. He'd backed Jing, the father of the current Emperor, during the Revolt of the Princes that had so nearly brought down the dynasty. He had fought bravely, if not too intelligently, against the rebels in the south during the campaign that followed the revolt. He had been part of the Wei faction ever since he married one of Lady Wei's sisters. Now his son was in disgrace and the old man's unexpected appearance gave Hwo Gwang one more thing to worry about. The old general must be planning to petition the Emperor for a pardon. Hwo wondered what else could possibly go wrong today.

The curtains behind the raised throne rustled. Two eunuchs stepped out from behind them. Silence fell. All but the general and a few other elders who had been granted exemption from the ceremony, dropped to their knees and bowed down till their foreheads touched the floor, performing the kowtow.

Li was tempted to raise his head so as to see what was happening, but as this was his first audience, he played things safe. Finally, with a surprisingly deep voice, one of the eunuchs called out, "Approach to the foot of the steps oh ye who have ought to transact!"

With as much dignity as they could muster, the crowd of mostly middle-aged courtiers clambered off their knees and to their feet.

Now Li could dart fleeting glances at the Emperor. So this was the man who ruled all that was civilized under Heaven. This was the Son of Heaven. All he saw was a tired old man who looked bored. The Emperor's eyes scanned the crowd, then fixed upon Li, who after a moment shifted his gaze toward the ground as was demanded by court etiquette.

"We observe, kinsman Hwo," began the Emperor, his voice surprisingly kindly sounding, "that you have brought someone new to the audience today."

"I have, Your Majesty. This is my assistant, Soong Li, the son of an old friend whom I have taken as a member of my staff. He has made an important discovery in the matter of the... passing on of the Korean girl, and I deemed it advisable that you hear his report directly."

A look of deep sadness passed over the Emperor's face. Li realized, with some surprise, that the Emperor had actually felt some genuine affection for his mistress.

Prosecutor Jyang stepped forward and bowed. "If it please Your Majesty," he said before stepping back to his place.

"Yes?" said the Emperor. "Speak, Jyang."

Jyang stepped forward again. "The death of the Korean girl was a result of witchcraft. Hwo Gwang, honorable though he might be, has no business in this matter, and any information he obtained should have been forwarded directly to me."

The Emperor turned his attention to Hwo Gwang. "Is this correct?" he asked. Jyang turned to Hwo, a sneer on his face.

"As I said, Majesty," Hwo continued as though he had not been interrupted by the Prosecutor. "My assistant has made some discoveries in this matter, and I deemed it proper to bring him before you so he might make his report directly."

"But Your Majesty," Jyang interrupted, not disguising his annoyance. "This is clearly a case of witchcraft. It is in my jurisdiction."

"It was not a murder by witchcraft!" All eyes shifted to Li, in astonishment at this breach of court etiquette. Li hastened to bow and shifted his eyes once more toward the ground.

"How so?" asked the Emperor. Hwo Gwang breathed a sigh of relief. The Emperor was apparently sufficiently curious as to overlook the breech of etiquette.

"Your Majesty," Li began. "Your servant has had some experience in medical matters. I was called to examine the body of the Korean woman when she was found this morning. This was at the request of my master Hwo Gwang and of the Prosecutor." Jyang raised his eyebrows at this but said nothing. Li continued.

"I noticed that the woman's skin was discolored. I had never seen anything like it. Even in the single case of witchcraft I saw in my village nothing of the sort appeared. Of course, at the time we first saw the body, there was no question of witchcraft. We all assumed it to have been a murder."

"How do you mean, discolored?" the Emperor broke in.

"Her skin was an odd shade of blue," Li said. "I've sometimes seen something like this in the case of the corpse of an exceedingly elderly man or woman, but this was much more pronounced. It was..." Li stopped when he noticed an uneasy look appear upon the Emperor's face.

"Go on," the Emperor said, quickly regaining control.

"As I examined the scene of the crime I happened to catch sight of a most unusual bit of writing," Li resumed. "The woman, as she died, had spilled some of her face powder on the floor. She must have done so deliberately, for she had then written a message in the powder."

"What?" the Emperor exclaimed. He turned to Jyang. "You said nothing of this to me." The muscles on Jyang's neck corded.

"It seemed of no importance," he said.

"What was the message?" The Emperor was looking at Li again.

"The woman had written the characters for 'murdered, not natural death,'" Li told him.

"And what conclusion did you draw from this?" the Emperor asked.

"None, at the time," Li answered. "I simply assumed the woman had somehow been murdered and had found a way to tell us that bald fact. I made no other assumptions until the doll was found."

"The shaman doll?" The Emperor shivered. Li nodded.

"So why do you come to Us now and claim that the woman was murdered, not by witchcraft, but by other means?"

"I come in the name of my Lord Hwo Gwang out of fear for the life of my Emperor," Li said. the Emperor sat up straight and stared fixedly at Li as a low murmur became audible in the throne room.

"How so?" asked the Emperor after a long pause.

"The Son of Heaven has been the target of many attacks through-out his exalted life," Li said. The murmurs, now of astonishment, grew louder. Such things were not to be mentioned. Li hurried on while he still could.

"As a result, I am sure Your Majesty takes precautions against witchcraft. All enemies are thereby confounded and All Under Heaven that is civilized prospers under His rule. But my fear is that someone has found a way to murder without leaving any traces, and that the real target of last night's attack was Your Majesty himself."

Again there were gasps in the room. That the Emperor often went to the Korean girl's bed was an open secret, but not one to be thrown into the Emperor's face. The Emperor seemed less disturbed than the courtiers by this breach of manners.

"How can you be so sure the woman was not the victim of witch-craft?" he asked.

"The appearance of the girl, for one," Li said. "Your Majesty's court is filled with learned men. Have any ever seen such an appearance in one who has been the object of witchcraft?"

"Let us find out," the Emperor replied. He signaled to one of the eunuchs, who immediately disappeared behind the curtains at the side of the throne, then reappeared a few minutes later from a door at the side of the throne room accompanied by several distinguished looking men.

"Put the question to these men," the Emperor told Li. Li described the appearance of the dead woman. The men consulted with each other, then faced the Emperor.

"Your Majesty," their spokesman began, "we must confess that none of us has ever before heard of such symptoms in a case of death by witchcraft." The savants began to leave, but Li spoke up.

"Begging pardon, Majesty," he said. "May we have these exalted men stay to supplement my meager knowledge?" Jyang snorted, but the Emperor motioned the men to stay.

"There's more?" the Emperor asked.

"Indeed there is, Sire," Li said.

"Get on with it then," the Emperor told him.

"The woman knew she was dying," Li said. "Those who die from witchcraft seldom realize they are dying until almost the very moment of their death." Li turned to the wise men. They exchanged looks and nodded in agreement.

"It doesn't take long to knock over a box of powder and write a character or two, if one has the will to do so," Jyang spat out. "That is hardly conclusive evidence."

"Agreed," Li said. "Not conclusive, but when added to the whole of the rest of the story, it makes for a strong indication."

"There's more?" the Emperor asked.

"Yes," Li told him. "Generally, witchcraft is accompanied by an issue of evil creatures from the body of the dead one. In the one case I ever saw, the body was covered by great sores from which crawled a multitude of noxious creatures. In this case, however, the body of the Korean woman was unmarked."

"Perhaps the poison remained within," Jyang remarked.

"I too wondered if that might be the case. That is why I went to the temple today. There I cut open the woman's belly, but found nothing untoward within." Now none of the courtiers bothered to mask their astonishment. Jyang all but roared his interruption.

"You dare to eviscerate one poisoned with witchcraft, and then face the Emperor," he shouted. "Take this man away and throw him into the eternal flames, lest he infect the Emperor with the poison he carries." Jyang all but pushed two of the attendant guards towards Li.

"Hold!" The Emperor was shouting now. The guards, who already had Li in their grasp, turned him loose and stepped back. Silence slowly fell on the crowd, though some murmuring continued in the back of the large room. The Emperor looked down at Li for a moment, then shifted his gaze to Hwo Gwang. Finally, his eyes rested on the prosecutor.

"I am the arbiter here," he said. Flushed, Jyang seemed ready to say something, but then thought better of it.

"Your will be done, Majesty," he finally said, bowing deeply. "Your servant was simply trying to safeguard the Imperial Person."

"We take no offense," the Emperor replied, more gently, and sat back once again. Jyang shot a look of pure hatred towards Li and his mentor Hwo.

"Now," said the Emperor. "Answer the question posed by the prosecutor. How do you dare deal with the body of one killed by witchcraft and then face your Emperor?"

"The woman was not killed by witchcraft," Li said. "I feel sure of that. There was no evidence of the gu insects within the woman's body and nothing about the way she died points to witchcraft."

"Go on," the Emperor prompted, waving away another protest by Jyang.

"The woman left a message," Li continued. "One who dies from the gu seldom knows the reason for their death. In fact, as Your Majesty well knows, one who suffers from the gu curse seldom even displays any overt symptoms until near the end. Various tests must be performed to discover the presence of the poison before then. This woman knew she was dying and left a message specifically stating that she was being murdered. That is hardly what one would expect from a person dying from the poisons of witchcraft."

"Can you really be so sure?" the Emperor asked.

"The woman obviously made a great effort to tell us of the nature of her death," Li replied. "That is not the act of someone dying of witchcraft. Add to that the fact that no evidence of gu poison was present in or on the woman's body, and our conclusion must be that she did not die naturally, but that it was not witchcraft that killed her."

The Emperor turned to Jyang. "What do you make of all this?" he asked. The prosecutor paused for a moment, seemingly to think.

"There is the matter of the image found buried behind the house where the girl died," he said, finally.

The Emperor turned to Li. "What of that?" he asked.

"I do not know," Li said. He too paused. "It could be that one who would kill the Son of Heaven and hide the fact, would use such methods to raise doubts and incriminate the innocent."

The Emperor turned back to Jyang. "Have you a reply to this?"

"I do," Jyang said, quickly now, and using his booming voice to good effect. "We have here a young man scarcely beyond the transition to manhood. He tells us a woman did not die in the manner supposedly appropriate to what afflicted her. The future of all the Civilized Lands may well rest on the truth or falsity of his claim, yet we are supposed to accept as conclusive the musings of this barely capped child. I suggest he may have had perhaps too much liquid refreshment while reflecting on the matter."

A ripple of laughter ran around the room at that. Even the Emperor smiled. He waved for Jyang to continue. "What proof does this child have? What fact does he bring before us?" Li flushed angrily at the emphasis Jyang had placed on the word "child" and started to interrupt. Simultaneous pokes in the ribs from the elbows of both Bao and Hwo Gwang brought him to his senses.

"Don't let him get to you," Bao whispered. "Use your brains." Hwo nodded his approval of this advice.

"I submit that the affairs of the Empire are too important to hinge on the words of so young a man," Jyang concluded. "We have ample evidence of witchcraft in this case. A thorough investigation ought to be made and the cause of this epidemic rooted out, even if this requires a general purge of the court." Hwo Gwang shuddered inwardly at this. He knew what such a purge would entail. Many thousands would die, the line of succession to the throne would change, and the prosecutor would do all that he could to extend the purge to every branch of the family of the heir apparent.

The Emperor turned to Li. "Do you have anything to say in reply?" he asked.

"Indeed I do, Majesty," Li said, projecting an assurance Bao was certain was feigned.

"Then by all means do so," the Emperor said.

"I repeat," Li said. "My cousin Bao and I went to the temple wherein lay the body of the dead woman. We investigated and found absolutely no evidence of gu poison. I ask Your Majesty to question the advisors. Has any of them ever heard of a case of wugu not accompanied by evidence of gu worms in the body of the victim?"

The Emperor looked to the old gentlemen. After a quick consultation the answer came. No one had ever heard of such a thing. The Emperor seemed relieved. After all, such things were highly contagious, and he'd been in intimate contact with the woman. He turned to Jyang.

"It would seem the young man has more of the truth on his side than you gave him credit for."

Jyang flushed. "Your Majesty," he boomed out. "Young Soong Li and your able servant Hwo Gwang have come up with some interesting theories, but I must still insist that precautions continue to be taken to protect against witchcraft. Through no fault of their own, Hwo Gwang and Soong Li have been misguided. They, and your medical advisors, are not familiar with all the varieties of wugu. I have heard, recently, of new forms having been brought in from the barbarian lands to the north. I really must insist that Your Majesty be protected."

"But Jyang," the Emperor chided, "the practitioners of the court have studied their discipline from repositories of medical lore reaching back to the days of the Yellow Emperor himself in the most remote of times. They have access to the lore of all civilizations since then. Surely you can not pretend to knowledge unknown to these practitioners of the court!"

"Your Majesty," Jyang replied. "You know, as does everyone here, that I have fought in the lands to the north. Some hold that against me, calling me a barbarian, but in this instance, at least, my knowledge may save the state. Young Soong is adept in the arts of our civilization, and I congratulate him on his keen mind and will to look to the good of the Emperor. He has, however, had no opportunity to learn the arts—or rather the devilish tricks—of the Huns who hammer at our frontiers." Jyang turned to Soong Li, but his malevolent smile was really directed at Hwo Gwang as he spoke to the young man.

"It may be that you will have heard more of such things after a longer period of service in the family of Hwo Gwang as there are many members of that clan who fight—or pretend to fight—on the northern borders." Jyang now transferred his nasty grin to the person of old Goongsun, who was in no position to reply to this slur against his son. Hwo Gwang stepped forward. He dared not remain silent in the face of this open assault on the family of the heir apparent.

"It is possible that our knowledge of wugu and how to use it against another is deficient," he began with a quick glace at the Emperor. "I will send the young man to your office where he is likely to gain a much more extensive knowledge of this hideous practice." Hwo paused and turned with a flourish towards Soong Li. It looked as though he was going to speak to the young man, but then stopped, thought for a moment, and turned back toward the prosecutor.

"On second thought," he said, loudly and with obvious malice, "those in your office may have entirely too much knowledge of this dangerous subject." Once again he turned to Soong Li.

"I forbid you to learn more of this subject than is necessary for the work of protecting the Emperor." Hwo Gwang swung back and fixed Jyang with a piercing stare. "Those who dabble in such arts tend to be seduced all too easily into their use." Jyang turned livid, the veins standing out on his forehead.

"Your Majesty!" he exclaimed. "Such accusations are beneath the dignity of..."

The Emperor held up his hand for silence. "Enough!" he commanded, "We are not here to squabble with one another. We are here to look to the safety of the Royal Person and so of the Empire." Both Hwo and Jyang bowed.

"Of course, Your Majesty," they said, almost in unison. The Emperor turned to Jyang.

"What do you suggest I do to resolve this matter?" he asked. Hwo Gwang flushed at this obvious slight. As a member of the royal family he should have been asked such a question first, but he dared not object at this point. Jyang smiled, but before he could speak Soong Li broke into the conversation.

"There is more, Majesty," he said. The Emperor looked down at him with arched eyebrows.

"Yes?"

"After leaving the temple wherein lay the girl's body, we were attacked by brigands who tried to kill us. If we had not made a significant discovery, why would someone have attacked us?"

"Why indeed?" asked the Emperor. He turned to Jyang. "You know of this?" he asked. Jyang shook his head no.

The Emperor turned back to Li. "Tell us of the events you have just alluded to." Li told the entire story, not omitting the identity of the leader of the assassins. As he finished, the Emperor continued to muse, hand on his chin.

"There seems to be more to this affair than meets the eye," he said finally. "I think I will reserve judgment until more proof can be offered by one side or the other." The Emperor turned to Jyang.

"You will continue your investigations into the matter as though Our Person had been directly attacked by means of witchcraft." Jyang nodded solemnly as he received the charge. The Emperor next turned to Hwo Gwang.

"You will continue to investigate the matter under the assumption that it was a murder of the common kind," he said. Hwo Gwang nodded. The Emperor continued. "This young man, Soong Li, is to remain at your side?"

"Yes Majesty," Hwo Gwang said.

"Good," the Emperor said. "I have been much impressed by his work in this matter." Li blushed. Hwo Gwang bowed low. "Now," said the Emperor, "to matters more nearly at hand. The man Ju Anshih is to be arrested. He seems to have something to do with this and I wish to know what that might be."

"There was a cough from the right side of the throne at this moment. The Emperor turned in that direction. Goongsun Heh was not ready to speak. He flushed, then worked up the nerve to begin.

"Your Majesty?" he began, his voice almost breaking.

"Yes Lord Goongsun?" The old man was stung by the formality of the Emperor's phrasing. In the old days...

"Your Majesty," Goongsun began again, determined to push on. "Warrants of arrest have been served on Ju Anshih before, and yet he's never been brought in. He has many friends—or rather I should say he has the goods on so many people—that he's always managed to head for the hills and evade capture until the storm has blown over." The Emperor was glaring at Goongsun, only too well aware of the close connections Ju had kept with the courtiers, but Goongsun was determined to have his say at all costs.

"The point is, Your Majesty, that I would like to lead a party of old military men of my acquaintance to capture this fellow who has always gotten away so smartly before. To be frank about it, I have a better chance than any of the rest of this crowd of young whipper-snappers." Heh glared at Jyang who merely responded with a polite smile.

"If I succeed in this task," Heh resumed, "I know Your Majesty will be merciful to me in this time of trouble for my family. I..."

"Very well," the Emperor broke in. "We remember well the service and loyalty you've given the Throne. If you succeed, We will forgive that silly young man who is your son, but take care, Heh old boy, that you and your family walk a straighter line in the future." The old man smiled broadly, responding more to the familiar tone into which the Emperor had lapsed than to the overt threat uttered in that tone.

"Thank you, Majesty," he said, bowing low. "Thank you. You may be sure that in the future nothing of the kind of thing that has befallen my family will happen again."

"I shall take that as a promise," the Emperor said. He rose, all but the elders bowed down to the floor, and he left the room.

CHAPTER FOURTEEN

Plotters

I don't know how, but the young fool seems to have figured most of it out!"

Jyang was raging.

The shaman watched the prosecutor patiently. Finally, his rage spent, Jyang sat down, poured himself a bowl of stillbeer and drank.

"He can prove nothing," the shaman said.

"He can upset everything," Jyang snarled.

"We can use him," replied the shaman.

"How?" demanded the prosecutor. The shaman smiled.

"We shall see," the shaman smiled. "We shall see."

CHAPTER FIFTEEN

Bagging A Bandit

"Will Lord Goongsun be able to catch Ju?" Li asked as he and Bao followed Hwo out of the throne room.

"Hard to say," Hwo responded, gloomily. "Ju is a slippery character with powerful friends. I shouldn't be surprised if old Goongsun has bitten off more than he can chew."

"It was a last chance for him," Bao said. "In his place I'd have done the same. What's the good of standing by and doing nothing when there's a chance for some action?"

"I suppose so," Hwo said doubtfully. "I'd have preferred to negotiate my son's freedom. One is more in control of a negotiation"

"Action gets results. Talk brings nothing but more talk," Bao said, rather more forcefully than was necessary. Hwo smiled grimly.

"You'll not last long at court with that sort of talk."

"Perhaps not," Bao replied, "but with the trouble your family is in, doing nothing will ruin them even more certainly."

Hwo's heavy eyebrows rose. He was not used to such direct talk from anyone, let alone from so young and undistinguished a man. But the main avenue of the court was no place to exert discipline overtly. "Perhaps you'd better explain yourself," he said softly.

"If you don't think the old general can catch Ju Anshih," Bao replied, "perhaps we'd better do something to make sure the man is captured."

Bao ignored Li's reproachful look and continued. "We know where Ju hangs out. Let's go in and get him."

"How do we know that?" Hwo asked, amused at the young man's brashness.

"Well," Bao replied, flushing, "we know what section of town he's likely to be hanging out in at least."

"And where might that be?" Hwo asked.

"In the east marketplace," Bao responded. "That's where all the rougher element hang out. Ju is the prince of the thieves, so it's reasonable to assume he'd go to ground there."

"That's easy enough to say," Hwo rejoined. "Probably it's even true, but finding someone who doesn't want to be found in the east marketplace is a risky business."

"We have no alternative," Bao said forcefully. Once more Li nudged his cousin in the ribs, but still to no avail. Bao merely paused long enough to rub his chin reflectively, unaware that Hwo was doing the same thing.

"What do you have in mind?" Hwo asked finally.

"A trap," Bao responded.

"To spring a trap you have to be able to first find the rat," Li broke in. "Ju knows half the city is searching for him. He also knows how to drop out of sight and stay there. He's been through this before and always come out intact."

"What are the alternatives?" Bao asked again. Neither Li nor Hwo Gwang could reply.

Some hours later two scruffy looking characters left Hwo Gwang's headquarters complex by the rear entrance. Anyone passing by might have mistaken them for employees going home for the day save for the fact that Hwo Gwang generally demanded a better appearance in his servants. The two made for the east marketplace, following instructions hurriedly given them. Their destination was a restaurant and saloon called the Rotten Cabbage.

"Well," Li said as the two paused at the door of the saloon, "here we are."

"I'm thrilled," Bao said dryly. He looked around, taking note of a figure sliding into the shadows across the way. He fingered his knife. Li directed a quizzical look at his cousin.

"This was your idea. Why are you so upset about being here?"

"We have to be here, but that doesn't mean I have to like the idea," Bao responded. He pushed past Li and into the Rotten Cabbage.

The stench of fermented cabbage was almost palpable. Heavy smoke filled the room, which was hardly brighter than the alley outside the door despite the several lamps scattered around the perimeter of the room. "Heaven above," Bao whispered. "What a stench."

"If it smells like that, think what it tastes like," Li whispered back. "I'm not so sure this was a good idea after all. I don't mind the prospect of our imminent deaths, but I think I may not be able to face a plateful of that stuff." By now the two had reached a small bar at one end of the room.

"Two Kim chi and a warmed jug," Bao demanded in as rough a voice as he could muster. The barman reached around and threw onto two dishes two scoops of the noxious concoction that gave the place its name. Li wondered which had more filth adhering to its surface, the barman's hand or the plate he'd piled the stuff onto. The two picked up their dishes and carried them to a low table off in one corner, well into the shadows. They squatted down and looked around the place. They saw no one familiar.

"What now?" Bao whispered.

"Eat up," Li grinned. "This was your idea. I suggest you take the lead." Bao looked down at the limp shredded cabbage and the unidentifiable red and green specks that dotted its surface. He made a face, then picked up a bit and tentatively tucked it into his mouth. He began to chew, and chew, and chew, seemingly unwilling or unable to swallow.

Li laughed, then attacked the food as though he hadn't eaten in weeks. Having wolfed the stuff down in a few seconds, he then sat back, smacked his lips, and rubbed his stomach. "Delicious," he said, somewhat unnecessarily, and belched. He watched Bao turn green, his own queasy stomach somewhat soothed by the sight of his cousin's obvious discomfort.

"What have we here? Two young birds ripe for the plucking." The two boys hadn't noticed the approach of the speaker, a short, heavily muscled man, who looked as though he could, and probably had, killed with his bare hands.

Bao jumped at the sudden intrusion and upset his plate of food. Li wondered how much this was an accident and how much an excuse not to eat any more of the stuff. Li himself looked up at the man as calmly as his throbbing heart would allow.

"Do I know you, sir?" he asked. A hard backhand blow sent him sprawling off the scruffy seating mat into the mess that passed for a floor in the saloon.

"You will speak when I ask you to speak," snarled the man.

Li rubbed a seep of blood from his lip, then looked up.

"I only wish…" This time it was a kick. He barely saw it coming, but managed to duck far enough away so that most of the force of the blow was lost. Still, he went sprawling again. This time he lay silent, waiting for the man's next move. Bao remained at the table, rigid and white faced. The other customers in the bar seemed oblivious to the drama being played out in the shadows. The man squatted down next to the table.

"You might duck arrows and lead us a merry chase through the city, but you've pushed your luck beyond the limits in coming here," he said. "You should have died this morning. Thank the spirits that protect you. You've gained an extra day of life, but now it's over." He reached into a fold of his cloak and pulled out a long, slightly curved and very sharp looking knife.

"Kill us and Ju will kill you," Bao spat out quickly. He braced for the blow he knew would be coming. He was not disappointed. One of the short man's confederates delivered it across Bao's back, sending him bumping along the floor to Li's side. He looked up to see the short man looking speculatively at him.

"Explain," the short man finally grunted.

"Thunderstone," Bao said.

"Thunderstone?"

"In almost unlimited quantities," Bao said. He nodded to Li, who reached inside his grubby garment. Instantly a half dozen knives were at his throat. The short man held up his hand to stay their final thrust. Li slowly withdrew the pouch he had shown Bao earlier that day.

"As you know," he said, bracing himself for another blow, "I work in the household of Hwo Gwang, mentor to the Heir Apparent."

The blow did not come and the short man nodded for Li to go on.

"I have found a way to obtain some of the thunderstone collected by the Emperor as a safeguard against witchcraft. My position in the household of Hwo Gwang allows me access to the palace and the course of my duties allows me access to the imperial storage chambers. The Emperor has more of the stuff than he'd ever be able to use, so I though it fair that a commoner from a small village to the north have a chance to improve his own position." Li looked around at the men who surrounded him and grinned. "After all," he resumed, "most of you have taken advantage of, shall we say, opportunities?" Several of the men grinned back and a chuckle or two was heard. Emboldened, Li wriggled up from the floor back onto the seating mat, not taking the trouble to dust himself off.

"I know of only one man who could make proper use of the materials I have managed to obtain," Li said after he'd poured himself a bowl of stillbeer. He hoisted the stillbeer and winked at the short man. "Ju would know what to do with my modest find," he said.

"And how do I know you aren't here to find Ju and turn him over to the authorities?" demanded the short man.

Li made an elaborate ceremony of looking around the room, then he laughed out loud. "I don't think I see too many authority figures here," he shouted merrily. Even the short man grinned at that. Several of his men laughed out loud. The short man stood, then made his way to Li's side.

"Come friend," he said. "There is always room for profit. If you can show the way to some, our friend Ju Anshih will reward you greatly. He reached out and put his arm around Li in a friendly gesture. Li winked at Bao, extremely pleased with himself. A moment later sweat was bursting from hi pores as he found himself pinned to the wall of the saloon by a powerful hand encircling his neck.

"On the other hand," snarled the man, "if you're trying anything funny, you'll die, slowly and painfully." The man shook Li once, then released his hold. Li slumped, then felt himself jerked erect as the man once more became jovial.

"Come," said the man. "Let us go to Ju and see what we can do with this gift you've brought us from the Celestial One." Li felt himself being propelled into the street, then pushed first one way and then another as the group moved through the winding alleys of the market district.

Perhaps ten minutes passed before the group reached its destination. They stood before a rough looking hovel, seemingly one of the poorest in the city. Li thought that Ju Anshih must be living in fear indeed if he chose to live in such a place. Ju was very rich. This place was a dump.

The short man gave some sort of a sign. Three men detached themselves from the group, made a reconnaissance, then reported back. The short man turned and knocked at the door of the hovel. A breathtakingly beautiful woman opened the door and ushered the three men into the front room. The short man disappeared into the back reaches of the house, leaving Li and Bao alone with the woman. Expensive tapestries covered the walls. Elegant furnishings were tastefully scattered about the floor. Every detail was where it should be. This was obviously not a house to be judged by its exterior.

"Welcome to my humble home." Accompanied by the short man, Ju Anshih had entered the room from the rear through some door behind the hangings. He made his way to the center of the room where he sat before a low, ornately decorated table. "Bring my guests refreshment."

At Ju's gesture the woman who had answered the door left the room, then quickly returned, carrying a tray with a variety of fermented juices in cups on it.

"I'm told you can obtain large quantities of thunderstone," Ju said after his two guests had been served. Li nodded, sipping on his drink.

"I can," he replied.

"You have proof of this?" Ju asked. Li turned to the short man who'd taken his pouch filled with the powdered material and held out his hand. The man gave him the pouch. Li carefully poured a bit of its contents into the palm of the gangster. Ju clapped the stuff off his hand with a careless gesture. Li and Bao stared at him in astonishment.

"Powder," Ju snorted. "Anyone may carry a bag of powder about. What kind of proof is that?"

"What proof do you require?" Li asked.

"Whole thunderstone," Ju responded. "Produce it now or they'll find you floating face down in the river tomorrow."

"I have none," Li said.

"Take them out and kill them," Ju said to the short man.

"Wait!" Bao shouted in panic. "We can tell you where to get some!" Ju held up his hand, stopping the short man.

"If you value your life, tell me now," he demanded.

"In our lodgings," Bao sputtered, ignoring Li's protests. "We have some hidden in our rooms."

"If you'll simply release us for a short time, we'll gladly go and get the stones," Li interjected. "You have nothing to fear from us. All we want is a small profit for ourselves and a large one for…"

"Silence!" Ju shouted. Li stopped abruptly and stood, head bowed.

"Where are the stones hidden?" the bandit asked after a moment's pause. "Perhaps we can do business after all. I am informed that no one followed you here. I was sure you were sent to ferret me out. Perhaps I was wrong."

"Oh, indeed sir," Li said in his most ingratiating tone. "I am nothing more than a poor boy from the country who…" Ju gestured impatiently and Li found himself once more sprawled on a floor, albeit a considerably cleaner one than before.

"Your friend talks rather too much," Ju said to Bao.

"A fault I've often commented on," Bao replied.

Li rubbed a sore elbow, then lifted himself up onto the mat again.

"Tell me where the stones are hidden," Ju said. "I'll send a man. If he finds them, all will be well with you. If not, you'll wish you'd never been born to woman." Bao quickly told Ju and his man where the thunderstones could be found and a man was dispatched to the place.

It was nearly half an hour before the man returned with another small leather pouch carefully cradled in his hands. He handed the pouch to Ju who opened it and spilled its contents—two small but clearly genuine thunderstones—into his palm. He whistled softly.

"You really were telling the truth," he said. "If you were to be caught with these in your possession, your heads would be on the block within the day."

"Of course I was telling the truth," Li replied.

"Profit is profit, and you're the one who can bring it to me." Ju looked at home for a long moment, then turned to the short man. "Kill them."

"What!" Li exclaimed. "Why?"

"You're dangerous to me," Ju said, his eyes glittering. The short man drew a knife and began moving towards the cousins.

"I thought we had a deal," Li said, pleadingly.

"I never make deals that can turn on me," Ju snarled. "You came to me. I did not come to you. We had no agreement." The short man was very close now. He raised his knife to strike.

Bao was quick as a snake. As the short man raised his arm Bao sprang onto him. Bao's knife flashed once, then disappeared into the short man's rib cage. The short man flexed his entire body in a spasm of pain, then threw Bao off, turned and went after him. They circled round the room, the one stalking, the other striving desperately to stay out of reach. Blood soaked the short man's clothing. Finally he managed to corner Bao and his knife was poised to thrust again when the door burst open and Hwo Gwang rushed in, sword at the ready. Hwo Gwang took in the situation instantly and moved rapidly. One sword thrust and the short man lived no more. He looked around.

"Where's Ju Anshih?" he shouted.

"This way!" The call came from the next room. It was Li. Hwo Gwang rushed to him, Bao on his heels. They had entered an empty room.

"Here," came the call again. A draft of cold air drew their attention to an opening in the side of the room. The den of the fox always has an escape route. Hwo Gwang and Bao rushed toward it. Li was doubled up on the door of the escape tunnel, gasping for air. He held a knife in his hand. It had blood on it. He pointed.

"After him," he croaked. Hwo Gwang motioned and a half dozen soldiers rushed down the escape passage. Five minutes later they dragged a limping Ju Anshih back up the passage into the room.

"Bad enough," the gangster snarled, "to be run to ground by a boy, but of all the foul luck it has to be one of yours."

Ju was speaking to Hwo Gwang, but glaring at Li. His ankle was bleeding profusely from where Li's knife had severed the tendon as Ju had run past.

"I caught him running away," Li explained. "He threw me to the ground and kicked me in the stomach so hard I don't think I'll ever eat properly again, but as I went down I managed to make one swing of my knife."

"You made it count," Hwo Gwang said approvingly. "You certainly made it count." He crossed over to Ju.

"So," he said, "the old fox is taken at last."

"You've taken me," Ju snarled, "but keeping me may be a different matter. I'll find a way to get loose and when I do I'll kill the men who were supposed to make sure no one followed from the Rotten Cabbage."

"But no one did follow," Hwo Gwang said, a rare broad smile splitting his long sallow face.

"How did you find me, then?" Ju asked, amazement on his face.

"A simple stratagem developed by our friend Bao here," Hwo Gwang said, smiling even more broadly. "He knows your reputation, both for taking pains and for greed. He allowed your men to capture him and his friend over here with the quick knife and to bring both of them to this house. No one followed, for they would surely have been discovered. No, Ju. Our men didn't follow from the Rotten Cabbage. They followed from the boys' lodgings. Bao figured you'd be unable to resist the chance of profit from the thunderstones. So he knew you would send someone to fetch them, and we waited for him there and followed your very own man to your den. He had no reason to suspect a trap, and so led us right to your door." Hwo Gwang was by now laughing aloud, as were his soldiers. He made a motion and Ju was dragged off.

"You're taking him to prison?" Bao asked.

"No," Hwo replied. "They're instructed to deliver him to the old general."

"Why?" asked Bao.

"By delivering him to the general, I gain an even stronger ally than

I had before, for I thereby save the general's son. I also remove a stain from one who is part of my family and that of the Heir Apparent. I gain everything and lose only a little credit. And even that is not lost, for there are those who will see that the Emperor learns of this. My loyalty to friends is proved, an embarrassment to the Emperor is removed, and the job is done. Who could ask for more?

The celebration lasted well into the night.

CHAPTER SIXTEEN

More Death, The Bandit Turns The Tables

"Ah," Li sighed, drawing deeply of the morning air, air that somehow as they strode along the main avenue leading to the audience hall. "Today should be a great day indeed."

"Oh?" grunted Bao.

"Of course," Li responded, choosing not to notice his cousin's sour mood. "We caught Ju Anshih, saving some of our patron's relatives, and will be heroes once Ju is exposed as the murderer of the Emperor's mistress. What could be wrong?"

"The way things have been going, I'm sure something awful will turn up," Bao grumbled.

"Don't be so sour," Li rejoined. "One would think you'd just bitten into a piece of fruit and found half a worm."

"Being around you too long seems to produce that effect," Bao groused.

"Oh, come now," Li objected with a grin. "Everything's worked out well so far, hasn't it?"

"So to speak," Bao rejoined, refusing to shed his air of gloom.

"Ah, brighten up," Li said, impatiently. "Nothing can go wrong on a day like today." After a final grunt Bao lapsed into a mulish silence as they approached the audience hall.

Today, as the young men came into the throne room there was a difference in the attitude of the crowd toward them. Their entrance, ignored the previous day, was now the occasion for a flurry of whispered comments, and a respectful path was cleared for them as they made their way toward the throne. They had just reached their assigned place when Ju Anshih was led in. The old gangster grinned towards the two young men as he was led past. "I don't like it," Bao whispered.

"You never like it," Li responded.

"Why isn't he more worried?" Bao asked, ignoring the sarcastic tone in his friend's voice.

Before Li could reply, the eunuch had entered the room and announced the Emperor.

Li, less impressed than he had been yesterday, risked a peek at the entrance after assuming the kneeling position with his forehead touching the floor. The Emperor swept into the room, a grim look on his face. Li knew why Hwo Gwang hadn't accompanied them to the audience when his employer slipped into the audience hall a few feet behind the Emperor. Once the Emperor seated himself, the two began to speak intently, obviously continuing a conversation begun in private earlier. Li saw the look of hatred Jyang fixed on his rival as the courtiers again rose to their feet at the eunuch's signal.

The noise caused by the Emperor's entrance had not yet subsided before the old general was speaking. "See what I've caught for Your Majesty," the old man cackled.

"We see," replied the Emperor, the coldness of his voice putting a chill on the old general's self-satisfaction. Though taken aback by the Emperor's manner, the old general was not to be stopped. His son's life hung in the balance, and any risk was worth that prize.

"I always… uh… do what I have promised for Your Majesty," the general stuttered. "Just as Your Majesty always keeps his own word," he added weakly when he detected no reaction from the Emperor.

"Indeed," the Emperor replied coldly after a long and embarrassing pause.

"So then," continued the general, his voice growing fainter, "my son will be released and restored to me?" Once again there was a long silence. The general, desperate now, continued speaking.

"Of course," he said, making his point with a desperate stubbornness, "my son and I will want to make sure there is no more disturbance caused by this unfortunate incident, so we will do something I have always wanted to do once my army days were behind me. I have made arrangements for my son and myself to retire to a little cottage in the countryside where I will enjoy the pleasures of retired life after long service to my Emperor. My son and grandchildren will remain safely by my side to comfort me in my old age."

Again there was a pause. Finally the Emperor spoke. "Just so," he said, his tone still cold, but the import of the words restoring life to the family of the old general. The general dropped heavily to his knees and knocked his head repeatedly on the floor.

"Thank you, Majesty," he said after each time his head struck the floor, then scrambled to his feet. "I pray that it will be possible to get to the bottom of this business and…" The Emperor held up a hand.

"Go! Collect your son and reap the rewards of your long and faithful service," he said. The general looked up at the man he had served for so long, began once again to speak, thought better of it, turned and walked away, tears over welling his eyes.

"Now then," said the Emperor after the old general had made his way from the room. "We must get on with the matter before us." He glared at Ju Anshih, who, to Li's amazement, seemed not the least bit worried. The Emperor turned to the prosecutor.

"Conduct the questioning," he ordered. Jyang bowed, then stepped forward and faced the wily old criminal. The two men stared at each other for a moment, neither of them backing down. Finally the prosecutor turned and with a dramatic gesture pointed to Li. "Our young friend here seems to feel you had something to do with the death of Kim Soo, a member of the household of His Majesty. What have you to say about that?"

"If this young man accuses me, he lies," Ju responded. The room buzzed with suppressed conversation.

"You can prove that?" asked Jiang.

"I can."

"Do so."

"I was with His Royal Highness, the Heir apparent on the night the young lady died. His Highness and several of his household can verify that fact."

"Indeed," Jyang said. Li could hear the gloating tone in the man's voice. "So if you are involved, the family of the Heir Apparent is also involved?" There was a gasp of shock from the courtiers at the boldness of this attack on the Heir Apparent.

"I am not involved," Ju shouted suddenly. "You won't frame me for this. I run errands for all you pretty people in the palace. I know who does what and who goes where. If you try to frame me for this, I'll talk like you've never heard anyone talk." Ju looked about him, fixing first one courtier, then another with a gaze that seemed to say, "Back me on this or you'll get yours alongside me." The old gangster swung back around to Jyang.

"Bring me writing utensils. You want to get to the bottom of things?" Ju glanced at the Emperor. "If I start writing, there won't be enough bamboo growing on South Mountain to make the writing slips I'll need to tell everything that's gone on in this court." Jyang could not suppress a cold smile at the obvious discomfort caused by Ju's words among the assembled courtiers.

"The lies of a gangster are of no consequence to us," he said. "For a few cash I can have any story I wish from one of the storytellers in the wine shops of the city."

Ju grinned back at the prosecutor. "I don't need to make up tales," he said. He patted his robes. "I know who ordered the killing and I have the proof."

"What?" Now even Jyang seemed to be thrown off balance.

"I have letters," Ju said with a leer. "I can prove the truth of my words." Jyang turned to the Emperor, who merely gazed levelly back at him. Nor did Hwo Gwang appear to be surprised.

"What do you mean, letters?" Jyang demanded of Ju. "From whom?" About what?" Talk, villain!"

"You couldn't stop me if you tried," Ju commented dryly. "The Princess Yangshih and the Princess Juyi, the daughters of the Empress Wei, mother of the Heir Apparent, are responsible for the crime, not I."

All eyes swung to the Emperor. Everyone at court was familiar with these two women. There was a chilly silence as everyone waited for the Emperor to speak.

"Hwo Gwang has warned Us that such might be the case," the Emperor said, finally. "It is with a great deal of pain that We learn of such matters, but justice must prevail." The Emperor's gaze rested on Ju. "Present your proof," he demanded.

Ju reached into his gown and pulled a scroll of silk from it. He handed the scroll to Jyang, who hastily unrolled and began to silently read the first of what appeared to be several sheets which it contained. Though he moved his lips, no sound issued from them. The Emperor loudly cleared his throat. Jyang started and then blushed.

"Pardon, Majesty," he said. "I merely wished to see that nothing had been inserted into the scroll that would bring harm to the Imperial Person."

"We understand, and approve," the Emperor said. "Approach, and hold the document so that We might read it." Jyang obeyed. The Emperor examined each of the letters in turn, but without touching them. His face darkened with anger as he read. Finally he spoke.

"Bring the women." Messengers hurried from the throne room. A few moments later there was a flurry of activity as one of the messengers returned, whispered something to Jyang, and then at Jyang's instruction, rushed to the Emperor, bowed deep and spoke.

"The two women in question are dead."

"Dead?" questioned the Emperor. "How?"

"They committed suicide, Sire."

"Suicide? Why?"

"A note was left, Sire." The servant handed the Emperor another piece of silk. The Emperor reached out for it, then stopped.

"Jyang," he called out. Before the prosecutor could respond, Hwo Gwang had stepped to the Emperor's side.

"Allow me, Sire," he said, grasping the piece of silk and holding it up for the Emperor. Jyang flushed but said nothing and merely shifted to a position where he too could read the note.

"They claim to have committed no crime," the Emperor said.

"Your Majesty has read the letters provided by Ju Anshih," said Jyang. "They clearly state that these sisters, maternal relatives of the Heir Apparent, had come to feel a hatred for the young Korean girl, Kim Soo, because of your love for her. By their own hand it is written that they feared lest your love for this girl lead to the displacing of the Empress Wei from your affections and the naming of a new Heir Apparent. They further state that they had asked Ju what measures could be taken against the girl."

All eyes turned to Ju. "And what was your advice?" Jyang bellowed at the gangster.

"I told them that nothing could be done which would bring harm to a person so near to the throne," Ju replied.

"Nothing?" Jyang echoed.

"Nothing that I could do, at any rate," Ju answered.

"And what was their answer to that?"

"They simply said they'd have to look into other methods, if I would not help."

"Methods such as witchcraft?"

"I didn't ask."

Hwo Gwang stepped forward to deflect the interrogation from this awkward topic. "May I suggest, Majesty, that we repair to the scene of the women's deaths. There is no profit in a discussion of such things at the morning audience."

"On the contrary, Sire," Jyang interrupted, pulling out all the stops on his powerful voice. "There is a question of treason here. If members of the family of the Heir Apparent have been guilty of plotting against a member of the harem, that fact must be discovered and all the plotters eliminated as soon as possible."

"I agree." Hwo Gwang's voice was less formidable than the prosecutor's but there was a quality about it, over and above his reputation for cleverness, that always compelled attention. "If these surmises be true, the conspiracy they point to must indeed be rooted out, but before all the facts are known, a formal audience is hardly the place to proceed. Surely the chief of all the civilized lands' prosecutors would agree?"

Jyang knew when he was cornered. "Agreed," he muttered.

"Then it's settled," the Emperor said. "We will meet, the three of us, in an hour. In the meantime you, Hwo Gwang, and your two assistants will accompany the prosecutor to investigate these new deaths."

"And what of Ju?" asked the prosecutor.

"Keep him imprisoned," replied the Emperor. "It appears he's had nothing to do with the matters before us, but we may need to question him further." The Emperor's aged eyes took on a sparkle of amusement for a moment, and from that the assembled courtiers could begin to understand what a formidable man he had once been.

"Besides," the Emperor added, "the old rascal's been avoiding much deserved trips to my guest rooms in the prison for years now. An extra night's rest in them won't hurt." With that the Emperor turned and left the room. Immediately afterward, Hwo Gwang, Soong Li, Chiang Bao and the prosecutor also departed for the dead women's rooms.

"I told you something would go wrong," Bao muttered to Li as they passed the guards and entered the harem.

CHAPTER SEVENTEEN

Terror In The Harem

A loud, piercing scream greeted the men as they entered the harem. Unseen feet scurried away followed by loud shouts for help.

Jyang broke into a trot, motioning the others to follow.

A crowd had gathered at the entrance to one of the innumerable rooms making up the harem's portion of the palace.

Jyang pushed forward, roughly elbowing his way through the women and eunuchs crowding around the door. Hwo Gwang, Li, and Bao followed, taking advantage of the wide gap created by Jyang's passing.

The scene that greeted them as they burst into the room was one of confusion. Two women were sitting on the floor of the room. They were attended by a number of serving maids. Hwo sucked in his breath. Li looked a question at him.

"The Princess Yangshih and the Princess Juyi," Hwo muttered, a grim look on his face.

"But I thought…"

"Obviously not," Hwo said. "This really spills the bowl of fat into the fire." He quickly walked over to where Jyang was observing the women, a bemused smile on his face.

"So," Jyang said, "you live?"

The two women looked first toward Jyang and then to Hwo Gwang. Their faces were a pasty grey color.

"Something happened," the elder of the two said.

"Indeed," Jyang coldly replied. "The letters you wrote to your lover, the young traitor Goongsun have been read in court." What little color they had now drained from the women's faces.

The youngest sister spoke. "Lover?" she said. "We have taken no lover. That would be a death offense. We have no wish to die. What are you talking about?"

"Ju Anshih has presented us with letters written by your hand," Jyang said. "There is no doubt about that." The eldest sister broke into sobs. The younger leaned over to comfort her. Jyang motioned to the harem guards who had followed the four officials into the women's chambers.

"Take these two," he said. "They will receive their punishment at the afternoon audience." The guards seized the women and led them off.

"Come," Jyang said. he wheeled and left the room, Hwo Gwang and Bao in his wake. Li lingered, then spoke to one of the serving maids who had been helping the women as the four men had entered the room. "What happened?" he asked. The girl gave him a frightened look. This was obviously the first time she had ever spoken to a man from the outside.

"Come woman," Li said impatiently. "What happened here?"

"We found them dead," the frightened girl whispered.

"Obviously not dead," Li said.

"Dead," the girl insisted. "They were dead." She made a sign to ward off evil. "They were dead, but now they live."

"How is that possible?" Li asked. The girl's face took on an even more frightened look.

"They turned blue and died," she said. "Then they lived."

"What are you doing here?" The roar of the voice from behind Li caused him to jump. The girl cowered into a corner.

Jyang had returned.

"No one may stay in the living quarters of the harem and live," Jyang shouted. "If you value your life, come. Now!"

The prosecutor wheeled and strode from the room. Li hesitated a moment more.

"Now!" the prosecutor shouted again, this time from the hallway. The girl bolted from the room. Li shrugged and followed Jyang out of the harem.

CHAPTER EIGHTEEN

Sentenced To Die. Again!

The afternoon audience was crowded. Word had spread that something important was afoot. All the important courtiers as well as those who had hopes of becoming important had done their best to wangle invitations to this audience.

The preliminary formalities were barely over when the two sisters, the daughters of Empress Wei, herself chief consort to the Emperor and mother of the Heir Apparent were led in. The assembled courtiers seemed to hold their breath as one man. The possibilities of this situation were imponderable. On this day the future course of the civilized world might be decided.

The women were still being treated with some respect, though it was evident that they had been tortured not long before. That was not true of Goongsun Heh and his son. They were dragged before the Emperor and thrown to the hard floor. The marks left on them by the official torturer were clearly in evidence.

The younger Goongsun lay quietly where he'd been thrown, his spirit apparently as broken as his body by the events of the day. The old man was less easily cowed. He dragged himself to his feet and stood before the throne, his head bowed in submission, but his back straight, as befitted a former general of the empire.

Prosecutor Jyang strode to the front, bowed to the Emperor and began. "Goongsun Heh," he barked at the old man. "Your son, the issue of your loins, has been accused by the man Ju Anshih of lying with the daughters of the Lady Wei, Yangshih and Juyi. He has letters to prove the matter. You are the man's father. You are responsible for this treason. Are you ready to die?"

Heh drew himself even more erect. "If the charges are true, I am ready to die. My son will have dishonored me and my family."

Jyang motioned to the guards who had brought the two men in. The guards took hold of young Goongsun and none too gently dragged him to his feet. The young man stumbled, caught himself, then stood, albeit none too erectly, a slack expression on his face.

"Is the charge true?" Jyang asked. For a moment the question seemed to make no impression on the young man, but then he suddenly dropped to his knees and tried to crawl toward the Emperor.

"Save me, Majesty! Have mercy! Save me!" he cried out. The old general looked at his son with disgust. The guards seized him and threw him back.

"At least die like a man," old Goongsun spat out when his son once again stood beside him. The young man stood, pale and cowed, but remained silent.

"Please forgive the behavior of my son," Goongsun called out to the Emperor. "We are ready to face the punishment we deserve. I no longer wish to live, for my family has caused inexcusable grief to the family of the Emperor. I ask only that His Majesty remember the service of his general, Goongsun Heh, and allow this disgrace to die with him." The old man bowed toward the throne, then stood silent.

The Emperor's face softened for a moment as he addressed his old friend. "We do indeed recall the service of the man Goongsun Heh. He served Us faithfully and well. But his issue has brought disgrace to his family. Nevertheless I will pardon him for that, and will allow a quick and painless death to him and his unworthy son." Heh bowed, tears in his eyes.

"And our burial?" he asked.

"We will see to your honorable burial," the Emperor said.

"Thank you, Your Majesty. I go willingly to my death, my thoughts full of the admiration I feel for the Son of Heaven." He dropped to his knees and presented his neck to the executioner, who stood nearby. The executioner looked to the Emperor, who nodded. The executioner took a knotted cord from a nearby rack, walked to the old general, wrapped the cord around his neck, and with a single, deft motion snapped the old man's neck.

The noise of his father's neck snapping seemed to do something to the son. He stopped shaking, pulled his clothing into some semblance of order around himself and stepped forward toward the executioner. A brief shudder passed through him as the cord went round his neck, but he was erect when the snap came. The prosecutor turned towards the two sisters, who had watched the executions wide-eyed but silently. "And now," he said, "you will die for the crimes of treason toward the person of the Emperor and of murder."

"Murder," responded Yangshih, the oldest sister. "We have committed no murders. We admit to bedding the son of Goongsun Heh. What of it? That is no more than is commonly done among our set as you, prosecutor, well know. But we have committed no murder."

"You are accused of the murder of Kim Soo, beloved of the Emperor, by means of witchcraft." The prosecutor's voice was harsh. Hwo Gwang stepped forward. This could not be allowed. A charge of witchcraft against the Heir Apparent's sisters would be the beginning of the end: Their mother, Empress Wei, would immediately lose direct access to the Emperor's person and in a matter of days the whole family could be extinguished, including the Heir Apparent, and the stability of the empire itself threatened.

"I would remind the prosecutor that the charge of witchcraft has yet to be proved," Hwo said. "To my people this affair seems to be nothing more than a simple murder."

"Hardly simple," Jyang replied. "But that doesn't matter. Members of your own family have conspired against the Emperor. That is treason whether done by witchcraft or simply by the hand of one who hates the Emperor. The question is not how the murder was done, but by whom."

"Indeed," Hwo responded. "By whom is the question." He paused and turned to face the Emperor.

"It can hardly surprise Your Majesty that there are those who feel the Emperor has made a mistake in the matter of succession to the throne. There have been many attempts over the years to dissuade His Majesty from his choice as Heir Apparent. Failing in that, is it not conceivable that some might try to change the succession by foul means?"

"How can that be?" Jyang demanded.

"Consider this, Majesty," Hwo resumed, not bothering to turn toward Jyang. "If the woman Kim Soo was killed by the sisters of the Heir Apparent using normal physical means rather than witchcraft, there would have been no reason for the shaman doll to have been placed outside the woman's house save for the single reason that someone wanted us to assume the employment of witchcraft and had already determined that members of the Heir Apparent's family would stand accused of the deed."

Hwo Gwang paused, turned to survey all those in the audience hall, then turned back to the Emperor. "On the other hand," he resumed. "Suppose someone wanted the girl dead before Your Majesty repaired to the Gan Springs Palace for the warm season. That would be necessary if the sisters of the Heir Apparent were to be blamed, since they are not scheduled to accompany you. Would not that someone find a way to kill the girl here and fake the circumstances of witchcraft? In fact, their deception would have succeeded had not the Korean girl realized that something was wrong and left us a posthumous message. I submit that the sisters of the Heir Apparent are guilty of nothing more than of having bedded the son of the late Goongsun Heh. That was foolish and wicked, and they deserve death for it, but no more sins should be attributed to them than those they have actually committed."

"Still beating that old ox, huh?" Jyang jeered. "You have no proof of simple murder."

"And you have no proof of witchcraft."

"Perhaps I can provide the proof of witchcraft you desire," Jyang retorted.

The Emperor leaned forward, obviously interested.

"How will you do this?" Hwo Gwang asked.

"The method is well known to the shamans of the north. An experiment could be arranged."

"What sort of experiment?" the Emperor interposed.

"I know a shaman who can evoke such gu," Jyang replied. "He is a man of true spiritual power. The same man who proved the guilt of His Majesty's supposed loyal servant the other morning. This shaman would never, of course, do something so wicked as to evoke gu on his own, but with Imperial permission and by Imperial order it could be done." The Emperor turned to Hwo Gwang.

"Have you any reservations about this, Hwo Gwang?" he asked.

"I do," Hwo replied. "But if so dangerous an experiment helps bring the truth to light, perhaps it had best be performed."

"Who shall the gu magic be aimed at?" the Emperor asked.

"The sisters of the Heir Apparent stand accused of treason," Jyang replied, licking his lips almost like a cat that had cornered an injured bird. "Why not perform the demonstration on them?"

"Let it be done," the Emperor ordered. "Tomorrow, when the sun has reached its highest point." There was a loud shriek of protest from the youngest princess, but at a signal from Jyang one of the guards placed a hand roughly over her mouth and the two women were dragged off. Jyang followed them, smirking at Hwo Gwang as he passed. Looking somewhat disturbed, the Emperor also departed, signaling the end of the audience.

CHAPTER NINETEEN

Suspicion

W e're in serious trouble," Hwo Gwang told Li and Bao as they left the audience hall. "Jyang has something up his sleeve. He wouldn't be doing this unless he was sure he could come up with something convincing. He'll have us yet. He'll see us all exterminated, and then serve as broker for the naming of the new Heir Apparent."

"And yet," Li mused, "something smells about this whole affair. Perhaps if we keep poking into it long enough, we'll find the dung heap that produces that smell. Then we'll see who is in trouble."

"One can only hope your optimism proves justified," Hwo replied.

"Sir, did you bring the items I asked for?" Li asked after they had walked a bit further.

"I did," Hwo replied. "I had the dragon's own time slipping them out without Jyang noticing, but I have them."

"Good. We may yet find a way out of this mess." Nevertheless, Hwo's air of gloom remained unchanged.

CHAPTER TWENTY

The Bandit Is Targeted For Death

"Ju Anshih must be eliminated," Jyang said. "He knows too much and can't be trusted."

"Agreed," the shaman replied. "I'll see to it."

"Make it spectacular," Jyang urged.

"You may count on that. Fear not. Within the month you will be helping to name the new heir apparent."

Jyang's triumphant grin would have sent shudders down Hwo Gwang's back if he could have seen it.

CHAPTER TWENTY-ONE

Supernatural Death

Wait," Ju Anshih said, suspicion in his voice. "This isn't the prison."

"Indeed," Jyang said. "Would you prefer the torturer's chamber to this comfortable house?"

"Perhaps," Ju replied. "Why am I being brought here?"

"The Emperor has ordered that you be held for a short time," Jyang replied. "There's no reason to assume that your stay will be long. Nor is there any reason for you to be uncomfortable while you're being held."

"You mean," Ju replied, sneering, "that I know enough about people in the court to cause the deaths of half of those beautiful people and the imprisonment of the other half, so someone wants to make sure I keep my mouth shut." Ju grinned wolfishly at the prosecutor.

"As you will," Jyang told him. "In any event, I have been instructed to see to your comfort while you remain in my charge." Ju said nothing more, but merely grinned and stepped into the small building up to which he had been led.

The interior of the structure was sparsely but richly furnished. Ju had not remained alive on the edge of the law for the past two and a half decades by blindly accepting everything he was told. He carefully moved his eyes around the small house, but detected nothing to rouse his suspicions. He grinned again and lay down on the well-padded couch that had been provided. "It pays to know things about the right people," he thought as he waited for sleep.

Evening turned to deep night. The guards stationed round Ju's prison remained vigilant. They had been told what would happen to them if Ju's gang managed to help their master escape. At midnight the change of the guard could be heard marching through the streets.

Jyang himself strode at their head. As the new guards came to a halt and began to prepare to replace their comrades, there was a shout.

"The sky! The sky!" One of the men in the relief guard was shouting. There was an edge of panic to his voice. All eyes rose to the sky.

"There it is!" Two voices cried out at once. Two streaks of fire were shooting across the sky.

"There's another one!"

"Another!"

"There're more of them!"

"It's an omen!"

"An omen!"

Now all the men were chattering excitedly. Some made the age-old sign against the coming of evil. They pressed against each other much as their ancestors must have clung to their fellows when strange forces sundered the sky.

"It's an omen!" This time it was the strong voice of the prosecutor filling the night air. "It's an omen foreshadowing things about which we know nothing. Bow down and pray to the souls of your ancestors. Pray that these things may be signs of good for the future of the kingdom." Jyang did indeed fall to his knees and bend his head to the ground. The rest of the relief guard followed his example.

Suddenly a streak of flame roared out of the night sky straight toward them. Fortunately, they were already on the ground, and so the flame passed over them at about the height of a man standing. For a moment there was total silence. Then the night air was torn as the house within which Ju was imprisoned exploded in a great ball of fire. The men of the guard were hammered into the ground as the force of the blast ripped through them. Three were killed by flying debris and all were bloodied. It seemed a scene from hell as the house burned, wounded men moaned, and the tall figure of the prosecutor rose and stretched arms out to the sky.

"An omen," the prosecutor intoned. "A great evil time is coming upon the empire. Let all men prepare themselves for service to the Emperor."

The men of the guard looked with awe upon this tall figure and by morning their story was all over the city, with embellishments. It was being said that the prosecutor even had the power to control the elements.

CHAPTER TWENTY-TWO

Forged Evidence

Soong Li was examining the letters Hwo Gwang had somehow obtained.

One missive was from the elder of the two sisters to Goongsun Heh's son, with whom she had been accused of sleeping and thereby committing treason.

"It's quite clear from this that the charge against the woman is true," Li said. "Is there any doubt as to the authenticity of the letter?"

"None," Hwo Gwang snapped.

"They risked so much," Bao said wonderingly. "Why?"

"It's not all that uncommon in the harem," Hwo Gwang replied. "The women are expected to eventually be married to men they've never seen to cement alliances they care nothing about. It should surprise no one that some of them will occasionally take such a chance. Usually the matter is simply covered up, with no one the worse for it. But this time Ju took advantage of the situation to save his neck."

"Perhaps," Li muttered. "Explain yourself," Hwo Gwang commanded. In answer Li handed the two letters over to his master. "These letters were not written by the same hand," Li said.

Hwo Gwang carefully examined the letters. "You're quite right," he said. "The hands are similar, but there can be no doubt. One of them is a counterfeit, a conscious attempt to imitate the first."

"Could one of the sisters have written one note and the other the second?" Bao asked.

"I suppose that is possible," Li admitted.

"No!" Hwo Gwang interrupted, a note of excitement in his voice. "That is not a possibility."

"Why not, sir?" Li asked.

"The younger of the two cannot write," Hwo Gwang replied.

"I thought every woman in the harem was educated," Bao said, surprise in his voice.

"That is usually the case," Hwo agreed, "but the Princess Juyi is a special case. She is afflicted with poet's disease."

"Poet's disease?" Bao asked. "What's that?"

"I've heard of that," Li said. "Something is wrong in the mind of the afflicted person. They cannot learn to read because the symbols seem reversed to them."

"Exactly," Hwo added. "Juyi could not have written either of the notes. Since neither sister would have trusted anyone else with such a matter, we are left with but one conclusion."

"One of these letters is a forgery," Li chimed in, with an air of satisfied excitement in his voice.

"That would appear to be the case," Hwo added, barely hiding his own enthusiasm.

"Which is the forgery?" Bao, ever practical, asked.

"We can find that out easily enough," Hwo observed. "As a member of the family, I handle most official matters for nearly all of its members, and so have many samples of the Lady Yangshih's handwriting." Hwo left the room, but quickly returned, with several official looking documents in his hand.

"Let's see here," he said, comparing the documents he had just brought in with the incriminating letters. Finally, he handed the letter obtained from Ju Anshih to Li. "This one is authentic," he said.

"So the suicide note is a forgery."

"It would seem so," Hwo observed, "and a bad one at that. I suppose it was assumed that no one would trouble to compare the suicide note with samples of the Lady Yangshih's true writing." He turned to Li. "Once again I am in your debt. I must admit that the thought of doing so never occurred to me either." Li bowed low, barely able to conceal his pride.

"So what do we do now?" asked Bao, pulling Li back down to earth.

"I think it would be well to question Ju Anshih in the morning," Hwo replied. "For now, I think we might as well repair to dinner. It's been a long day."

CHAPTER TWENTY-THREE

Disbelief

The next morning was dreary. A light rain was falling and clouds had closed in round the capital.

Li rose early, dressed his wound and hobbled about the small "apartment" trying to loosen up. He was surprised by how little the wound hurt.

Finally the two young men reluctantly left the cheery warmth of "home" and made for the offices of Hwo Gwang.

As he'd done the previous day, Bao made sure he was armed. When Li objected, Bao reminded his cousin of the previous day's adventure and insisted Bao at least accept at least a short dagger too.

The narrow streets were nearly empty, and so the two made quick work of the short trip. Hwo was at the outer door, apparently awaiting them, a grim look on his face. "Let's go," he said and abruptly stepped out onto the street, leaving Li and Bao to follow. A small group of bodyguards fell in behind them. As Hwo normally walked the streets unprotected, Li was alarmed, exchanged glances with Bao, and then hurried to catch up with Hwo.

At first Hwo ignored his two assistants. Finally he spat out a single sentence: "Ju Anshih died last night."

"What?" Li exclaimed.

"How?" the practical Bao, straightforward as usual, asked.

"He seems to have been struck down from on high."

Hwo's dry tone contrasted wildly with the import of what he said. He then went on to tell them about the explosion of the previous night.

"How convenient for the prosecutor," Li mused at the story's conclusion. "No more problems for him from Ju Anshih."

"And so much for our questioning the man," Bao added dolefully.

"So," Li resumed, "that leaves only the two princesses. We must hurry to question them before some strange 'omen' strikes them down too."

"Don't speak so impiously," Hwo Gwang warned him. "An omen from the Heavens is not to be taken lightly. The gods do not strike without reason, or merely to inconvenience us. Their purpose is to guard and protect the person of the Emperor. If the Heavens have spoken, we can but obey."

"If, indeed, the Heavens have spoken," Li insisted, frightened but determined to press his point. "It seems too much a coincidence, in the end. Too many of those who know at least a part of the truth in these matters have either died or come into danger. It was only luck and Bao's quick thinking that saved the two of us. Perhaps Ju ran out of luck, or into a more efficient executioner."

Hwo Gwang remained silent. The smoking ruin that had been Ju Anshih's house of imprisonment lay in front of them.

"What could have caused that?" Bao wondered aloud.

"Nothing in my experience." Hwo shook his head and turned to Li. "But then I'd never heard of anything capable of turning the corpse of a young woman blue either."

"Not one, three young women," Li said.

"Three?" queried Hwo. Li moved forward and began poking about the charred ruins as he spoke.

"I was going to avoid mentioning this until we had talked with the two court ladies. I wanted more to go on before I presented my suspicions to you. I managed to briefly question the serving maid who had found the bodies of the sisters after they'd supposedly committed suicide. She was all but frightened out of her wits, but she did say that the two had turned blue, then died, and then come alive again. Wouldn't you consider that an odd coincidence?"

"Li! Master Hwo!" Bao had also been poking around in the ruins of the house. Now he was holding a piece of wood high up in the air.

"What is it, Bao?"

"Something strange," Bao replied.

"Isn't everything about this case?" Li murmured. Hwo frowned but said nothing. The two hurried over to Bao.

"What have you got?" Li asked again.

Bao gestured toward the piece of wood he was holding. "This must have been a piece of the sleeping couch," he said, and handed the object to Li. "Look at this carefully."

The wood was heavily charred, but traces of elaborate carving were still evident as was some foreign object embedded within it. Li pointed out the foreign object to Hwo.

"What is it?" asked Hwo.

"An arrow," Li replied. "Or at least what remains of an arrow. Notice what is attached to it."

"It looks like a piece of hide-rope," Hwo said as he bent closer to the object.

"That's exactly what it is," Bao interjected. "When I was a youngster I used to hang about the garrison barracks near my house. The soldiers would show me how they did things. That is part of a fire arrow."

"A fire arrow!" Hwo Gwang examined the fragment again with more interest than before. "Why a fire arrow? And why here?"

"Perhaps it's another omen," Li observed irreverently.

Hwo ignored the impiety in his excitement. "But the house! Look at it! No fire arrow could have done that. Only a bolt from Heaven itself could have done such damage."

"We still can't prove a thing," Li said, a puzzled frown on his face, "but I'd stake everything I own or hope to own that Ju Anshih was the victim of something quite a bit less exotic than a bolt from the Heavens."

"I'm not sure if I want your guess to be correct or not," Hwo said.

"Why not, sir?" Li wondered.

"If you are right, someone in the court has powers far beyond any known here before. Such power would be difficult enough to control if it were in the hands of someone who meant well. In the hands of a person evil enough to have done these things..." Hwo shuddered, and not from the chill of the dank morning. "Well," he resumed, "however it turns out, we've got work to do this day. I think, friend Li, if you are correct in your deductions, that we had better interview those two wayward sisters quickly, before anything further happens to them."

CHAPTER TWENTY-FOUR

Danger and Exile

Hwo Gwang was surprised by the amount of coming and going and the air of subdued excitement evident as they approached the Inner Court. "What's going on?" he asked an acquaintance who was hurrying by. The man stopped, looked quickly about as though making sure no one had noticed him, then stepped backward so that a small arbor shielded him from direct observation from anyone but Hwo on the pedestrian path.

"The sisters, your kinsmen, are being put to the test by Jyang," the man said, then turned abruptly away as someone passed, pretending to adjust his sash of office.

Hwo Gwang felt a knot of fear growing in his stomach, more from what the man did than from what he had said.

"Now?" Hwo prompted once the path was again clear.

"At this very moment."

"Why was I not informed?" But Hwo knew the answer to that one, and also knew he could expect nothing further from this man and, thus, was not disappointed.

"I must go," the man muttered, not meeting Hwo's eye as he stepped back onto the path, turned, and quickly walked away.

Hwo faced his two young companions.

"You two had better run for your lives. It appears that an ill wind is blowing against the fortunes of my family. Those caught in that wind are likely to be sucked dry by it and then left for the wolves."

"We'll stay, sir."

Bao's avowal took both Li and Hwo Gwang by surprise.

"Look here, Bao, you've been in my service but a little while. There is still time for both of you to change allegiance with little harm to your careers. You've both shown promise. I'm sure the prosecutor would take you onto his staff in a moment."

"No sir, we stay," Bao insisted. "We've promised you our loyalty. Anyone can be loyal when fair winds blow. The real test comes with ill winds. If I thought you yourself were disloyal, I'd take you up on your offer, but it appears to me that someone is trying to twist the Emperor's will. We will stay."

The speech was the longest Li had ever heard from Bao. Hwo was nearly as astonished by the proclamation as Li.

Hwo turned to Li.

"Of course we'll both stay, sir. There's never been any question about that."

"I'll do what I can to protect you," Hwo said, squaring his shoulders. "The battle isn't over yet. Let's go."

A piercing scream greeted the three men as they entered the Hall of Interrogations. They saw the sisters being led bound to the central dais, the same dais on which the Emperor had watched a man burst into flames and die just a few days earlier. Hwo shuddered inwardly at the memory of that scene.

The two bound women were forced to lie down upon the platform.

The shaman stepped forward.

Those nearest the dais recoiled. If wugu was to be practiced here, they had no wish to be infected.

The shaman began his dance. The two women writhed as much out of fear as pain, but the gags Jyang had placed in their mouths kept them from making much noise.

Gradually all movement halted and the women's skin took on a pasty grey shade. Jyang held up his hand as he turned toward the throne.

"Your Majesty can clearly see that the women are dead, just as the Lady Kim Soo was killed but a few days ago." There was a loud murmur among the courtiers. No one had ever seen such a thing. The gu poison worked by means of vile insects placed into the body by magic, but several days of illness normally preceded death.

Ever the showman, Jyang let the uproar continue for some time before he roared out a command for silence. He was obeyed instantly. "Fortunately, Your Majesty," he resumed, "I can counter such gu poison. I do not know why the gods have so favored me, but I have learned something no one has ever learned before. I can cure someone—even someone who has already died—who has absorbed this poison." Jyang motioned to one of the court physicians standing nearby. The color drained from the man's face, and he looked to the Emperor as though for mercy. The Emperor remained motionless. The physician reluctantly moved next to the two bodies, made a quick check, then rushed back to his place. His colleagues backed away from him in turn.

"Well?" Jyang's voice boomed.

"The women are dead, both of them."

"For now. Only for now." Jyang moved next to the bodies and bent over. He removed the gags from the eldest sister's mouth and bent still more closely over her. No one could see what he was doing as his robes fell, purposely Li was sure, over both their heads.

For a time nothing seemed to happen, then there came a rasping gasp and the woman's body heaved up and down as she began breathing. Her skin returned to a more normal color.

"The woman lives," Jyang shouted. "The woman lives," echoed through the hall. Even the Emperor did not try to control his astonishment. Li breathed a little easier. Perhaps he would have a chance to question the woman after all.

"A moment," Jyang shouted. He placed the gag back in the woman's mouth and pushed her down. At first she struggled, but a quiet word from the prosecutor, spoken too softly for anyone else in the hall to hear silenced her. Jyang moved away and nodded to the shaman, who resumed his dance. Within a few minutes, the first sister again lay quietly on the platform, apparently as dead as before, as dead as her sister.

Jyang looked toward Hwo Gwang and Soong Li. Slowly he winked, then turned toward the Emperor. "Your Majesty," he said. "The sentence of death has been passed on these women. I trust it stands?" The Emperor, seemingly unable to speak, nodded. Jyang stepped up to the two bodies, then snatched a knife from his belt and with two quick motions slashed their abdomens open. Some in the crowd gagged, but none turned away.

"Soong Li!" The prosecutor's voice rang out. "Come forward." At a nod from Hwo Gwang, Li rose and made his way forward to Jyang's side.

"Witness, Soong Li, oh you of the many questions. Are the gu worms present inside the women of the House of Wei?" Li moved to the women's side, bent over, carefully but quickly examined their exposed bowels, and shook his head no. There were no worms. A faintly sour odor, but no worms. He had no time to brood on what that odor might be, but perhaps so freshly dead a body might exude such a smell.

"So you see," Jyang shouted. "The so-called murder is solved."

Li was sickened by the sight of the disemboweled woman lying in front of him but the prosecutor's shout of triumph brought him back to his senses. "No!" Li shouted, wanting to make sure he was heard. "No."

The crowd's buzzing ceased. The courtiers were mesmerized at the prospect of a young nobody challenging the great Jyang at the zenith of his power as a result of the just concluded demonstration.

"What?" roared the prosecutor. He turned to the Emperor. "Your Majesty, there can no longer be any doubt. Have I not conclusively shown that evil abounds in this kingdom? Is it not clearly necessary that something be done to contain the infection?"

The Emperor turned to his old adviser. "What do you say, Hwo Gwang? The boy is, after all, your disciple."

"Be careful, Hwo Gwang," Jyang rumbled, menace in every phrase. "It is obvious that witchcraft is being practiced. Perhaps this young Li of yours is somehow involved. He certainly seems to be doing his best to hinder my investigation of the matter. Or is it possible that the great Hwo Gwang himself is…"

Jyang was careful not to extend the pause for too long. "No," he resumed. "Not Hwo Gwang. No matter what the involvement of his family, the great Hwo Gwang would not stoop to such things." The prosecutor's tone of voice projected more uncertainty about that proposition than did the face value of his words.

Hwo Gwang's deep laugh boomed out. "Besides," he chuckled, "if I were involved, the prosecutor knows I'd not waste my time killing innocent girls. I'd do something about the man most likely to cause me trouble."

There was a brief silence as the courtiers took in the import of Hwo Gwang's words, then a scattering of laughter grew into a collective roar of appreciation at the prosecutor's visible discomfort. To Jyang's dismay, the Emperor himself had been the first to laugh at Hwo's sally.

Finally the laughter subsided. Jyang used the time to regain his composure. "A neat turn of phrase," he bowed to Hwo, "but it fails to answer the question."

"And that question is?" Hwo prompted.

"Just what involvement this young man of yours has in the..."

"Enough!" Hwo Gwang's powerful bass dominated the hall. He turned to the Emperor.

"Your Majesty. My assistant was charged by the court to do all he could to discover the truth of the matters surrounding the death of the girl Kim Soo. Is he now to be accused of treason by the prosecutor simply because he discharged his duty to his ruler?"

The Emperor looked confused. "But is it possible that what the prosecutor suggests is true?"

"No, Your Majesty. The lad operated on my instructions. His motives cannot be called into question." Hwo paused, then walked to the side of one of the public executioners. "Unless I too am suspect, as the prosecutor would seem to imply." He reached down and grasped the hand of the executioner. He raised the man's arm and bowed his own head. "If that is the case, let me die now, serving my Emperor in death as I have served him in life."

Jyang began to speak, but the Emperor, no confusion in his voice now, spoke first.

"No one can doubt your loyalty, Hwo Gwang," he said. "It was you who first brought to Our attention the possibility of treason within the court and even within your own family. You have served me too long and too well for me to have any doubts about you."

"I am unworthy," Hwo murmured, bowing low. "As to my assistant, it is possible that he, in his youthful enthusiasm, came to some wrong conclusions, but for these he deserves forgiveness. He is resourceful and bright. His was the plan that led to the capture of Ju Anshih. In the future he is sure to be of great service."

"We take no offense at the lad's error. Well then, Jyang?"

"My Lord?"

"A most impressive demonstration. We must consult further on this."

Jyang bowed low, a smile on his lips. A eunuch entered and gave something to the Emperor's attendant. The attendant unrolled what appeared to be a scroll, then bent to whisper into the Emperor's ear. The Emperor took the piece of silk into his own hands and read it himself.

"Jyang. Hwo." He motioned for the two to approach the throne. "A report has just arrived from the southwest, from Shu. A portent has been observed."

"Of what sort, Your Majesty?" asked Hwo.

"An explosion in a mine."

"Is that not a common occurrence, sir? Jyang asked. "Why should such a thing be considered a portent?"

"It is common enough in the pits where the black rock that burns is mined," the Emperor replied. "But this explosion was in the shaft of an iron mine. Has anyone ever heard of such a thing before? Surely such an event is a portent."

"Indeed," Hwo said. "If authentic it would indeed be a portent of significance."

"Authentic?" The Emperor was genuinely surprised. "How could such a thing be falsified?"

"I do not know," said Hwo. "It may well be that those who reported the incident lied, or some exaggeration could have taken place as the story travelled towards us, or someone could have deliberately caused such an explosion."

"Have you reason for saying such a thing?" the Emperor asked.

"I have none," Hwo conceded. "But it would be well to remember some of the happenings during the life of my former teacher and master, Doong Joongshu. Once Master Doong taught us all his new ways of interpreting portents, remember the trouble caused by unscrupulous men willing to counterfeit reports of earthquakes, eclipses, and flying stars. Such portents, like the one with which we are now confronted, are valuable, though difficult to interpret, but they are still more difficult to authenticate, and until that is done, their value is in question."

"Indeed, We do remember," replied the Emperor. "Those frauds cost Us dearly. You are right. The incident must be investigated."

"Your Majesty." Jyang was visibly agitated. "Surely you must recognize the importance of tending to matters here. You are scheduled to repair tomorrow to the Gan Springs Palace, and this witchcraft must be attended to. This infestation within the Imperial Household itself must be rooted out. Surely the portent of the fiery sky which killed Ju Anshih added to the portent of the iron mine explosion, and the proven use of witchcraft within the Imperial Household should be enough to convince even the most skeptical that Heaven is speaking to us."

The Emperor looked toward Hwo Gwang.

"These events must be investigated," Hwo replied. "But if it becomes evident that any of these events have been counterfeited, those promoting such falsity must be discovered, rooted out, and destroyed. If these events be true portents, they must be studied for what information they may yield so that we may better interpret the meaning of the portents. In either case, investigations must be carried out."

The Emperor looked pensive. "We cannot spare you, Hwo Gwang. You have been a strong right hand. You are needed." The Emperor turned to Jyang. "We cannot spare you either. Someone may have dared to practice witchcraft against the person of the Emperor. You are correct. Such things must be rooted out and destroyed."

Much to Hwo's delight the prosecutor looked pained at the Emperor's comment, a comment indicating the Emperor had not fully bought into the scenario Jyang was trying to set up. Hwo quickly moved to take advantage. "I have a solution, Your Majesty," Hwo Gwang put forward.

"What might that be?" the Emperor asked.

"My assistants, Soong Li and Chiang Bao could go to the south-west," replied Hwo. "Even the prosecutor will agree that they have about them the proper degree of skepticism."

A ripple of laughter ran around the hall. Even Jyang himself echoed Hwo's and the Emperor's smile.

"Are they to be trusted in such an endeavor?" asked the Emperor.

"Completely," Hwo replied.

"You can be so sure?" boomed Jyang.

"I can," Hwo quietly replied. He turned to the Emperor. "The prosecutor did not bother to send for me this morning. I was not told of the demonstration just witnessed."

There were audible gasps at this revelation. Not to invite a man like Hwo Gwang to an audience as important as this one was a serious breach in court etiquette. It could only mean one of two things: Either Hwo Gwang himself was under suspicion or the Emperor had personally decided that Hwo was no longer in favor. Almost as surprising as the omission itself was the fact that Hwo was admitting to it.

Even the Emperor leaned forward in curious anticipation. "You were not invited?" he asked.

Hwo tried not to let his relief show. He had correctly surmised that the Emperor had had nothing to do with this snub.

"It was worse than that," Hwo said. "I was told the event was to take place several hours from now."

"Explain." The Emperor was looking at Jyang, a stern look on his face. Jyang spread his upturned hands as though to say he was as surprised as everyone else.

"An oversight perhaps," he said. "I will take care such a thing doesn't happen again."

"Indeed you will," the Emperor said. "Hwo Gwang has shown his loyalty too often to be held under suspicion. Such a thing will not take place again without Our knowledge."

Jyang's face blanched as he bowed his acquiescence.

"At any rate," Hwo Gwang continued, "my assistants were made aware by me of the events of the morning before we came to this chamber. I gave them leave to abandon my service and seek out the prosecutor as their patron. Both responded that they would stay with one who served the Emperor."

All eyes swung to Li and Bao. Respect was evident on the part of some courtiers, but most wondered at the intelligence of two young men who would choose to cling to a seemingly discredited master in preference to one whose star was so obviously on the rise.

"Such loyalty is worthy of respect," said the Emperor. "Especially in two so young. Send the young men to Shu."

With that, the Emperor rose and made his way from the hall.

Jyang seemed about to make a protest, but thought better of it. For the moment he had been outmaneuvered and he was too skilled a courtier to risk pressing the issue here and now. Hwo Gwang motioned to Li and Bao to follow him. As they left the room Bao looked at Li, arching his eyebrows. "What have you gotten us into now?" he asked.

Li said nothing, but merely hurried to catch up to Hwo Gwang. They found their master conversing with the same fellow they had met on their way into the audience chamber. The man was professing eternal allegiance to the house of Hwo, obviously trying to patch up any damage that might have been done by his craven actions earlier in the morning. Hwo finally managed to disentangle himself from the man. He was almost grinning as he turned to Li and Bao.

"So," he said. "You two are going on a long trip."

Li protested. "Master Hwo," he said fervently. "I was about to expose the falsehoods that have taken place. Ju Anshih was not killed by Heaven. He was put to death by the hand of man. The Lady..." Hwo held up a hand.

"How did Jyang put the Ladies Yangshih and Juyi to death?" he asked once he had the boy's full attention. "Was it by means of wugu or was it a simple execution?"

"I don't know," Li admitted.

"How was Ju Anshih put to death?"

"I don't know."

"How was the Lady Kim Soo put to death?"

Li hung his head. "I don't know," he said once again.

"Perhaps you are mistaken about all of this," Hwo Gwang said. "Perhaps the prosecutor is correct. Perhaps forces are at work here that we simply can't understand. Perhaps witchcraft is at the bottom of some of it, and Heaven's warnings and retribution underlie the rest."

"No!" Li shouted. "I cannot believe that."

"Cannot? Or will not?"

"Both," Li conceded, anger born of frustration still in his voice.

Hwo raised a placating hand. "I agree," he told the boys. "By whatever means, and for whatever purpose, the prosecutor has involved himself in something that threatens My Lord, the Emperor."

"Then why do you send us into exile in Shu?" Li asked. "We should be here to help you."

"Stay here and you both die," Hwo said. "Can't you see that? You are the only ones questioning the prosecutor. You are the only ones likely to inquire into matters he doesn't want uncovered. You must leave for a time. Jyang has the ear of the Emperor. That demonstration this morning has guaranteed that the Emperor has at least considered accepting at least the outlines of Jyang's explanation of events. His Majesty has not turned against me only because he wants to assure himself an alternative in court to Jyang. But my safety does not assure yours. Stay here and you die. Go and you may yet learn something of value. In any case, you live to fight another day."

"And you?" Bao asked quietly. "What of you?"

"I must stay," Hwo answered gravely. "The prosecutor has decided to eliminate my family from the face of the earth. He may well succeed, but as a matter of filial obligation I must do what I can to stop him and I can only do that here."

Li and Bao spent the rest of the day preparing to leave.

CHAPTER TWENTY-FIVE

Deaths Are Ordered

Those two still suspect something but have been able to prove nothing." Jyang was reclining on a couch, relaxing after the strain of the Imperial Audience.

"And the Emperor?" The shaman crouched in a corner without benefit of furniture. "He is the only one who counts."

"We've got him eating out of our hands," Jyang chuckled. "Thanks to your theatrics, he's convinced that witchcraft is rampant in the land and that I'm the only one who can save him."

"Then we have nothing to worry about," the shaman said. "What can two boys do to discover us."

"I don't know," Jyang said. "I don't like it though. Did you know they were poking about this morning in the ruins of the house where Ju Anshih died?"

"So what?" asked the shaman. "What is there for them to find?"

"Nothing, I suppose," Jyang said. "I know I'd feel a lot better if they were dead. Dead people don't ask questions."

"So, kill them," replied the shaman. He rose and walked across to Jyang. He poured a cup of stillbeer from a jug on the low table next to Jyang's couch. He drank it off in one gulp.

"Take it easy with that stuff," Jyang told him. "We can't have a drunken shaman running about the court."

"I'll be glad when we don't have to keep up this pretense anymore," laughed the shaman.

"Nevertheless, for now we have to be careful."

"Don't worry so much. Kill those two and you can relax.

"Not yet," Jyang replied.

"Why not?"

"There have been enough suspicions raised," Jyang replied. "We've got the Emperor right where we want him. Soon we'll be rid of that bitch, the old lady Wei and her snotty murderous son. Then we can rig the succession to favor ourselves. For now, though, we'd better take it easy. We'll have them followed and killed well away from the capital. A lot can happen on the road to Shu."

The shaman laughed. "Well, that takes care of that! You seem to have thought of everything."

Jyang laughed as well. "I have to," he said. He called one of his men into the room and issued instructions about the death of Soong Li and Chiang Bao.

CHAPTER TWENTY-SIX

The Journey Begins

The Emperor was going to the Gan Springs Palace. He was feeling his years and weight of rule. The hot baths at the palace would, he hoped, refresh him. Hwo Gwang had been ordered to attend him. Jyang was being left behind to pursue the investigation into witchcraft.

"Why all the secrecy?" asked Bao, looking around. The imperial procession stretched out along the full length of the main avenue leading north from the central palace complex.

"Master Hwo feels someone may have been assigned the job of seeing that we don't come back from our journey," Li replied. He too looked about at the gathering throng. It was still short of midday. The drizzle of the previous day had dissipated. It was a cool, crisp, clear morning.

"I knew it," Bao declared, rolling his eyes to the heavens.

"Knew what?" asked Li.

"That you'd find some way to get us into more trouble," Bao answered. "Why couldn't I have stayed home and led the nice, quiet life of a common man with not a care in the world?"

"Because you don't like stacking manure," Li said with a grin.

Bao laughed. "You've got that part right at least," he said.

"So stop grumbling," Li told him. "Look at all the excitement you're getting now."

"Any more and I may decide I like stacking manure after all," Bao said. "At least you can stay alive that way."

"If you call that living."

A flutter of motion spread through the crowd. The enormous Imperial palanquin was taking its place at the head of the column.

The two young men saw Hwo Gwang being escorted into a palanquin directly behind the Emperor's own.

As the procession got under way, Li and Bao, as instructed by Hwo Gwang, fell back into the ranks of the many clerks and lesser officials who always accompanied the ruler on his trips through the empire. Such men were, in terms of social dignity, superior to palace servants, but inferior to the men of station, with access to palanquins and bearers. They carried their own baggage and had to straggle along behind the last of the imperial guardsmen, keeping up as best they could. It was expected that many of these lesser officials would fall behind. Those whose services would be needed immediately at the Gan Springs Palace had been sent on ahead the previous day. By the time the Emperor reached the Gan Springs Palace, some of these lesser beings would still have half the road to cover and might not reach their destination for two or three days after the Emperor himself had arrived.

Li and Bao were to straggle along, losing themselves in the crowd as best they could. When they felt safe, they were to disappear from the column and begin making their way south. It was some time before the people around them began to stir and take their places in the procession. The two young men used the delay to scan the crowd around them for familiar faces. If Hwo Gwang was correct, someone would try to follow them. They wanted to identify this person as quickly as possible. Finally, they joined the procession. The man with the scar on his cheek smiled as he watched them go. He joined the column some distance behind them, far enough back to avoid notice, close enough to keep track. As he walked his right hand occasionally caressed the hilt of the short dagger he carried at his side. He had killed many men with it, all at his master's bidding. Soon, two more names would be added to his list of victims.

After eight hours on the road, Li and Bao felt much the worse for wear. The morning sun had dried the road so, by noon the long procession was stirring up considerable amounts of dust, most of which settled on those making up the procession's elongated tail. By early afternoon the two looked like actors covered with tan make-up.

"Let's stop," Li croaked, his throat dry with dust. He led the way to a small stream near the road. A couple of dozen of their fellow travelers had had the same idea. They were setting up camp near the stream. Others straggled over behind them. Among these was a man with a scar on his face.

Li stooped at the edge of the bank to begin washing himself, but Bao was more direct. He dropped his pack and waded into the stream, turned, then fell backwards. He came up with a "woosh," then whooped for Li to come in.

A few minutes later the two were reclining beneath a tree, talking. "Do you think anyone's following?" Li asked.

"Hard to say. I kept an eye out as best I could, but there's so many people about that I couldn't be sure."

"Same with me."

"So what do we do?"

"I think we ought to sneak out tonight and go back on our tracks," Li replied. "We crossed the Three Bridges cutoff about an hour ago. If we wait until late tonight, we can retrace our steps and be off on the road south before anyone is the wiser."

"Agreed," Bao replied. He tucked his pack under his head and promptly fell asleep. Li lay back and thought. The man with the scar on his face watched the two for a time, satisfied himself that Li and Bao were settled for the night, and then rejoined the nearby crowd immersed in betting on the stone throwing game.

Bao awoke at twilight. Li was still awake, his back against a tree, thinking.

"What's up?" Bao asked.

"I wonder how he did it?" Li asked quietly.

"You still think witchcraft had nothing to do with those deaths?" Bao asked. "You have to admit the facts seem to be against you."

"I know witchcraft had nothing to do with it," Li insisted, still quietly. "Someday I'll find out how Jyang did it, and then we'll have him."

"Well, maybe you're right, and maybe you're wrong," Bao said. "Right now, though, you'd better get some sleep. It's going to be a long night."

"I suppose you're right." Li stretched out and tried, unsuccessfully, to sleep.

The two rose again as the sun went down and made a sparse meal of stale rice cakes and water. Within a few minutes of night's onset most of their fellow travelers were asleep. Clerks used to the soft life of the court had succumbed to the rigors of an eight hour march. Only one fire remained lit, near which several men were playing the stone throw game.

"Let's go," Li whispered.

"Wait," Bao said. He went behind the tree, and reappeared a few moments later carrying some loose brush which he arranged into some semblance of two recumbent bodies where they had originally lain.

"Now let's go," Bao whispered. No one glanced up as they made their way out of the camp.

A quarter moon rose and lit their way as they retraced their steps. Li was stiff and sore. The soft life of the court had done him no more good than it had most of the other clerks. Bao, however, seemed quite unaffected by the day's exercise. Li knew that Bao exercised daily, following the teachings of one of the schools that stressed the importance of a healthy body in keeping up a vigorous mind. Though he had tried to entice Li into joining these exercise sessions Li had always declined. Now, Li admitted, he was paying the price for his sloth.

It took them an hour and a half to get back to the turn onto Three Bridges Road. There they rested for only a moment before starting onto their new course. Back at the camp, the man with the scarred face left the stone throw game and made his way to his sleeping pad. A quick glance at the two dark shadows under the tree to his left told him that his prey remained available. His instructions were to eliminate the two young men on the second night out. He fingered the hilt of his dagger, then lay down for the night.

Li was ready to stop soon after they had set out on the Three Bridges Road. "Surely," he said, "no one could catch us now." Bao merely grunted and kept walking.

"I can't go another step," Li finally said, and matching his actions to his words, he sank to the ground under a roadside tree and leaned back.

"The best way to avoid a problem is to make sure it never catches up with you," Bao grumbled.

"Do you really think someone was following?"

"When I travel with you, I just assume the worst," Bao replied. He remained standing. Li managed a weak grin.

"Even if someone eventually noticed we were gone, they couldn't catch up with us now, could they?

"The more ground we put between ourselves and them, the better off we'll be," Bao insisted. He reached down, and with a weary sigh, Li allowed himself to be pulled to his feet. Bao allowed no further halt until the town of Three Bridges appeared before them, illuminated by the moonlight.

The scar-faced man awoke suddenly, knowing he had overslept. He turned convulsively to his left, onto the dew dampened portion of his sleeping mat, then relaxed when he saw the two forms on the ground under the tree. He couldn't see them very clearly through the low patch of brush growing between him and them, but he could make out the motionless forms of the two young men. That was enough. They must have also overslept.

As he hastily folded his sleeping mat, the man began to visualize the ways he might lure those two to their deaths. Movement near the still sleeping forms of his prey attracted his attention. He turned.

A pack animal was grazing on the bodies of the two young men! He stood, stunned, then the truth suddenly flooded in over him. His prey had escaped!

CHAPTER TWENTY-SEVEN

Free And Clear

Bao woke at sunrise. For a moment he lay savoring the cool morning air on his face and the contrasting feeling of warmth provided by the light covering of the bed clothing. After a time he stood, then walked through the dew-moistened grass to the far side of a tree. Having attended to the needs of nature, he moved back to the affairs of men by moving to a position where he could see back along the road on which he and Li had travelled the night before. There was no one on the road. Bao flexed his muscles and began stretching in the slow, methodical way he had been taught since childhood. Then he began a series of exercises designed to strengthen, but not exhaust the sinews of his body. Li had not yet wakened when Bao returned to the campsite.

The heat of the sun was already raising a low mist when Li finally rolled over and yawned. He began to rise, then sank back with a groan.

"My body," he moaned.

"What's wrong?" Bao asked.

"I don't believe it works anymore," Li replied. He made another pitiful attempt to rise, then sank back.

"Getting a little soft?" Bao mocked. A groan was his only reply. "Come on, lazy. Up and at them."

"You go on," Li told him. "Just send back the funerary priests for my poor dead body."

"I shall mourn you deeply." The glee in Bao's voice belied his words. He leaped to his feet in a single spring, touched his heels together in mid-air, and landed near his prostrate partner. "Come friend Li. I will help you, for you are my lifelong friend, and I cannot allow you to die of self pity." With that he reached down and grasped his friend's feet, then pulled him abruptly into a vertical position, but standing on his head. As Li snatched for his ankles, Bao jumped lightly back. Li wobbled, then balanced on his hands and head, and finally turned a twisting summersault, ending up on his feet, nose to nose with his cousin.

"Aiii," he screamed. "Are you trying to murder me?" He staggered about, then fell against a tree with a good deal more theatre than was necessary.

"No," Bao replied. "Should you die, it would be the fault of your own soft living, which is now about to end. We need to get back on the road before we've squandered whatever lead we may have gained over Jyang's men."

"Then you think someone's really after us?"

"Of course," Bao replied. "You don't think the prosecutor is going to forgive your attempts to bring him to grief?"

Li turned a quizzical look on his friend. "Then you believe I was correct in my suspicions?"

"Of course." Li looked relieved.

"I was beginning to doubt myself. No one seemed to believe me and everything was going wrong. Jyuang was frustrating me at every turn."

"All the more reason to believe that your suspicions are correct," Bao said dryly. He was breaking camp as he spoke.

"How so?"

"Why would the prosecutor work so hard to confound you, if he truly sought truth? If he really believed all that witchcraft nonsense, he'd have let you go ahead and be proved a fool. Instead, obstacles are placed in our path at every turn. Something's going on. So why shouldn't I believe in your suspicions?"

"But how?" Li asked. He was moving around again, albeit somewhat gingerly. "How could he have done all these things?"

"I'd suggest you answer that question soon. If you don't, we'll both be meat for the carrion birds."

Bao looked around and satisfied that all traces of their stay had disappeared. After one last check back along the road, they set off towards the town of Three Bridges.

"Perhaps I was wrong after all," Li muttered, walking rather stiffly.

"Perhaps the sun will rise in the west tomorrow morning," Bao grunted.

CHAPTER TWENTY-EIGHT

Renew The Pursuit!

You lost them! How can you lose two snotnoses who aren't even old enough to grow a few whiskers?" Jyang was turning purple with rage, the veins at his temple pulsating.

"I'm sorry, sir," the scar-faced man said meekly.

"You'll be more than sorry," Jyang howled. "I can promise you that." The scar-faced man stood, his head bowed, and waited for the storm to run its course. He knew the dangers of speaking too soon. Finally, Jyang's anger began to abate and the man saw his chance.

"They can still be caught."

"How?" a still angry Jyang demanded.

"They had to have gone to Three Bridges. They figured, somehow, that they were being followed, so they pulled that trick and left. Three Bridges is the only place they could have gone if they were going to set out south for Shu."

Jyang considered for a moment. "Go then," he said abruptly. "Those two must die."

"I shall see to it." The scar-faced man bowed out of the prosecutor's presence. He knew all too well the prosecutor's range of penalties for being wrong. In less than an hour the scar-faced man and three companions were in hot pursuit.

CHAPTER TWENTY-NINE

Incognito

Li and Bao were chattering like children as they came abreast of the city gate of Three Bridges, but the deep shadows cast by the inner walls surrounding the several wards into which the town was divided, quickly subdued them.

"I assume we're heading for the county offices," Bao asked.

"No, we aren't. Lord Hwo has made other arrangements."

"Oh?" Li chose to ignore the edge to Bao's voice which indicated that he realized he had not been included in that bit of Lord Hwo's plan, and was not pleased by that fact. At one point Li stepped away from Bao to make some inquiry of a gateman who pointed toward a narrow gate further down the same lane.

"Am I permitted to know what our mission here is?" Bao asked rather pointedly as Li knocked at the gate.

"Of course," Li answered, responding to the substance of the question rather than its tone. "This man is an old friend to our master. I have a letter of introduction to him and a request for his help." A peephole was opened and a pair of eyes appeared within it.

"Yes?"

"Two visitors for the Merchant Gao," Li answered. "We carry a letter from an old friend of his."

The disembodied eyes regarded the two for a moment, then disappeared as the peephole was slid shut. After an interval the gate swung slowly open. An elderly gatekeeper invited the two in, then closed the gate behind them.

"Please follow," the gatekeeper said politely enough. He set off across a large courtyard.

The boys looked around. This was obviously the home of a man of substance. The courtyard was filled with carts and bales of goods heaped up alongside the carts. A ripe odor identified a building to the right as a stable.

The two were led across the courtyard and through a corridor-like room on the side opposite the gate. From that room they emerged into another courtyard. This one was smaller. The rooms fronting it appeared to be warehouses.

The old gatekeeper led them through yet another corridor and into still another courtyard. Now they were in the residential section of the mansion. This courtyard was the smallest of the three, but had been carefully landscaped and the buildings surrounding it had been neatly plastered and whitewashed. A servant stepped out of one of these buildings. The old gatekeeper led the two towards him.

"These men to see Master Gao," he said.

Having turned over responsibility for the guests, the old man said no more, turned, and headed back in the direction from which he'd come.

The servant, a young man hardly older than Li and Bao themselves, looked the two over carefully. "Might I inquire as to your noble family names?" he asked politely.

"I fear that our business with Master Gao is confidential," Li replied. "We must present our letter of introduction directly into his hand."

The servant raised his right eyebrow quizzically. "Well," he said. "In that case you'd better follow me." He turned and led the way toward a room across the courtyard. As they walked, two armed men stepped quietly out of the same building from which the servant had come and fell in behind. Neither Li nor Bao turned to take formal notice of them. A smooth operation, thought Bao. *I never noticed whatever signal this young fellow must have used to call forth these dogs. No one will get away with much in this household.*

The young man knocked at the door of the room toward which he had led them, then opened it and entered, followed by Li and Bao. He greeted the man within, then motioned towards the two.

"Uncle," the young man said, demonstrating that he was no servant after all. "Two travelers are here to see you. They give no names. The slim one says he has a confidential letter of introduction."

Li slipped the letter, a carefully wrapped square of silk, out of his robe, stepped forward, bowed deeply and with both hands passed it over to the merchant.

Master Gao was seated on a mat behind a low table at the north end of the room. The room itself was luxuriously furnished but did nothing to diminish the splendor of the clothing worn by the trader. He seemed to radiate the very essence of what it was to be a rich merchant.

Master Gao's robe was of rich brocade, and his fingers were covered with gold and silver rings, many of them inset with the red, green and yellow glass imported from a distant civilization to the West called Great Chin by the Chinese, but known to its own citizens as Rome.

Some said that the knowledge to create glass had once existed in China, but if so, this craft had long since disappeared and now glass, particularly colored glass, though cheap in Great Chin, was as valuable as diamonds, rubies, or emeralds in the empire of Han.

The merchant, who had grown wealthy through such knowledge, was a large, fleshy man. His corpulence only added to the aura of wealth and power which emanated from him. His face displayed neither friendliness nor unfriendliness as he accepted the small silken packet from Soong Li. He fingered the seal for a moment, then nodded and broke it. He unfolded the packet into an oblong piece of silk and began, silently, to read it. As he read, he ran his finger quickly down each line of characters. Li was impressed. Most people, even of the upper classes, normally read aloud, or at least moved their lips as they read. Only a few intellectuals had in the last couple of generations mastered the art of rapid, silent reading. Somehow, this merchant had learned this trick of the bureaucrat's trade.

Gao finished reading the message, then looked up to Li and Bao. He stared intently at them for a moment, his brow furrowed into a frown. Abruptly he shifted his gaze to his nephew. "Hu-han," he said. "These gentlemen and I must speak in private for a few moments. Please arrange for a room and places at our table for them and then wait outside. I will send for you when we have finished."

Hu-han shot another quizzical look at the two young men, but said nothing, nodded in obedience, and left the room. The merchant turned back to his guests and smiled. He gestured towards the table in front of him. "Please, gentlemen. Do sit down and allow me to pour a little of this warmed stillbeer for you."

Li and Bao bowed, then settled down opposite the merchant in front of the low table. Gao poured the golden stillbeer from a small flask into three of a set of matching drinking cups, each hardly larger than a thimble. The cups sat upon a tray, lacquered with the same design they themselves bore.

After pouring the liquor, Gao shifted the tray towards his guests. Each took a cup. Gao then took a cup for himself, lifted it in silent toast, then sipped at the liquid.

"It's good to hear from the son of my old friend," the merchant began. Noticing the blank look on the faces before him, he chuckled. "Hwo Gwang's father gave me my start as a merchant," he said by way of explanation. I am deeply indebted to him and, through him, to his son." The merchant paused for a moment, a faraway look in his eyes, obviously lost for a moment in old memories, but he quickly recovered himself and once again peered intently into the eyes of the two young men before him.

"Master Hwo requests that I lend you two strong horses and a travelling kit, and that I give what advice I may that will help you to arrive safely in the iron mining districts of Shu."

The merchant paused and once more searched the faces of his guests. "Lord Hwo could surely place official facilities at your disposal, yet he has not. No doubt it would be indelicate of me to inquire as to the reason?"

Li bowed his head, but remained silent. It was the merchant who finally sighed and broke the silence. "Ah well. You must forgive a poor merchant's natural inclination to gather any and all information. It is information, you know, not goods, that gives us our wealth. Without the information we would not know what goods to send and where and when to send them." Ever hopeful, he paused again. Li silently bowed again. "But enough of that. You will, of course, be provided with all that you might need. How soon must you set out?"

"Tomorrow at first light, if that is convenient, sir." Li was grateful to finally meet a question he was permitted to answer.

"Certainly," said the merchant. "I will personally see to whatever arrangements must be made." Both Li and Bao bowed low this time, Bao glancing sidelong at his friend to make sure of the correct protocol. The merchant poured more stillbeer, then continued.

"If you wish company along the way, you could travel with an unladen pack train led by my nephew. It will be leaving for Chengdu at first light tomorrow."

Li and Bao exchanged glances. "We must move fast," Li said. "I think we'd best travel alone."

"You need have no concern about all that," replied the merchant. "The packtrain will carry nothing but a few ingots of silver intended as payment for the lacquerware with which it will return. It will move as quickly as you could by travelling alone." The merchant stopped, seemed about to add something, thought better of it, but continued anyway.

"And, of course, a half-dozen well armed men will form its escort. Silver is a tempting target for brigands." Something appeared to embarrass the old gentleman. He clearly wanted to say something more, but was constrained by the demands of good manners as well as the need for the young men to be reticent about their mission. This was evident when he finally decided to say his piece: "If it seemed expedient, you two could be outfitted to form a part of that escort. It might be a good disguise for you and," here he chuckled audibly, "it would save me the hire of two extra men for the journey."

Li looked to Bao doubtfully. Bao nodded enthusiastically. Li reconsidered the matter. "We'd be most happy to accept your gracious offer, Merchant Gao," he said finally. "Such an arrangement would indeed be of much use to us."

"Excellent." The merchant clapped his hands. Hu-han, at once entered the room.

"Nephew," said Gao, jovial now that the business of the day was concluded. "Please show Master Soong Li and his associate Chiang Bao to the guest rooms." Gao turned to Li and Bao. "Gentlemen, this is my nephew Gao Hu-han. His name means 'protector of Han,' and he is as good as his name." The three young men smiled and bowed to one another.

"These gentlemen," Gao resumed, "will join your pack train as guards. Please arrange for several changes of clothing to be packed into their saddlebags. As well provide a pair of swords for each, along with bows and arrows. Give them the new dappled Fergana horses." Gao turned to Li and Bao.

"Have you gentlemen ever ridden horses from the far western lands?" the merchant asked. Bao nodded, not counting it a lie so long as he did not actually say yes aloud. His eyes sparkled at the thought of actually riding such great beasts that he had only seen from afar being ridden by imperial cavalrymen and the more adventurous of the court aristocrats. Li looked more doubtful, but also said yes, equally untruthfully. "They are both big and fast," Hu-han assured them. "Riding them can be more like flying than riding."

"Good," merchant Gao exclaimed. "You go along with Hu-han then. He'll get you set up in your rooms and arrange everything for your departure tomorrow. This evening you will dine with me."

Li and Bao rose, bowed, and turned to follow Hu-han out the door. Old Gao nodded in response, but did not rise, which signaled Hu-han that these young men, though on some kind of special mission for an important personage, were not themselves of a status higher than his own.

After his visitors' departure, Gao again let his gaze fall to Hwo Gwang's letter. Gao made it his business to stay informed on court gossip. Hwo had said little that was specific in his letter, but the aura of secrecy about the whole affair and the fact that Hwo was willing to humble himself enough to ask for a merchant's aid said much to a man trained in the ways of intrigue. Gao knew how vulnerable the family of the Heir Apparent was at this moment. If it was anyone else in such trouble who had made this request, Gao would have prudently turned him down no matter how heavy the obligation he had incurred to the man, but Gao had long ago learned not to count Hwo Gwang out of any game, and this was the biggest game imaginable.

Gao sat and thought for a long time, weighing the pros and cons of the situation. Finally he stirred. A signal called in a trusted messenger. After a short conference the messenger left for the capital city. Then another messenger was summoned, briefed, and then set out for the Gan Springs residence of the Emperor. A prudent man of commerce had to cover his flanks.

CHAPTER THIRTY

Betrayed By An Ally

"They're in Three Bridges." Jyang was holding a message cloth. One corner of the cloth was missing. "They will be accompanying a trader's caravan disguised as guards. I'll send word to our people and see to their elimination."

"No." The shaman stirred. "I have a feeling about these two. They mean real trouble. I'll go take care of the problem myself."

"They're little more than children," Jyang replied. "My men on the spot can take care of them."

"Your men haven't done so well thus far," the shaman said sarcastically.

Jyang flushed. "You're needed here. I'll have my men do it."

"I will go." The shaman stood up and left the room without another word. Jyang watched him go.

"Someday," the prosecutor muttered. A shiver ran up and down his spine when the shaman appeared to pause, as though ready to turn, but the medicine man continued on after all. Jyang relaxed, realized he had been holding his breath, and exhaled loudly.

CHAPTER THIRTY-ONE

Strategy

It was dark when Hu-han came to their room to escort Li and Bao back to the dinner table. The two had spent the day wandering through the town, Li, at first, with the excitement of a born adventurer who had yet to experience much that was adventurous, and Bao rather glumly, frequently glancing back over his shoulder and muttering about the need for haste and the loss of a day.

In truth the blank ward walls lining the main streets of the town offered little to feed Li's anticipations, and even the single market ward the town boasted offered nothing to compare with the three great markets of the nearby capital. By the time they shambled back to the Gao compound Li was almost as glum as his companion.

"I gather you two will be joining my caravan to Shu tomorrow morning," Hu-han said as he sized up his two guests as they completed their simple toilets.

"Indeed we are," Li answered, his tone carefully bland.

"Are you sure you wish to travel as guards?" Hu-han asked, meaning are you sure you are up to that work?

"Oh yes," Li assured him, deliberately not rising to the bait. "We wish to remain as inconspicuous as possible, and such a disguise will certainly do the trick."

"Can you handle a sword and bow?" Li and Bao glanced at one another. Bao, of course, was expert with both. With either weapon Li was more a danger to himself than to any one else.

"Of course we can," Bao broke in to cover Li's hesitation. Hu-han grinned. "Welcome then," he said, "to the ancient and honorable profession of knight errant. Let's go and dine. You'll find our food to be excellent. I recommend that you eat your fill tonight, for it's the last decent meal you'll consume for some time." He turned and led the two out across the courtyard to the banquet hall.

"Have you ever been to Shu?" Hu-han asked as they walked.

"Never," Li replied.

"If you have questions, feel free to ask. You'll find it's still something of a foreign country down there, though it's been a part of the empire for centuries. If you have anything specific you want to know, I'm sure I can help."

Bao eyed the young merchant suspiciously, but Li appeared to see nothing wrong with his offer. "Thank you," he said. "Perhaps we will have some questions once we get on the road. I have read about Shu in the narratives of the chroniclers."

"Then you've read some of the chronicle records?" Old Gao was standing courteously by the low table as the three young men filed into the banquet hall.

"Only since coming to the capital," Li replied. "Back home in Pingyang we'd never even heard of such men as Master Sehma, much less of the new style chronicles he wrote."

"Sit, sit," said their host, ushering them over to the floor mats arranged around the broad low table already set for four.

"I am not surprised," Gao resumed once all had squatted down around the table, "that the Pingyang folk had not yet heard of the illustrious Sehma Chyan. Even now his fame hardly extends beyond the palace precincts, though he's certainly well respected there."

"How do you come to know of him, sir?" Li asked. He meant no disrespect, but both the substance and tone of voice with which he asked his question revealed that he did not expect a mere merchant, even one with contacts in the capital, to be aware of the existence of so great a scholar, the founder, along with his father, of the science of history.

Gao laughed. "Ah, young man. Learn from your mentor Hwo Gwang, and do not make the error that most who govern fall into. Because the court is the center of government, those who live there seem to consider it the center of all knowledge. They think of those of us who live outside its precincts as little more than barbarians. Believe it or not, as you will, some small fragments of knowledge do leak out from the sacred precincts and find their way to Three Bridges." His uncle's speech had choked off an angry retort from Hu-han, but the nephew now settled back with a smile. Li flushed, but Bao had to mask his own ear to ear grin with a silk napkin.

"I meant no disrespect," Li assured his host. His face was burning with embarrassment. "It's just that so few, even at court, have read his work, though he is greatly respected."

"No doubt he is most respected by those who read him least," Gao observed. "If the leaders respect him, the sycophants loudly proclaim their allegiance to him too, but they take care never to actually read him lest they be tempted to contradict their superiors when they mis-quote the great man."

Li gazed in astonishment at his host. The man was talking the way old Sehma sometimes wrote. Gao simply smiled at him. Finally Li managed to stutter out a few words. "I have often felt the same way, though I've found it better to say nothing on such matters, as no one's mind seems ever to be changed and one only draws antagonism. I sup-pose that means I am turning into a sycophant, but I have taken care to read Lord Sehma's work. I was advised to read as widely as possible if I was to understand the nature of politics as practiced at court."

"Then how come he can't stay out of trouble?" Bao muttered under his breath. No one noticed.

"That was a good piece of advice," Gao said. "It sounds like the kind of advice my old benefactor would give. Indeed, he gave the same advice to me and it was through him that I first met Sehma Chyan."

"You knew Sehma Chyan at court?" Li asked excitedly.

"Not at court," came the reply. "I met him here in the company of Hwo Gwang. Sehma Chyan was a remarkable man and an honored guest. After our first meeting I asked him back. He was kind enough to stop here often as he began one journey or another in search of the information he chronicled on the warring states of the ages before the empire."

"I must apologize," Li said. "I had no idea learning was pursued so assiduously outside the capital itself. No one in Pingyang ever thought much about learning."

"Don't give me too much credit," Gao laughed. "Knowledge is of great use to merchants. We have far greater—or at least a far more immediate—need for such knowledge as was gathered by Master Sehma." The old man paused and beamed at his guests with more than the hint of a twinkle of mischief in his eyes.

"Why is that, uncle?" asked Hu-han with a smile. He had no objection to playing straight man to his uncle.

"All those in government need to know about local customs is who has how much money, cloth, and grain, and where they hide it," Gao resumed, still smiling. "Once that is known, the prefectural militia can be sent to carry away as much of this wealth as the officials have persuaded themselves they need."

"Whereas merchants," chimed in Bao, who found himself enjoying this old man greatly, "have to convince the suckers that whatever you have to offer is better than what you take."

"You are exactly right," Gao said, beaming.

"So you must be even more clever than the officials," Li said. Gao chuckled.

"No one is that clever," he said. "A merchant would be hung for attempting to do the things an official considers his right. No, we must simply be more aware of local customs and desires than officials have to be, since we must offer people what they want while officials need only offer them what the officials themselves have decided the people should want."

The conversation was interrupted by the entrance of three servants. "Let us pause for a few moments in our discussion," Gao said. With a sweep of his arm the old merchant indicated the several trays of lacquerware dishes that had been brought in by the servants. Steam and attractive odors escaped from under the covers of these dishes.

The servants busied themselves distributing the dozen odd serving dishes around the central portion of the table. Some of the dishes had their lids removed and taken away. Others remained covered, though the servants lifted the lid of each in succession for a moment so as to display the contents of the dishes and to allow the striking odors to mingle. Lacquer bowls were filled with mounds of pure white rice and placed before each diner.

"Please, begin. Help yourselves to a bit of everything," urged Gao. "But first try a bit of this," he added, placing a rather black, limp, elongated vegetable onto the top of Li's rice bowl with his own ivory chopsticks. He quickly did the same for Bao. "Careful now," he cautioned. "It's a bit spicy for some palates."

"Bao popped the whole thing into his mouth and began chewing before he caught the glance Li shot his way. Li carefully picked up the thing and even more carefully bit a small piece off the end hanging down from his chopsticks.

"Why are you taking such piddling bites, cousin?" Bao asked. "This isn't half bad, and at the rate you're going you won't finish dinner before it's time for breakfast. Surely you'd…"

Bao had been talking between chews on the odd vegetable. Now he suddenly stopped both talking and chewing. His expression turned thoughtful, then alarmed. His face reddened. He manfully began to chew again, then decided to be done with the horrid thing burning a hole in his mouth. He swallowed, but almost immediately regretted having done so. His eyes bulged as though they were about to pop out of his head.

"A little stillbeer to wash down your first taste of Szechwan black pepper?" Hu-han suggested, trying to keep a bland expression on his face.

Bao, still popeyed and red faced, turned toward the young merchant and struggled to produce a ghastly grin as he accepted the small cup of amber colored liquid being offered him. He threw the stillbeer down his throat with a single toss. The liquid did little to still the gnawing fire in his vitals. He abandoned all pretense of good table manners and let his mouth hang open, noisily inhaling and exhaling through it.

"Such a waste of fuel, warming that stillbeer," Li mused, grinning widely. "I'm sure it was hot enough to cook dumplings in before it half reached your stomach."

Bao turned one last open-mouthed exhalation into a loud groan, then joined feebly in the general laughter. Gao beamed at the two young men.

"Good," he said. "One of you is prudent and one brave; and neither is quick to anger. You will both need a sense of humor and at least one level head if you are to keep your heads attached to your necks in such times as you will have to face from hence forth."

"At least nothing more can harm us now," Bao gasped.

"Oh?"

"If anyone tries anything with us, I'll simply belch and melt everything within miles," he said, a wan smile on his now ashen face.

"Well," Gao laughed. "Now you're aware of the primary danger you are likely to face on your journey;—Southwestern cooking!" With that, Gao extended his hands again to take in the rest of the dishes steaming atop the table. "Help yourselves. Help yourselves." None of the three young men needed further invitation.

The four ate in silence for a few minutes, the two hosts occasionally placing a special morsel atop either Li's or Bao's bowl, or refilling their cups with a remarkable kind of stillbeer.

Finally, Li set down his chopsticks. Gao followed. When Bao and Hu-han had finished, the old man waved to the servants to clear the table.

"Now," Gao said once the four were alone. "Let us discuss your mission in the south." Li and Bao made their faces blank. The old man waved a hand.

"No need for such discretion," he said. "Hwo Gwang is an old friend. His letter told me something of the mission you are on. Indeed I may just know more about your problem than you do." Bao and Li exchanged glances. Gao turned to Li.

"So you think there's more to this matter of the death of the Korean girl than meets the eye?" Li looked still more uncomfortable but remained silent. Bao loosened his cloak, ready for action. Before Li could be embarrassed by refusing to speak Gao extracted an oblong piece of silk from his sleeve and gave it to Li. Li read Hwo Gwang's letter for the first time, then passed it on to Bao. Bao glanced at the elegant characters brushed onto the cloth, then passed it back to the old merchant. He would follow Li's lead.

"Apparently my master Hwo Gwang wishes me to speak freely with you," Li said, quite formally, bowing slightly as he spoke.

"Come, come," Gao chuckled. "We need not stand on ceremony here. Hwo Gwang and I are old friends. You shouldn't be surprised that he'd trust me, and have me test your discretion by waiting until now to let you read his instructions."

"Would he trust all in your household?" Li asked. Hu-han tensed in anger.

"Of course," Gao replied. "I trust Hu-han with all that I have or hope to have. To trust me is to trust him." Li bowed towards Hu-han.

"I hope there is no insult taken," Li said.

"Wouldn't you be insult…" Hu-han was silenced by Gao's raised hand.

"Of course there's no insult taken," the old man said. Your question is only to protect the interests of your master. You would be unforgivably lax if you did not ask. Hu-han would do no less if your roles were reversed." Hu-han relaxed.

"Now," Gao continued. "Let's get down to business." He turned to Li. "Do you realize how much is at stake here?" he asked.

"I do," Li replied.

"I doubt it," Gao said. "It is more than a matter of justice and honor. On the events of the next few months rest the fate of the empire for tens of years to come." Gao leaned forward, his voice took on an urgent note and the muscles in his neck tensed.

"The prosecutor Jyang is a man consumed with lust," he continued, "not for women, but for power. He yearns for power and will do anything to gain it. The murder of the Korean girl is less than nothing to him. It does not matter whether he did it or the Heir Apparent did it or had it done for some silly reason that seemed appropriate to that foolish young man. Either way her death was simply a tool in the prosecutor's drive for power. Her death can be used to eliminate the Heir Apparent whatever is the truth of the matter. That and cementing the hold of the prosecutor over the mind of the Emperor. Prosecutor Jyang wants nothing less than total power."

For a moment there was silence as the three young men digested the old man's words.

"How can such a vulgar man hope to control the Emperor himself?

Li asked finally. "There have been struggles for power before, and I realize how serious this matter is to the life of Master Hwo Gwang, but surely no one can hope to control the Emperor himself?"

"The shaman," Gao whispered.

"The shaman?" Li asked, puzzled. Bao made the sign against evil.

"Jyang is a manipulator," Gao said. "He lusts for power and pulls the strings available to him so that he might have it. In that he is no different from those who have struggled for power before and will do so again in the future. The shaman makes the difference. The shaman is the one you must unmask. Even if the Heir Apparent is involved somehow, directly or indirectly even that will turn out to have been the work of the shaman. Unmask him and you will have the key to everything."

"The shaman. Do you think it is witchcraft, then?"

"No. This is wickedness of this world, not the netherworld. So it is not witchcraft."

"I thought no one believed me."

"Hwo Gwang believes you," Gao responded. "So do I."

Li looked relieved. "I was beginning to doubt myself."

"Why does the shaman make a difference?" Bao asked.

"The Emperor is growing old," Gao answered. "He is frightened of death. He thinks his total power entitles him to live forever. Jyang seeks to convince the Emperor that the shaman is powerful enough to extend life. In return, Jyang wants to be named Chief Counselor to the Emperor."

"But when the Emperor dies Jyang will be eliminated by the enemies he's making now," Li said.

"Not if they're dead," rejoined Gao.

"Someone must be Emperor," Li said. "Jyang's lust for power will be obvious to whoever becomes Emperor. Any new ruler will force him from office."

"Perhaps," Gao said, pouring tea. "Perhaps not. Evil men have been allowed to remain in power before, but Jyang has no intention of relying on that possibility."

"What can he do?" Bao was listening rather more carefully than he seemed.

"What if Jyang gains the confidence of the Emperor through the power of the shaman, and then installs a child on the throne?"

"Of course!" Li exclaimed. "Jyang would be regent. He would have the power of an Emperor!"

"Indeed," Gao replied.

"And Hwo Gwang thinks we can do something to stop Jyang Choong?" Bao, ever the practical one, asked.

"He does," Gao replied.

"What can we do?" Li asked. "We're being sent to investigate a mine explosion in Shu. We are to determine whether the explosion is a portent worthy of the Emperor's attention or is merely some trick or natural phenomenon. We can't do much to help in Shu."

"There you are wrong," Gao said.

"How?" asked Hu-han. While much that had gone before was obviously familiar to him, this was not.

"Shu is the ancestral home of Jyang's shaman," Gao said, the smile on his face belying the seriousness of the discussion. "If it is agreed that this is not a question of witchcraft, where better to find out what worldly trick is being played here than in the regions frequented by the shaman while he learned his trade?"

"And I thought we were being sent to Shu to get us out of the way," Li said, shaking his head.

"You have much to learn about your master Hwo Gwang," Gao observed. "He seldom does anything for no reason, or," here Gao permitted himself to smile again, "necessarily for either a simple or a complicated reason alone."

"So we are to find out in Shu how the shaman does the things he does," Li said softly.

"Just so," Gao said.

"But what if we cannot?"

"Then don't bother to come back, for there will be nothing living here you would be interested in coming back to," Gao informed the boys, a grim tone to his voice.

CHAPTER THIRTY-TWO

Hot Pursuit

In the dark alley outside the gate of merchant Gao's compound, a lean figure huddled back against the wall. In the faint light of the moon, a scar could be seen running across the man's face. He cursed the shaman for not remaining in the capital where he belonged and instead coming here to bedevil him. Surely, at this hour, even the two young scamps who had given him such trouble would not be going anywhere.

The man looked up and down the street, then turned to relieve himself.

"Are they inside?" The voice suddenly sounded at the scar faced man's side. The shaman seemed to have materialized out of nowhere. The shaman smiled coolly when the stream that had been splashing against the wall stopped suddenly and the scar faced man involuntarily made the sign against evil before turning to face him.

"Yes sir," the scar faced man stuttered almost before he had confirmed the identity of his chief. "Where else would they be at this time of the night?"

"I can name several places," the shaman said, his voice deadly.

"No. They're inside. I swear to it on my life," the man said, suddenly panicked at the thought the two men might not be inside after all.

"Good," said the shaman. "Then you have no problem." The scar faced man shuddered.

"They'll be leaving in the morning," the shaman continued. "I want them followed."

"Shall I kill them?"

"Do nothing until I speak to you again. There's a pack train leaving at first light. They will be with that train. Simply follow it."

"Yes sir." The scar faced man made the sign against evil once more as the shaman dematerialized into the night. He shuddered again as he heard the echo of low laughter disappearing into nothingness.

CHAPTER THIRTY-THREE

The Battle At The Pass

The curses of merchant Gao's teamsters cut through the darkness of the pre-dawn world. Lanterns lit the courtyard but dimly. The packs were being assembled and loaded onto the animals—so far as Li could tell—in an atmosphere of confusion. Actually things were going quickly as practiced hands performed tasks done hundreds of times before. The small, round-muzzled ponies stood quietly, only occasionally launching a random kick in the direction of one of the handlers.

Hu-han and his uncle seemed to be everywhere at once in the large courtyard. Li and Bao, the sleep still in their eyes, stood and watched, helpless in their ignorance. Bao fingered the hilt of the long sword with which he had just been equipped. "At least we can defend ourselves now," he said. Li adjusted the scabbard thrust into the somewhat garish sash of his robe.

"Perhaps you can," he retorted. "I think all I could manage to do is stumble over this thing."

"We're going to have to work on that," Bao said dryly. "You get us into so much trouble, you'd better learn how to manage that thing."

"Hey! You two. Get over here and lend a hand!" The overseer's shout ended the conversation and finally launched the two into joining the last of the preparations for the trip.

Finally, after a solid hour's work, there was a pause. Bao wiped the sweat from his eyes. He nudged Li who was breathing hard after his unaccustomed exertion. "Those must be our colleagues," Bao said, nodding toward the far side of the courtyard.

"They look pretty tough," Li conceded. "I hope we aren't getting into something more than we can handle."

"If they weren't tough, they wouldn't be of any use as guards."

Led by old Gao, the three men in question sauntered into the courtyard with the ineffable air of men who lived by their strength and bravery rather than by their ancestry or their wits. They were dressed in much the same overripe style as Hu-han had used to fit out Li and Bao, but any similarity ended there. They did indeed look tough. They wore their costumes with a panache that Li and Bao knew the moment they saw it they themselves could never match. The swords swinging from their sashes looked as though they had grown there. The three men were of varying heights and weights, but all had large, heavy-fingered hands, and well-muscled forearms showing under the broad sleeves of their robes.

"Gentlemen, gentlemen!" Old Gao seemed to be almost bubbling with nervous enthusiasm. "Let me introduce you all to each other." He turned to the three men he had escorted into the yard.

"These young gentlemen are Soong Li and Chyang Bao." With a wave of his hand, Gao then indicated each of the three guards. "These men are Mr. Chyou, Mr. Foo and Mr. Lwo." The five men nodded to each other.

"You connected with the Chengdu mob?" asked Foo, the biggest of the three. His booming voice matched his physique.

"Mr. Soong and Mr. Chyang are from the north," interjected Gao. "They're from my old home town. I am under some obligation to their families and, as they had some trouble with the local authorities back home, I offered to undertake their training in various aspects of my business."

"Little boys playing at soldiers and robbers," observed Lwo, the smallest and nastiest looking of the three gangsters.

"Oh, come on," Foo wheedled. "You were once wet behind the ears too. If this pair have had problems with the authorities, we can teach them how to handle the situation next time."

"I think we deserve a bonus on this trip," Lwo said. The sneer seemed a permanent fixture on his face.

"For what?" asked Gao.

"We've got more to protect. We've got to watch out for your silver on the way out to Shu, and the lacquerware on the way back—which is no problem since you've already negotiated a price for that—but what about these two? They'll be more trouble than either the silver or the lacquerware from the looks of them, and unless I miss my guess, you do want them to return intact."

Li flushed in anger. He began a sharp tongued retort, but stopped short as Bao gave a sharp tug at the back of his robe. For his part, Bao said nothing. He simply examined Lwo's face speculatively.

"I agree." Chyou, the third of the guards, spoke. "These two look as though their swords are more danger to themselves than to any robbers. If you'll let us pack the lads up in the saddlebags with the rest of the luggage, we could see a reason not to charge for the extra freight, but with them up and about and always in the way, we really ought to get more."

"A big bonus," Lwo said. "At least baggage holds still during a fight." He put on a broad smile, obviously intended to be one of jolly good fellowship, but the effect was decidedly sinister. Now Bao finally spoke up, his hand conspicuously on the hilt of his sword.

"If the good Mr. Lwo wishes a demonstration of our ability to take care of ourselves, I'd be most happy to accommodate him. After I've done so, he may not have to worry about a trip to Shu." Lwo's hand darted to the hilt of his own sword. It was quickly covered by the huge ham that passed for Foo's hand.

"Oh ho," Foo boomed. "There's no need for any trouble. Why mess up a perfectly good day?" Foo's booming laugh was infectious. Lwo grinned, or at least turned his sneer into a grimace, and withdrew his hand from the hilt of his sword. Bao grinned and did the same.

"Brother Lwo doesn't mean to look the way he does," Foo continued. "He was born that way. He's really much nicer than he looks, and a far finer person than he sounds. The poor wretch just never learned how to behave in civilized company. Why, poor fellow, they had to tie his mother down before she'd suckle him!" At that, everyone burst out laughing.

Old Gao looked relieved. Li, who had started forward, either to restrain Bao or back him up—whichever seemed most practical—let his arm drop from his own sword hilt. He too smiled, though he failed to see much that was funny in the rough humor of the big gangster. Foo slapped Bao and Lwo simultaneously on their backs, and swept them forward.

"Come on," he said. "The teamsters almost have things ready to go. Lets step over to the wall and get acquainted over a bit of breakfast."

The sun was just above the horizon by the time the caravan had formed itself out of the apparent chaos of the merchant's outer courtyard, unwound through the alleys of Three Bridges, and trotted out the western gate. Li felt an odd sense of exultation. At last! The journey and their quest had begun. Somehow the uncertainty of the future and the grim feeling that his own future actions might well determine the course of the empire merely added to the feeling of exultation. Heady stuff indeed. The road west led them between the sere, tan soil of the broken hills to their left and the slow, dark waters of the Wei River on their right. The land appeared bleached, its pale expanses broken only by occasional dark clumps of small trees on the steeper slopes of the hills. The river's dark hue was more frequently highlighted by bright streaks of sand.

"The river's low," observed Bao. He and Li were astride two medium sized ponies, and had been positioned roughly mid-way along the line of the caravan.

"It always is this time of the year," Li replied.

"That's odd. You'd think it would be higher now."

"Not so." Li was happy to have the upper hand for a change. The past couple of days had done nothing for his self-esteem. "Winter's already begun way out west where the Wei has its headwaters. Most of the water that would normally feed it is already frozen."

"No water. No wonder it looks so dry around here."

"Not much like Pingyang, is it?" Li mused. "Look how few trees there are. And so small!"

"That's what comes of planting a city of nearly a million souls on the edge of the desert." Hu-han had ridden up from the rear of the caravan. He nudged his horse in the side to match its pace to that of Li's and Bao's animals.

"They say this land was heavily forested in the days of the Sage Kings," he continued. "There were thick forests even as late as the times of Kings Wen and Wu of Jou, but winters are cold, and the capital grows year after year. Even here, fifty miles away, the trees have been stripped, except from the steepest slopes. By tomorrow evening we'll start to hit forests as heavy as those that used to grow here, even though the country there is even drier than this."

"Out of the reach of the woodcutter's axe?" asked Bao.

"Just so," responded Hu-han.

"What will they do when all the trees within range of the city have been chopped down?" Li asked. "Things must be nearly at that point already." Li was saddened by the implications of his own question. Despite the brilliant blue sky, this bare landscape was beginning to get to him.

"Move the capital, I suppose, or maybe dig for those black rocks that burn like charcoal. But that's another story for another day." Hu-han waved, then spurred his horse and rode up toward the head of the caravan.

"A cheerful liar, isn't he?" observed Bao.

"That kind always is," Li said sourly. The land around the capital is denuded for fifty miles in every direction, and all he can do is airily suggest that either the capital will be moved when no one can afford to pack charcoal into it or tell some cock and bull story about burning rocks! Doesn't he worry about ruining the land?"

"Some of us have enough other worries," Bao said, glancing back along the trail.

"You still think someone may be following us?"

"I do."

"Have you seen any signs of that?"

"None," Bao admitted. "I don't know why, but I feel it in my bones. Someone is following us."

"Then I guess we'd better stay alert. There's too much at stake for us to let our guard down."

"You've got that right, anyway. My head has no wish to be parted from my body at my tender age."

"That's the least of our worries," Li said. "We've just got to find some way to stop Jyang Choong. If he takes over the empire, Hwo Gwang's family, Lady Wei, the Heir Apparent—they're all finished."

"And we won't last much longer," Bao added.

"It's far more than that. Far more. The empire will run with blood!"

"Our blood!"

"Every foul and noxious superstition the Sages and their pupils have labored to put down will ride onto the throne with the imposter!"

"We should only live to see it!" Bao's grin broke through his mock piety. There was a shout up ahead. The caravan stopped and Foo was waving the two boys forward. They put spurs to their ponies' sides and rode up to the head of the caravan.

"What's wrong?" Li asked as they came abreast of the head of the stalled pack train.

"Dead Horse Pass," Foo grunted, as though the name explained the problem.

"It's a favored place for ambush," Hu-han explained. Bao's hand went to his sword.

"Someone has to scout it out," Foo said. He reached into his cloak and took some colored sticks out. He chose three and held them out to Lwo and Chyou.

"What are you doing?" Li asked.

"Someone has to scout out the pass," Lwo sneered. "Since no one in his right mind is going to volunteer to put his butt on the line, we have to allow the gods to decide who gets to go."

"Why three straws?" Bao asked. "Am I not part of the guard?"

"Ho," Foo laughed. "Our little rooster is a fighting cock."

"Not me," Bao said. "But fair's fair."

"I think not," Foo replied. "Merchant Gao made it clear. You're to be cared for."

"I'll care for myself," Bao said. "Count me in." Foo looked a question at Hu-han.

"I think not," Hu-han said.

"Our young cock is for decorative purposes only," jeered Chyou.

"A capon," laughed Lwo.

"Perhaps," Bao said. "But one with enough manhood to reject chance as a way to determine the path of his life." With that he kicked the side of his horse, and galloped towards the pass." Li watched him go, gulped once, then set off after him.

Foo wheeled his horse around.

"Let them go," Lwo said. "If those two manage to find their way back, we'll know for sure the pass is safe."

"Can you imagine anyone stupid enough to go up there willingly?" asked Chyou. He and Lwo chuckled.

"Once we'd have been men enough to do something like that," Foo said. "That we haven't the courage any more has nothing to do with intelligence. It's our loss, not theirs." Lwo's and Chyou's laughter died away. Gangsters and private guards still affected what they took to be the manners of the long gone age of knight errantry, but in their bones they knew that only a few of the younger men, including some from the official class, still really believed in its values enough to act as these two boys had done. The three watched the two boys with new respect as Bao and Li cantered into the pass.

As he came up to the pass Bao looked back over his shoulder. The sight of Li bobbing along astride his pony, struggling to stay mounted while maintaining what he thought was a gallop was funny enough to make him forget the possible consequences of his rash act. He slowed his horse so that Li might catch up.

"So," he called out as Li approached, "you decided to tag along?"

"Someone's got to take care of you," Li gasped, trying to catch his breath as he talked. "You'd probably get lost if I let you go in there all by yourself."

"Probably," Bao laughed. They rode side by side into the pass.

"What are we looking for?" Li asked once they had entered the pass proper. "Bandits?"

"Fortunately, we don't have to look very hard. If they're here, they'll find us quick enough, and you'll find out what it is to really set a horse into a gallop."

"It's not bandits you're worrying about, is it?"

"Who's worried? But I do think this would be a perfect place to get rid of two meddlesome agents of an out-of-favor family."

"You really think the prosecutor's men know where we are?" Li asked. "How do you know they don't still think we're still on the way to Gan Springs to get our final instructions?"

"I'd bet a month's pay they know just where we are. If anyone was following us—and I'd bet two months' pay someone was—they'd have known by the next morning when we sneaked out of camp the other night. It wouldn't take a lot of brains to figure out where we'd be headed."

"Well," Li said. "We'll know for sure in a few minutes. You're certainly right. If someone wants us, here's where they'll try for us." Almost as the words left Li's mouth, his horse screamed and reared as an arrow pierced its side. Li was thrown clear as the animal went down. It quivered spasmodically, then lay still, blood dripping from its nose and red foam bubbling on its mouth. Bao was in motion before Li realized what had happened. Li was just staggering to his feet when he felt himself dragged bodily onto the neck of Bao's pony, and then just as suddenly thrown to the ground near some rocks. Bao jumped off the animal and pulled it to the ground. He pulled his sword and quickly slashed the animal's throat.

"Why did you do that?" Li demanded. "We should have galloped back as quickly as we could." Bao merely pointed, first to the trail they'd just travelled, then to the trail ahead. Men were climbing down from rocks and out of trees on both sides. There were at least seven or eight of them. All had bows and arrows.

"You're right," Li conceded. "They'd have nailed us any way we went." Bao said nothing. He was surveying the situation.

Bao's first action on seeing the arrow slam into Li's horse had been to pull back on the reins and drag his own animal over to where his friend had fallen. He had reached down and dragged Li up in front of him and prepared to flee only to see the trees and rocks sprout the enemies he had just pointed out to Li. He quickly looked around and chose a place to make a stand.

The pass was bounded on the east by a high cliff. Something had created a slight hollow at one point near the base of the cliff. Bao had spurred his animal to that place. Now at least no one could shoot arrows at them from above. The nearest tree large enough to support a man was forty paces away. Anyone trying for a good shot from there would be open to return fire. Some large rocks just in front of the depression in the cliff offered them some protection from arrows shot from ground level. The place seemed ideal for defense, but poor as the base for an escape. But, Bao reflected, escape didn't seem likely anyway.

"How many arrows do you have," Bao whispered.

Li did a quick count. "Eight," he replied.

"I've got nine. Not much for making a stand."

"If we can hold out for a few minutes, we should get some help."

"From that bunch?" Bao snorted. "None of them would rescue their own mother if she fell into a shallow stream with no current. Or if they did, by the time they'd finished that game of pick-up-sticks of theirs the old lady would have drowned."

"How about Gao Hu-han?"

"All he's worried about is his uncle's silver," Bao said. "I think we're going to have to get ourselves out of this."

"How are we going to do that?" Li asked.

"Maybe we can bluff them off until nightfall. Then we can slip away."

"I don't think so," Li said. "Look."

Their attackers had wasted no time taking random shots at their position. They had quickly put together a plan and were busily preparing for its implementation. Three men had taken up positions flanking the redoubt and were nocking arrows to bow strings. The rest had discarded their bows and unsheathed their swords.

"Uh oh," Bao muttered. "You're right. They aren't going to give us until tonight. They're coming now." He unsheathed his sword, set it down by his side and picked up his bow. Li mimicked him. Squatting back to back, each faced one of the flanks. "Don't lose track of where your sword is," Bao said. "Let's just hope no one comes at us straight from the front."

"Can we hold them off?" Li asked, already sweating as though he had fought through the entire afternoon.

"Are you kidding?" The wisecrack Bao was formulating was lost in a shout from outside their redoubt followed by the screaming whisper of the flight of an arrow.

Whoever had planned the attack had planned well. The three bow-men assigned to keep Bao and Li under cover while the rest attacked with swords did not all fire at once. First one arrow came, then one from a second bow, then one from the third. By that time the first bow-man had another arrow ready to go. The result was a steady stream of arrows hissing through the narrow opening between the rocks behind which the boys crouched. There was no chance for them to take any shots at the advancing swordsmen.

"Better take your sword," Li said. "They'll be on us in a few sec-onds. I'm sorry about all this. If it hadn't been for me, you'd be back home now with a small farm, a fat wife and a bunch of sons to carry on your line."

"What! And miss all this fun? You just get ready to fight. Nothing's over yet."

With that, there was a scream as one of the swordsmen, who had been boosted to the top of the rocks leaped down upon them. Bao had expected this and put an arrow through him before he reached the ground.

"Here they come," Bao shouted as he snatched up his sword. In a moment the two were fighting for their lives.

To Li it seemed as though the next five minutes lasted for half a day. He had thought himself incapable of the kind of fight he put up. The space between the rocks let only one man at a time come through at him. The narrowness of their little battlefield also helped even the odds as his opponents could not swing their swords freely enough to take advantage of their superior skills. Still, Li fought with a savagery he would have considered impossible for him before the fact.

Bao fought more soberly, but with grim determination. His supe-rior skill was somewhat offset by the need to keep watch for another attack from above. What he expected soon came about. He caught a quick movement out of the side of his eyes. He swung twice, forcing his opponent to back off, then quickly whirled. The knife he had held in his left hand flew through the air and slipped into the throat of the man standing atop the rock aiming an arrow at him. Bao was back in battle with the swordsman facing him before the man above had slumped to the surface of the rock, and then slid down into the narrow battlefield.

Li had been hard pressed by his opponent. His strength was ebbing. The last flurry of blows had resulted in a slash across his chest. He knew it was just a matter of a few more exchanges before Bao would be left alone, his rear uncovered. Still, he did not give up. His opponent leaped forward just as the archer Bao had killed slid down to the ground and the dead body struck Li's attacker just as Li made a thrust. Li felt the impact of sword on bone as he completed his move. The man's death shudder nearly shook the sword from Li's hand. Li reached out with his free hand, his instinct being to comfort the man, but the appearance of yet another enemy caused him to jerk back and set himself for another encounter.

Bao knew the battle was nearly over. He had killed two men besides the archer, but as each fell another leaped in to join the battle. He and Li were pressed back to back. He was surprised that Li was still fighting, but knew he could not last long. Again a flash of movement caught his eye. Another archer was sighting down on them from atop the rock, but this time Bao had no knife left to throw. He lunged forward desperately, forcing his opponent to jump well back out of range, flung his own sword up toward the archer and prayed he could reach the sword of one of the men he had killed before his current opponent could reach him.

The archer above screamed, then toppled, the shaft of an arrow protruding from his back. Bao's opponent was also down, and behind him Foo appeared, leading several horses.

"Hurry!" Foo shouted, turning away and swinging his sword at some unseen opponent. "I can't hold them off all day."

Bao acted instantly. He had already picked up a fallen enemy's sword. He turned and threw it across the few feet separating him from Li's attacker. The man went down, not mortally wounded, but at least incapacitated for the moment. Bao took hold of Li's robe and pulled his friend back out of the other end of the defile to where Foo still held the horses. He threw Li aboard one of them, leaped up on a second one himself and saw that Foo had already mounted a third animal.

"Let's go!" he shouted.

"None too soon for me!" Foo bellowed, a roar of laughter now amplified by battle lust coming from his throat. The three men wheeled their horses around and kicked them into a full gallop, riding low on the backs of the animals so as to present as small targets as possible. As he rode by one of the attackers Bao saw the man duck as an arrow sliced in from somewhere and embedded itself in the tree trunk the attacker had used for shelter.

"Eiiiiii..." Foo's battle howl rang out as they broke into the open outside the pass and made for the pack train, which had been secured for battle. Answering shouts came from the cliffs flanking the pass as Lwo and Chyou rode their ponies down to join them. Gao Hu-han stood waiting, armed and ready for a fight. The teamsters crouched nervously, fingering weapons they had not anticipated having to use. "Get ready to fight," Foo shouted as he reined in his pony. "They're likely to be right behind us and as mad as a bunch of hornets after someone's stirred up their nest with a stick."

Li almost fell off his horse. He felt sick. He had never worked so hard. He would have faded out behind a bush to vomit, and very likely swoon away, if the teamsters had not been watching him with what he still did not realize was admiration in their eyes. He drew himself up, and forced himself to walk over to where Hu-han, Bao and Foo were discussing their battle plan.

"How many were there?" Foo asked.

"Eight or nine that we saw for sure," Bao replied.

"How many are left?" Hu-han asked.

"I don't know," Bao answered. "Li and I took care of five, though one of those is only wounded. I know that whoever was shooting from atop the cliff got one of them, though how he managed to hit anything with that overhang in the way I'll never know. But I thank him."

By this time Lwo and Chyou had arrived. "Once he stood up on that rock to aim at you," Lwo said, "there was a clear enough shot."

"It was still a great shot," Bao said. Lwo bowed slightly to acknowledge the compliment.

"That means they may not have enough of a force left to mount an attack on us," Hu-han said.

"They don't want us anyway," Lwo said.

"What do you mean?" Hu-han did not sound surprised.

Lwo turned to Li and Bao. "Did you see anything when you went into the pass?" he asked.

"Nothing," Bao said. "They were well hidden."

"Then why did they attack you?" Lwo asked. "If they wanted to attack the pack train, they'd have waited until it entered the pass." He paused, then chuckled. It came out a rather sinister cackle. "It would seem, my friends, that you are worth more to someone than a pack train full of silver.

CHAPTER THIRTY-FOUR

The Watcher

The shaman sat back on his haunches and watched the pack train travel through the pass. He was absolutely motionless. A fly landed on his cheek, crawled up and across an eyelash without evoking so much as a blink. Like some color changing lizard, the shaman seemed to have taken on the characteristics of the background against which he rested. Watchful eyes from the pack train scanned the canyon walls, yet saw nothing.

A hint of a smile flickered across the shaman's face as he watched Li and Bao ride their ponies past him. "These two have a flair for survival," he thought as he watched them go. "It's almost a blessing to have worthy opponents for a change."

The incipient smile turned to a sneer as the shaman thought of the events that had put him on the trail of the two young men. "That fool Jyang," he thought. "He thinks to control me. One day he'll learn better."

The pack train passed on. The shaman followed.

CHAPTER THIRTY-FIVE

The Age Of Philosophy

The only reason anyone would want to kill us is that we're onto something," Li argued.

"But what are we on to?" Bao asked. "It isn't much use to know something, if you don't know what it is."

"Nevertheless," Li replied. "Someone wants us dead, and that means we're onto the right track somehow."

"Even if we are, is it worth the risk we're taking?" Bao asked. "What have we got to gain?"

"At this point, what have we got to lose? We're too darned far into this mess to back out at this point. If Lord Hwo's family goes, we'll go down with it no matter what we do now. And the dynasty. How long could it last under Jyang's domination?"

Li paused. Something more seemed to be required. "At least we'll be on the side of right," he added, his voice rather more firm than he had expected it to be. "That's enough to justify any risks."

"What is right?" Bao asked.

"Loyalty and faithful service. Our master's teacher, Doong Joongshu, knew that. So did our ancestor, Lord Chi, and so must we, if we are to honor his name."

"Do you think that old story is really true?" Bao asked. "Do you really thing the founder of Soong was one of our ancestors?"

"I do," Li said softly.

"Why?" asked his cousin. "Even the learned men seem to know little of him beyond a few old stories, and isn't it mainly because Soong territory was where our clan came from that you pay attention to that old stuff?"

"There's more than that. Old Sehma Chyan devoted some space

to him in his history, so he must have thought those old stories had something to them. Beyond that, though, I feel a kinship with Lord Chi in my very bones. In fact…" Li's voice trailed off.

"In fact what?" Bao spoke much more gently than usual.

Li blushed. "The fact is, I sometimes dream of him."

"And what does he say in these dreams?"

"It's hard to explain." Li's voice was now practically inaudible over the jangling of the harness. "He doesn't really say anything of consequence. He just… He sort of…"

"Yes?"

"Well, I'm always left with the impression that there is some great thing I must accomplish with my life. He gives me encouragement, and presses me to prepare for this thing."

"What thing?"

"I don't know. I simply know that I must stay on the road that leads to right, and that if I do so, I will accomplish the task destined for me."

"And what about me? Does ancestor Chi tell you what part I play in this piece of theatre?"

"A friend that can be trusted with one's very life is a treasure beyond all value."

For a moment both were too embarrassed by the depth of their own feelings to say anything.

"And why did we get into this mess in the first place?" Bao asked, clearly eager to shift to some less embarrassing aspect of their problem. "The Emperor is old, and sometimes I wonder if he is still capable of rule. The Empress is a former dance hall girl, and probably something worse. Her daughters were caught awhoring with a pasty little pimp like Goongsun, and from what I hear the Heir Apparent is not the brightest two legged animal at court. Is it for that collection of bipeds that we are risking all that we are or hope to be?"

"Yes," Li replied. "We risk everything for the Emperor, and for the imperial family. He is Heaven's Son, its representative on Earth. We owe him our very lives."

"Him, maybe," Bao grudgingly conceded, "but we owe his family nothing."

"What about Hwo Gwang?"

"What about him?"

"Have you ever known or heard of anyone more honest and upright, or a shrewder judge of men? Surely such a man deserves our loyalty. Without such ministers, how could the Emperor serve Heaven?"

"But why serve anyone, Heaven included? Why do we owe allegiance to anyone or anything beyond ourselves?"

"Because we just have to serve some higher good," Li replied.

"To what purpose?"

"To promote that which is right, and defeat that which is evil. If we serve nothing, there is no point to life."

"I suppose," Bao conceded. "Myself, I've never figured it all out, and I suppose I never will."

"Do you believe there is good and evil? That it's proper to love children, and not serve them in a sauce for breakfast?"

"Of course," Bao snorted. "Anyway," he grinned, "it's not healthy to eat anything complicated enough to require a sauce for breakfast."

"Aside from your tendency to make a joke of serious matters, you obviously must believe in something higher than yourself. It's just as Confucius said, if Heaven didn't want me to risk all for the good, and fight against the bad, why do I find within myself so irresistible an impulse to act along those lines? I know what justice is, and I know that Hwo Gwang is a just man. So do you. And I know we will both serve him any way we can."

"My friend the philosopher," Bao snorted. "You'll get me killed yet, you and those books of Master Doong's that old Hwo has filled you full of. Still, the sun is high and my bruised bones are warming up, and I haven't anything better to do, so I suppose I'll follow along for a time."

"Good." Li's spirits were restored. "Now let's get to figuring out what's been going on, and who is causing events to flow the way they have been."

"Not my department," Bao grinned. "I'll watch your back, but you are the philosopher. You do the thinking." With that he slapped the rump of Li's horse, sending the animal into a spirited gallop. He laughed as he watched his friend bounce about on the horse's back, then set spur to his own mount and raced to catch up.

For two days the pack train moved briskly along the banks of the Wei River, heading almost directly west. Gradually the villages and towns became more scattered and smaller. The trees, as Gao Hu-han had predicted, became larger and more numerous. On the left, the foothills of the great Chinling mountain range also bulked larger, and seemed ever closer to the low, pale, sandy hills which lay to their immediate left, on the south side of the river road.

Bao and Li were riding at the head of the caravan with Gao Hu-han as the late afternoon sun approached the line of the hills to their front and left. The sky was clear and intensely blue and the weather dry and cold.

"Look," young Gao pointed.

"Baoji?" Bao asked. "It certainly doesn't look like much of a town," he added as Gao nodded in affirmation.

"It isn't much," admitted Gao. "It's little more than an overnight stop at the junction of the roads leading west and south. Take the road going west, and you'll eventually end up on the great caravan routes to the far off lands of the Hindus or even the lands of the Persians and the empire that some say lies beyond that of the Persians."

"'Great Chin they call it, don't they?" asked Li.

"So we call it," answered Hu-han. "Some say its proper name is 'Lo-ma,' but no one knows for sure. Even the great explorer Jang Chyan never got beyond the eastern reaches of the kingdom of the Persians."

"Some say there is no such kingdom," Bao said.

"Some will doubt that the sun rises in the east," Hu-han rejoined. As he gazed toward the west a far away look came into his eyes before he abruptly turned back to his companions.

"Ah, well," he said. "It's of little importance. Here is where we turn to the south. Tomorrow we'll be entering the mountains and going up Powder Pass. It should be quite an experience for the both of you. Tonight we'll sleep under a roof in Baoji. Tomorrow we'll spend the night under the open sky atop a mountain."

CHAPTER THIRTY-SIX

A Night On the Town

I hope there's something going on in Baoji tonight," Li said. "That hole in the wall we stayed in last night was hardly better than camping in the open air!"

"You've been spoiled by the easy life of Chang-an, my friend," Hu-han chuckled. "You'll have to get used to the austere pleasures of the travelling merchant's existence."

"Pleasures?" protested Li. "A cold supper, cold drinks, and a still colder bed atop what looked like a masonry stove, but whose insides must not have seen any charcoal since the middle of the last reign!"

"It seems we are abusing the body of our tender prince," Bao laughed as he entered the conversation. He ducked Li's backhand slap.

Hu-han laughed too. "Believe me, even the simplest roof over one's head can sometimes be a genuine pleasure in our sort of life. But don't despair. Things will be somewhat better in Baoji. It's a bigger place, and boasts an excellent place to eat, drink, and… erh… satisfy other appetites."

"Indeed it does," Foo grinned as he rode up abreast of them.

"You'll have to stand one of the watches over the pack animals," Hu-han told the two cousins, "but I'll assign you to the last one, so you can take in the entertainment at its peak hour."

"I'll take the first watch," Foo laughed. "I don't mind letting the young bulls dally with the cows before I get to the pasture. They'll wear themselves out early, and I'll have the rest of the night to myself."

The company continued towards Baoji in high spirits, and no one noticed the solitary figure following well behind them.

The sun was long since down before the pack animals had been unloaded and the personnel of the caravan assigned to their quarters.

Li, Bao and Lwo walked briskly away from the tumult of the inn's courtyard.

"You're sure you know how to find this place?" asked Bao.

"I said so, didn't I?" snarled Lwo. The two young men took no offense now that they realized that Lwo snarled on all occasions.

"There's a lot of foreigners here, aren't there?" Bao commented.

"What do you expect in a place like this?" Lo nastily rejoined. "A bunch of sissified wimps like you'd find in the capital?" The cousins smiled at him and kept looking around as they walked.

The narrow street on which they found themselves was crowded, and in fact the faces that slipped past them did tend to be longer of nose and more hirsute of jaw than was the norm among the Chinese of the capital, though a few such were sometimes to be seen in Chang-an's markets. Here, though, they could much more often even catch sight of a pair of blue eyes below a thatch of yellow, or sometimes red, hair. Even some of those whose faces looked Chinese were dressed in the garb of one or another of the nomadic tribes or oasis towns of the western frontier region. Everywhere there resounded the strange sounds of even stranger sounding language from some far away place.

"On the other hand, there are a few familiar faces," Bao muttered softly after poking Li in the ribs. "Take a glance at that fellow on your right."

As Li turned to look, Bao jerked at his elbow. "Don't be too obvious," he whispered. "Just a glance. Do you remember him?"

"No. The man looks familiar, but I can't place him."

"He was one of Ju's men. At the Rotten Cabbage."

"Rotten cabbage?" interjected Lwo. "Nah. There's none of that Korean garbage out here. We're too far from the capital for that. This place specializes in the Shu style of cooking. Hot stuff!" Lwo pointed to a gateway. "Come on," he said. "Here we are."

He pushed the two young men into a wide gateway, across a cobbled courtyard, and up a narrow flight of steps. At the top they found themselves in a large, well-lit, and pleasantly warmed room containing low tables and soft, clean-looking mats placed at wide intervals along the floor. There was a low stage at the far end of the room. Less than half the tables were occupied, most of them by men who appeared, like themselves, to be Chinese merchants in travelling clothes.

The waiter seemed to know Lwo. He led the three to a table just to the right of the stage, and as they squeezed down onto the mat beside it, the waiter held a whispered conference with the little gangster. Bao glanced at Lwo, who took the hint.

"The fellow says there'll just be time for some preliminary snacks and a warmed bottle of booze before the first show begins. I've ordered you a set of Shu-style dishes for your dinner. Don't worry."

At that moment the waiter reappeared with a large, fully loaded tray, which he set down beside the table, and began to unload. Some of the dishes were hot, some cold, but all were colorful. In a few moments the table was full, and the elegantly carved ivory chopsticks they had each been issued were darting experimentally among the many items. The two cousins were alert to the presence of the hot, black peppers in some of the dishes, and were so absorbed by the variety of the feast set before them they missed the arrival of warmed stillbeer.

Lwo did not, however, miss such an important event. He poured a small cup of the fragrant liquid for each.

"This is good stuff," Bao said, smacking his lips after downing his second cup of the brew.

"This is good booze country," Lwo assured him. "And it gets better after we cross the mountains. Shu is the best place in the empire for booze, for food, and for winter weather."

Suddenly, Lwo broke off. "Hah," he said, pointing to the stage. A woman, clearly of middle years, but still handsome, had appeared on the stage and was kneeling beside the zither-like stringed instrument she had brought on with her. Her head was bent modestly down as she tuned it. Then, without looking up, she began a song which seemed to grow out of the random chords of the tuning process.

The ballad she sang was of the early days of the dynasty: Of how the founder of the Han at first took the old capital, and then yielded it up to his great southern rival, whose troops proceeded to loot the place before they returned south, where the founder finally ran them down and defeated them. She ended with the lament of the southern general's consort as she saw her lover off for his last fatal battle.

At the end of the song there was an instant of silence, and then the audience began to applaud enthusiastically.

"She's pretty good," said Li. "She actually got the history part of the song down pretty exactly.

"So?" Lwo seemed less than greatly impressed. Li misunderstood him, taking the comment as a question.

"It's pretty unusual," he explained. Bao rolled his eyes towards heaven. "I've just finished Sehma Chyan's history, and her lyrics are very close to the story he gives."

"Sehma Chyan?" asked Lwo. "Then there's no mystery in the woman's knowing a bit of history."

"Do they read Sehma Chyan here too?" Li asked, with some excitement. Lwo sputtered, he was laughing so hard.

"Not quite," the little gangster finally got out. "She got her history right from the fellow himself, though she doubtless was having a better time while she got it than you did groping your way through a scroll of bamboo slats."

"What do you mean?" Li asked, the blush on his face suggesting that he was beginning to understand at least part of what the now leering Lwo was hinting at.

"That Sehma fellow spent some time here about twenty five years ago interviewing merchants passing through. He became quite the favorite of this one." Lwo nodded towards the stage. "The story goes that she didn't even charge him for her favors. Took it out in trade, I suppose. If he visited her as often as they stories say, she must have gotten enough material out of him for a lifetime supply of ballad lyrics." Lwo leered again as he refilled his cup.

"Sehma Chyan... and this lady?" Li was taken aback. "One somehow doesn't associate his name with that sort of thing."

"Well," grinned Bao. "The man had to do something to break the monotony of writing that colossal book of his." He and Lwo burst into loud laughter at the look on Li's face.

"Ah," Lwo interrupted. "Here comes supper!"

The "snacks" Lwo had ordered to begin with had seemed to Li and

Bao enough to constitute an entire meal, but the number and size of the dishes now arriving at the table were enough to make the earlier repast truly look like a snack.

The meal and the entertainment made the evening fly by, though Bao made a point of scanning the faces in the room from time to time. The female singer did two more numbers, both of which Li could trace to chapters of Sehma's history book, though he was too embarrassed to resume his lecture on that subject.

Lwo eventually became very drunk, and the other two, though less inclined to that vice, found themselves not far behind him, since their capacity seemed to be less than that of the hard-bitten little gangster.

The night was well gone by the time they staggered back to their inn. After decanting Lwo onto his pallet, Li and Bao made their way back to their end of the large sleeping room.

Bao staggered to his bedding and deposited himself onto it without bothering to remove his outer clothing. "Boy," he whispered a bit more loudly than necessary for Li to hear him. "It hardly pays to go to bed it's so nearly time to get up again. This is turning out to be quite a vacation."

"So far, anyway," Li replied, slurring the words. He had undressed before settling inside his bedding.

"You know we're still being followed, don't you?" Bao said, not as drowsily as before.

"If you say so, it must be so," Li replied. "Every time I doubt you, I turn out to be wrong. The question is: Why?"

"Maybe Jyang wants revenge," Bao said. "You made him look pretty bad a couple of times back there."

"Maybe. But more likely we know something we shouldn't."

"Like what? What could we possibly know that Jyang would go through all this trouble for?"

"If I knew the answer to that question, I could save us a lot of time and trouble, couldn't I?" Li said, sounding cranky as well as drunk.

For a time they remained silent.

"Maybe…" Li began. He paused. "Oh, never mind. Let's call it a night." He was answered by loud snores from Bao's throat.

CHAPTER THIRTY-SEVEN

An Ally

S tart digging a grave," Bao said plaintively. "I'm certainly going to be in need of one soon."

"I can't," Li replied. "My head hurts too much."

"Good morning, young gentlemen." The booming voice of Foo, cheerful though it might be, evoked winces from the two suffering cousins.

Foo grinned at the obvious discomfort the two young men evidenced. "Up and at 'em," he said heartily. "Chyou and I took mercy on you. We took your watch and let you sleep in. But there's no more time to dally. We've got a long day ahead of us. One you're sure to enjoy, as there'll be lots of extra bouncing as your ponies trot up the pass."

Foo's grin widened as Li and Bao groaned at his words.

"What's the matter with these two?" Lwo asked as he sauntered back in from the courtyard. He stretched and yawned luxuriously, and then, for the first time since they had met, smiled broadly. "These two look as though they'd died, but then came back."

"They probably wish they had died and hadn't managed to come back," Foo observed. "Well, to work." He gave each of the boys a helpful clap on the back as he walked out towards the pack train.

Li and Bao were beginning to feel a bit, but only a bit, better by the time the pack train moved onto the road.

Almost immediately the track began to take the train higher and higher into the pass.

Signs of human intervention on the landscape, other than the narrow path, nearly disappeared soon after the train left Baoji behind in the dust. Though the weather was clear and the air sharp, progress was slow. The trail was well worn, but steep and irregular, forcing the ponies to pick their way. Now and again all had to dismount, and lead their ponies on foot. This slowed their progress even more.

"I'd have thought we could see more," Li commented. "There's so much brush, a squad of men could be hiding ten feet from the edge of the road, and we'd never know it."

"There'll be plenty of empty space to view soon enough," Foo said. "Have you ever heard of the roofed roads?"

"The roofed roads?" Bao asked. "What are they?"

"I've heard of them, but I don't know much about them." Li said. "What are they like?"

"You'll see soon enough," Foo said with a grin.

The pack train reached the summit of the first pass early the next morning, and spent the next several days zig-zagging across the Chinling Range, at times dropping deep into valleys, at other times traversing the edges of long, high ridges.

The weather had begun to change by noon of their second day in the mountains. Clouds piled up atop the peaks that afternoon. By the next morning the hollows were filled with fog, and though the sun burned off some of the mist, the skies never quite cleared thereafter.

They were marching along through the usual rough, brush-filled terrain when a sharp turn in the road revealed a sight that caused Li and Bao to gasp in astonishment.

The road ahead appeared to have been cut out of a nearly vertical wall of rock which curved to their right beginning a quarter of a mile ahead. Just past the beginning of the curve there was a long, low building attached somehow to the face of the cliff. The road disappeared into the narrow end of this building.

"What on earth is that?" Bao asked.

"A roofed road," Lwo replied.

"The roof keeps landslides off the road?" Li asked.

"It does that," Hu-han affirmed, "But there's more to it than that. Take another look as we get closer, and then guess again as to the reason for the roof's existence."

"What do you suppose he means?" Li asked Bao as they trudged toward the strange looking structure.

"I don't know," Bao replied. "To me it just looks like a shack built over the trail."

Though they had reached a relatively high altitude, the road was no longer climbing, so it was only a matter of a few minutes before they had come close enough to the bridge to examine its whole length, just before the road turned sharply to the right to enter its short end.

"Why it's not just a roof," Li exclaimed, once he could see the construction of the thing. "The whole road is cantilevered out from the face of the cliff."

"The roof is simply to keep the weather from rotting out the timbers supporting the road," Hu-han explained.

"No wonder Sehma Chyan made so much of the construction of these things in his chronicle of the rise of Chin," Li said, his eyes wide with wonder.

"Where does Chin come into the picture?" Bao asked. "Chin fell more than a hundred years ago. This structure is old, but it's not that old."

"It was Chin that first built this road right after he conquered Shu and Ba," Li replied. "They had to invent the roofed road so as to complete this highway across the mountains. It enabled them to ship grain up from Shu and Ba and soldiers down in that direction very quickly. That put them in a position to conquer all the states downstream on the Yangtze River from Shu and Ba by barging an army down the river to fall on their flanks." Li looked up at the structure. "I knew building this road was a great exploit, but I never imagined something like this!"

"Look at the size of those beams!" exclaimed Bao. "And the carpentry of the trusses that hold them up. Can you imagine how much work went into building these things?"

"And even with the roof, the climate here is so damp that the timbers have to be replaced every fifty years or so," Hu-han told them. "Even so, you sometimes wonder if you're going to make it across. This one's brand new, but wait until you see the condition of some of those further down the road."

"Do they ever collapse?" Li asked, his voice echoing as the pack train entered the structure.

"Sometimes," Foo said, loudly and cheerfully, the man-made cave amplifying his voice alarmingly. "It's a real mess when they go. There's not much left of whoever's inside one of them when it breaks loose." The hollow thud of the horses' hooves punctuated his remark. Li could not tell whether the low rumble was the echo of their movements or the beginning of the structure's collapse, but he was sure he could not wait to be through the roof road and back onto good, solid rock again.

"This whole road closes down for weeks at a time when one of the roofs goes down," Hu-han continued. "The inns in Baoji get so crowded that you'd think you were living in the slums of Chang-an, except that the food is better."

Everyone was still quiet as they reemerged into the open to see a great vista of hills, mountains and fog-dotted valleys unfold before them. Two more roofed roads were visible at intervals ahead.

"Whew," Bao said. "I don't know whether I like those things or not. How many more of them are there?"

"Between three and four dozen, depending on the route we take," Hu-han replied.

"In that case, I suppose we'd better get used to them," Li observed.

"If we can," Bao chimed in. "As for me, I doubt whether hanging out over several hundred feet of open air will ever hold much appeal."

By the time the caravan had passed through the mountains, Bao had proved himself wrong. Everyone, himself included, had become used to the idea of the strange bridges. Nevertheless, everyone was relieved to come out of the southern foothills of the Chinling Range a few days later. Even the animals seemed to enjoy the flat, green expanse of the great southwestern plateau.

Bao leaned back against the rear of his saddle and stretched. "It's nice to be able to ride these beasts on the flat for a change," he said. "It sure beats leading them on foot up and down those damned mountains."

"This early Spring is nice too," Li observed.

"This is no early Spring," laughed Foo. "It's still Winter up north where the road enters the mountains. If we were still in Baoji, you'd be freezing your tail off."

"You mean we've come that far south?" Li asked. "I'd have thought it would take longer to go far enough south to make that much of a change."

"It's more than a matter of distance," Foo replied. "The Chinlings are now at our backs, so the cold northern winds are blocked. The weather will probably be pretty mild from here on, but there'll be clouds and drizzle most of the time. You know what they say, 'When a dog from Shu sees the sun, he barks at it.'"

Foo paused, and looked keenly at Li and Bao, then seemed to come to a decision.

"You'll be leaving the pack train soon?" he asked. Actually he made it more a statement than a question.

"What makes you think that?" Bao said, an edge to his voice.

"Someone's following you," Foo said. "I assume you'll be wanting to duck out and give them the slip, if you can."

"Whatever do you mean?" said Li, blandly.

"Oh, come on, young fellow," Foo said, not at all impressed by Li's bluff. "Don't try to kid me. That ambush last week wasn't any big try to steal our silver. They were after you two. More than that, someone's been following us, as you already know. I managed to see the man's tattoo. He's one of Ju Anshih's gang. I don't know who's running them now that old Anshih is dead, but I'm willing to bet it's not someone you two would like to meet in a dark alley."

"If we assume that all you say is true," Li said, his voice more uncertain than his words called for, "what would it be to you?"

"Despite the line you tried to foist off on us back at old Gao's place," Foo said, "there's no way you two are crooks of my kind or any other kind."

"So you say," Bao rejoined.

"So I say," Foo chuckled. "You wouldn't last a minute among a real gang of thieves."

Foo held up his hand as Bao began to protest. "No, no. You're plenty brave, and fight pretty well, but you haven't learned to watch your backs, or to stab someone else in his, if you have to. And if you haven't learned that by this time, you're not crooks, and aren't likely to learn how to be crooks hereafter."

Foo paused a moment, his face screwed up in thought.

"At any rate," he resumed, "I'd be willing to help you give the slip to whoever's following you, if you want me to. I know people in the towns we'll be passing through. They all owe me. If you need a hand, call."

Li looked carefully at the huge bodyguard. "How do we…" A sharp jab in the ribs delivered by Bao interrupted him.

"What my friend means is that we'd be pleased to call on you for help. We haven't forgotten that it was you who saved us at the first pass. We're honored by the offer, and we'll call on you when we have to make our move."

The big man nodded. "Enough said. You've got business to tend to same as we do. I'll ask no more about it, but I only ask that you remember me when you've come through it all."

"Count on it," Bao said.

With that, Foo turned his horse, and trotted off towards the rear of the pack train.

"You think we can trust him?" Li's voice conveyed his doubt.

"Who can tell?" Bao answered. "But yes, I think we can, and besides, what choice do we have? Don't forget, he really did save us back at the pass, and why would he have done that if he was in with that crowd?"

"There's more than one faction at court. He could have had good reason to save us then, and still not have our best interests in mind."

"If you look for an enemy behind every face, you'll never see a friend," Bao sighed. "I say we trust the man until we know better."

"And watch our backs."

"And watch our backs," Bao agreed, grinning.

CHAPTER THIRTY-EIGHT

The Emperor Speculates

"Hwo Gwang," the Emperor asked. "Have you heard anything from those two young protégés of yours?"

"Nothing, Majesty," Hwo replied. "I've had no contact with them at all. I thought it best, if they are to be allowed to make an impartial investigation of the portent."

"You still think there was something to what the young man—what's his name—had to say, don't you?"

"I do, Majesty. Soong Li is his name."

"But how can what he said be?" The Emperor's age showed in his voice. "How could such a thing be done right in front of us?"

"I don't know." Hwo Gwang looked frankly into the Emperor's eyes. "I can only remind Your Majesty that others have in the past sought to claim supernatural powers so as to obtain some measure of Imperial favor. Such a thing is possible again."

The emperor stroked his whiskers as he thought. Their dyed blackness only emphasized the lines of age on his face. "If what you say is true, then Prosecutor Jyang would have to be a part of it. Is that not true?"

Hwo Gwang inclined his head a fraction of an inch, whether in agreement or merely in polite acknowledgement of his words the Emperor could not tell.

"You accuse the prosecutor?" the Emperor prompted.

"I accuse no one, Majesty. I simply point out that many people would like a part of the power the throne possesses. If they can not obtain it for themselves, they would obtain it for another, hoping for some hold on the future of the one they work for."

"But your own family has a part in this struggle."

"Indeed it does, Your Majesty."

"So where does Hwo Gwang stand?"

"I would like to do all that I can to protect my family and its interests. No filial son could wish to do less. On the other hand, my loyalty is sworn to the throne. As my teacher, Master Doong, always taught, loyalty is the higher form of filial devotion. If my family is involved in any betrayal of the throne, I shall stand on the side of the higher form of filiality."

"Hmmm," said the Emperor. He had never known what to make of old Doong's teachings. The old schoolmaster of his youth had preached this higher form of filiality right enough. The trouble was, the very highest form of filiality turned out to be owed by the Emperor to Heaven, and Doong claimed to be the only fellow who really knew what Heaven wanted! "Let me know if you hear anything from those two young fellows."

"Indeed I shall."

As Hwo Gwang left the Emperor's side, a curtain parted and Jyang entered the room. He smiled as he passed Hwo.

"Jyang," said the Emperor, greeting his prosecutor eagerly. "What news do you bring from the capital?"

"There are deadly forces at work, seeking to undermine your Sagely Rule," said Jyang, his face having turned somber again as he turned to face the Emperor.

"You have found something?"

"Nothing yet," the prosecutor admitted, "but rest assured. We will not stop until we have rooted out any who would bring harm to the Ruler of All Under Heaven."

"Good," said the Emperor, looking speculatively at Jyang. "Keep Us informed."

CHAPTER THIRTY-NINE

Speculation

In the following days the landscape of the Szechwan plateau unfolded before them. The grasses of the plain were green, even though it was Winter, and the land was flat, or on occasion, gently rolling. The caravan frequently passed through prosperous villages. The larger towns were neatly laid out and clean.

Now the caravan was neared Hanjoong, the largest city encountered since leaving the capital.

Li had been silent all day. Bao kicked his horse up abreast of his cousin's.

"What's up?" Bao asked. "You've hardly spoken all day."

"I've been thinking," Li replied.

"About what?"

"Things."

"What things?" Bao persisted.

"Everything," Li answered, obviously not wanting to talk. Bao ignored the hint.

"Still trying to figure out how he did it?" Li nodded, but said nothing. Bao rode alongside in silence for a time. Finally, he spoke.

"It won't help to just keep going over it in your mind time after time. It'll just get more confusing each time you think about it."

"How else am I going to figure it out? The future of the Empire for tens of years to come is at stake, and you tell me it won't help to try to think things out? Have you a better suggestion?"

"Just let things happen," Bao answered. "If we are meant to find out, something will happen, and that will take care of it. If not..." Bao shrugged.

"That's easy for you to say," Li snapped. "You don't care what happens."

Stung by the accusation , Bao said nothing. He tugged at the reins of his horse, and dropped back. Before long Li dropped back too.

"I'm sorry," Li said. "It's just that I've been tearing my mind apart trying to figure out what happened back there. It's so important. I'm the only one who seems to be convinced that Jyang is responsible for the Korean girl's death, but I simply can't see how he did it."

"That's the first time you've said that you know."

"Said what?" Li was surprised. "I've said all along that someone killed her."

"Sure, but you've never said what you obviously believe—that Jyang is behind the whole thing." Li thought for a moment.

"You're right. I do think Jyang killed the girl."

"So you see, we're making progress. Now we not only suspect that the girl was murdered, and that witchcraft had nothing to do with it, but we also have a suspect."

"So?"

"Now you can examine the evidence in the light of that new idea. You've been beating your head against a stone wall trying to discover how a murder was done. It's obvious we don't have enough evidence to solve that part. So why not attack the thing in terms of why and by whom it was done? Maybe we can get some answers about that."

"The why is obvious. Everyone in the harem, from the most humble serving girl to the Empress herself, hated the Korean girl. Even my skin crawls a bit at the thought of the Emperor bedding a barbarian. There was even a chance, I suppose, that the Emperor might make her the official consort. Or at least he might use her as an excuse to demote the Empress, and later on replace her with yet another harem lady. Either way, the Heir Apparent would be out. And if it was the Korean, and she had a boy child, some half-barbarian could become Heir Apparent. Disgusting! That's what old Master Doong warned would come from conquering all those strange countries where Heaven and Earth come together. Even Jyang would have to stop such a thing from happening. The Empire would be ruined."

"Thinking as Jyang might think," Bao prompted, "why would that be so ruinous?"

"Why… Why… Barbarians can't be allowed to rule," Li stammered.

"Yet Jyang will do anything for power. You said so yourself," Bao smiled. "Isn't that right?"

Li looked at Bao thoughtfully. "Well?" Bao prompted. "Isn't that the way you feel?"

"Yes," Li conceded, "It is."

"Then wouldn't the simple way to power lie in becoming a friend to one who has no friends, and thus a friend to the one who will rule?"

"You mean you don't think this whole thing is an attempt to discredit the Heir Apparent and his family, including Hwo Gwang?"

"That's part of it, I'm sure," Bao said. "But it may be that we're missing something in assuming that the whole thing is a part of an attack on the family of our patron."

"Missing what?"

"Where is that attack coming from?" Bao asked.

"I thought we'd decided to assume it was Jyang," Li barked. "Would you stop speaking in circles, and tell me what you're getting at?"

"Someone's out to bring down Hwo Gwang's family all right. They want to do that because the next ruler of all the civilized world is part of that family. They want to do that because they want to rule next themselves."

"You think Jyang is representing another family?" Li asked.

"No."

"Then what? What are you trying to get at?"

"I think someone controls Jyang," Bao replied. "That someone probably represents another family, one of the families likely to produce an Heir Apparent should Empress Wei's family be discredited. I think we should stop worrying about Jyang, and do something about searching out the fellow who controls him."

Once again Li lapsed into silence. "You may be right," he said finally. "Do you have any ideas about who might be controlling Jyang?"

"I sure do. Think about it for awhile yourself, then we'll see if we agree."

With a grin Bao wheeled away and rode to the head of the column.

Li thought about this conversation all day, then pushed it aside during the night spent at Hanjoong.

Bao had been apprehensive about Hanjoong. He had expected another attack under cover of the city's crowds. Perhaps the fact that Foo had accompanied them as they sampled the delights of the place had something to do with the lack of action, but Bao suspected not. Their enemies must have something else in mind.

After leaving Hanjoong the caravan made its way through several interlocking river valleys, moving in a generally southwesterly direction. They were on the road for seven days this time, but as the weather remained mild and the terrain level, their passage was an easy one. River crossings on ferries were the only obstacles to rapid travel encountered. It was on one of those crossings that Li finally returned to the subject of their earlier conversation.

"I should have seen it earlier," Li began. "You made perfect sense the other day. It's quite obvious that Jyang can't be working for himself. If he were, he would have attached himself to the Korean girl's cause, just as you said. Someone else is calling the shots."

"Any idea who?" Bao asked.

"Yes."

This time it was Bao's turn to be impatient. "Well, let's have it," he demanded as Li grinned.

"It has to be someone Jyang is afraid of," Li resumed, once he had milked the silence as much as he dared.

"Why?" Bao demanded.

"You were correct the other day, but I think I was right too. Jyang would do anything to have a part in the rule of the empire. He would not attach himself to a family, and leave the opportunity offered by the Korean wench to go begging unless someone had some kind of a hold over him. His obedience must be enforced."

"Who could get a hold over a man like Jyang?"

"Don't you already know?"

"My guess is based on a gut feeling," Bao answered. "I'm not smart enough to figure things out like you do. I'd like to know if your guess is the same as mine."

"I can't imagine as shrewd and powerful a man as Jyang making enough mistakes to allow any individual court family to get a hold over him. Whoever has that hold must maintain it by means of a direct threat, and the only one who could conceivably exert that kind of power is the shaman, even though on the surface the shaman seems to be doing Jyang's will."

Bao looked at his cousin with respect in his eyes. "You figured all that out?"

"Not quite," Li replied. "I never even thought of the possibility until you started me off on this track the other day. Before that I just assumed the shaman was working for Jyang."

"Still, I'm impressed," Bao said, shaking his head.

"And you?" Li asked. "Who did you think was behind this whole thing?"

"I thought it was the shaman too," Bao answered. "I didn't have anything to go on, though. I just thought that as witchcraft seemed to be involved, it had to come back to him somehow or other, and he just seemed a whole lot tougher than Jyang."

"That makes sense too," Li mused. "But it doesn't get us that much further. We still have to find out which family he is involved with, and show how he did all those crazy things."

CHAPTER FORTY

An Empress Concerned

The signs are ominous."

"Yes, my lady. They are."

The Lady Wei was lying back on a low platform. Hwo Gwang was seated, facing her.

Even at her age, Hwo Gwang could still see why the Lady had remained the Emperor's favorite for so long. Though her beauty had now faded, she remained at least the equal of most of the denizens of the harem. Of course she had always depended more on her talent as a dancer than on her good looks to keep the Emperor's attention. That was part of the problem. With the years that talent had quite disappeared. It was, however, his aunt's mind that had always impressed Hwo Gwang the most, and it was that mind which now stared out so intently through her coal black eyes.

"You have some suggestions, Hwo Gwang?"

"None that would be of much use right now, I'm afraid. Your daughters' conviction, and the strength of the evidence against them, did us an immeasurable amount of damage."

"Nothing can be done about that now. What's done is done."

Hwo Gwang was reassured. The old lady had not gone soft. Most of the women of the harem would have whined out some excuse to the effect that his cousins had done nothing that any one else in their position had not done, and so were hardly guilty of any meaningful wrong. But Lady Wei understood that in the world of court politics right and wrong counted for nothing. Only power mattered.

"You should see to it that everyone who might cause us more harm by such foolishness is either stopped or sent away," Hwo Gwang said.

"That's already been done."

"Then we can only hope that my two young protégés manage to find something that can help us."

"Is that possible?" Lady Wei seemed genuinely curious at the prospect.

"Anything is possible."

"Is it likely, then," she probed.

"I've sent them into the eye of the storm. If Heaven wills it, we may yet emerge from this trial."

"The eye of the storm?" Lady Wei raised one eyebrow. "Whatever do you mean by that?"

"Someone is out to destroy us. That someone is using Jyang."

"And that someone is…?"

"The shaman, though he seems to merely be Jyang's servant."

"And how will sending those two young men so far away help us trap those who wish us harm? The shaman comes from the north, doesn't he?"

"True," Hwo conceded. "But he came to the capital by way of Szechwan. That is where we will pick up his trail, if there is one to find."

"Let us wish them well," said Lady Wei as she motioned to a serving girl."

"Let us wish them well, indeed," echoed Hwo Gwang.

CHAPTER FORTY-ONE

To The Mines

The caravan reached Chengdu early in the afternoon. "It's a beautiful city," Li said as they approached the city from a slight rise in the ground.

"You've heard the old saying," Bao said, grinning. "See Chengdu and die contented."

Li looked askance at his cousin. Bao laughed out loud once he realized the second meaning for them of the old saying. "Of course," he added, "I'd much rather help our enemies to so contented a death than take that route myself."

"Let's hope we don't have to do either," Li replied. "If we're lucky, we'll be out of this place and on our way before anyone realizes we're gone."

"What good does that do us? They know where we're going. If we give them the slip here, they'll just find us at the mines. After all, it was hardly a secret that we were sent down here to investigate that mine explosion portent."

"So let them find us at the mines. In the meantime we can do some snooping around without an escort."

"If you say so," Bao said doubtfully.

"Do you have a better idea?" Bao shook his head. "Well, then," Li resumed. "Gao Hu-han will be busy here for the better part of a month buying up lacquerware. Aside from our stints guarding the goods, nobody is going to care what we're up to. After a day or two getting the lay of the land, we'll just take off one morning, and not come back. If we can't lose a couple of petty gangsters in a town this size, we deserve whatever we get." Bao pulled his sword from its sheath, and ostentatiously began to test its sharpness against his thumb nail.

Chengdu lived up to its reputation. The inn was the largest and cleanest the cousins had seen. The weather remained mild, the restaurants were both good and cheap, and—or so Foo told them—the girls were all willing and equally cheap, though neither found time or opportunity to test the truth of that statement despite, as young men will, talking about it a great deal.

The cousins drew guard duty the first night, but were given the second night off. Foo would have accompanied them to serve as their guide as they sampled the nightlife of the city, but he had taken too large a sample himself the previous night and had volunteered for guard duty tonight, feeling not fit for anything better. Holding his head, and moaning at intervals, he urged caution on his two young friends.

"Those fellows are still following you two, and they aren't taking much trouble to hide the fact."

"Which means they probably don't intend to make their move just yet," Li said, grinning at the big gangster's obvious discomfort. "They probably have to wait for instructions before making another try at us."

"Well," Foo groaned, "watch your backs. Don't trust anyone, even for a moment, or you'll find yourselves out of moments and into your graves."

"We'll be careful," Li assured him. "For now, though, we're off to the teahouse you recommended."

"Right. Little Chen's. Don't forget. On the east side of the market. And for the girl…"

"Ask for Aunty Chen's niece from Jyang-ywan County," chimed in Bao. "Don't worry. We couldn't possible forget such exact instructions, though to hear you tell the story, the girl will still be tuckered out from last night and full of contempt for amateurs like us after seeing what you could do for her." Foo laughed aloud, then grabbed his throbbing head. Li feigned a look of disapproval at this indelicate conversation. "At any rate," Bao concluded, "we'll see you in the morning."

"If I live," Foo groaned.

"If you don't, we'll see you the day after tomorrow," Li laughed as he dragged Bao off.

It was still light, though just barely, when they stepped outside the gate of the inn. As they walked off, two men who had been squatting on their heels at the mouth of a nearby alley lurched upright and strolled in the same direction a few dozen paces behind them.

"I wonder what it feels like to walk down a street all by one's self, with no one following," Bao mused.

"We'll find out before the sun sets," Li assured him.

"You really think your scheme will work?"

"Absolutely. I found a place this afternoon. Unless those two really know the town, or have hired a local fellow to help them out, we can shake them without any problems. They're the same two we've been seeing for the entire trip, and I think I've got their number. We should have a pretty good chance of a clean getaway."

"You sure you don't want to try out 'Little Chen's' first?" Bao snickered. "Foo's likely to be sore if we don't try out his idea of paradise."

"Right," Li grinned back. "And Aunty Chen's niece from Jyang-ywan County? That's all we need! That coincidence bothers me. Somehow I don't think that niece can give us much information on portents in her own home town."

The two laughed and joked their way through town, giving every appearance of being bound for a riotous night out. After a while Li led them down a dark alley. He paused in front of a small, run-down tavern. A decrepit signboard reading "Uncle Soong's" was attached, barely, to its front.

"A branch of the family?" Bao asked, gesturing at the signboard.

"If it is, it's not one that anyone cares to include in the clan genealogy," Li smiled. "Shall we enter and introduce ourselves?"

They sauntered up to the door, Li opened it, and they stepped inside, Li quickly closing the door behind them. Li strode purposefully toward the rear of the tavern, just slowly enough to avoid attracting attention. Bao, not knowing what was going on, followed.

At the rear of the tavern there was another room at right angles to the first, and at its far end yet another long room extended to the alley opposite to the one from which they had entered.

Without breaking stride, Li moved smoothly through all three rooms and led the way out onto the other alley, which a quick look in either direction proved to be empty. Bao broke into a broad grin.

"Why Mr. Soong," he said, "I do believe you're getting pretty sneaky in your old age." Li was too preoccupied to respond with a wisecrack.

"Come on," he snapped. "Off to the left, then up to the north gate."

"I thought we were heading west!" Bao easily matched Li's brisk stride.

"We are. I want to go out the north gate because they'll likely first try to pick up our trail outside the west gate."

The cousins soon merged into the usual large crowd heading toward the city wall to leave town before the sundown closing of the gates. Most were dressed as farmers, but there were enough gentlemen in the crowd to keep Li and Bao from standing out.

They made it out the gate in plenty of time. Bao thought it would have been better to time things a bit closer to sundown, on the chance of leaving their unwanted companions locked up inside the walls, but decided to hold his piece. They moved along with the crowd for a bit, then Li slipped to the side of the road.

"Now what?" Bao asked.

"The rest is up to you," Li said. "I got us out of the city. You studied the maps back in the capital. You take us to the mines." Li wore his smug smile like a flag.

"Pretty proud of yourself, aren't you?"

"Shouldn't I be? I got us out of town, and managed to lose our tail in the process."

"True enough." Bao's tone suggested that he was less impressed than Li would have liked.

"So what's wrong?" Li asked.

"I'm hungry. I'd also like to get some sleep some time tonight. Do you have any idea where we're supposed to get some food, or where we can lay our heads? The maps in the capital weren't that detailed."

"I hadn't thought of that." Li looked as deflated as he sounded.

"Oh well, at least we're out of the city, and I guess no one is on our tails yet, so let's make the best of it." He led Li back onto the road. Soon they came to a well-travelled turnoff to the left.

"Let's try this road," Bao suggested.

"Do you think it'll take us to Jyang-ywan?"

"Who knows? But at least it's going in the right direction, and it's big enough to maybe have an inn." Before long they indeed came to an inn.

"What did I tell you? This should do us for tonight."

"No it won't."

"Why the devil not? I don't know how many more inns I can deliver up out of the void tonight. I'm not the shaman, you know."

"We're going to be on the road all night," Li insisted. "We went through all that trouble to give those fellows the slip. They must know we're on our way to Jyang-ywan, so they'll catch up with us there. I'd like as much time on our own there as possible, so we'll walk all night. With luck, and if you can figure out the roads, we'll get there by mid morning.

"All night? In the dark?"

"What's the matter? You afraid of ghosts?"

"Nah. The only ghosts around here would be sissified southern ghosts anyway. I'm just a little surprised at our cultivated gentleman of the ruling class being willing to walk all night."

Li smiled, a bit of satisfaction in the grin. It had only been something over a month since the two young men had left the capital. Li remembered he'd barely survived the overnight walk then.

"At any rate," Bao continued, "Let's at least stop and get some food. I don't think I could make it through the night without something to eat."

"I'm with you there. My stomach is snapping at my backbone."

The meal they purchased at the inn was as plain as Szechwan food ever gets. It may have seemed a bit hot to the neophyte but Li and Bao were long used to spicy fare. They ate the main part of the meal but saved a few balls of rice for them to nibble at on the road.

The delay for food only slowed the two by a few minutes. The moon was little more than a sliver high in the sky, but it lit the way plainly enough.

"What do we do at Jyang-ywan when we get there?" Bao asked.

"Find Old Stone Hill, to begin with. According to what Hwo Gwang found out, the iron mine there is one of the most profitable in the Empire. There're supposed to be chunks of ore the size of garlic bulbs in that mine which are so pure you don't even have to set up a blast furnace to smelt them. Just heating them over a hot fire gives you liquid iron good enough to cast into swords. That's why the Emperor values that mine so highly."

"And why he was so impressed by an explosion in it as a portent. Do you think we'll be able to find anything in there. Neither of us knows anything about iron, much less iron mines."

"Who can say?" Li replied. "It's enough for us to know that the Emperor himself wants this checked out. That alone should be enough honor for a lifetime."

"Maybe so, but the way things have been going, I'm more worried about having enough lifetime to enjoy the honor."

"Very funny. At any rate, I think there must be something someone doesn't want us to find out down here. If not, why all the fuss? Why follow us? Why lose several men trying to get rid of us and make it look like a simple raid on a trading caravan, and why be so open about following us now?"

"You sound like a parrot with all that talk about why anyone would come after us," Bao chimed in. "I think you've opened every conversation for the last week with that. We're hundreds of miles from the capital. What could we possibly find here that would bother anyone? And what about that silly portent?"

"If that explosion was a genuine portent, we're supposed to establish the fact, and see if there is some clue as to what it actually portends. I wish I had read those chapters in Master Doong's book more carefully. It's our main job here to unravel that portent, and I've only an amateur's knowledge of how to do so."

"Our main job here is to stay out of the roadside ditches," Bao grunted as he stumbled and made a show of wobbling toward the edge of the road.

CHAPTER FORTY-TWO

The Shaman And The Prosecutor At Odds

The stupid fools can't even follow two kids who aren't old enough to shave regularly. Is that the best you can do!" The shaman was as angry as Jyang had ever seen him.

"It doesn't matter," Jyang said. Though seething within, he maintained a calm exterior. "What can they find inside a mountain?"

"Who would have thought that two fuzzy faced boys could come so close to destroying everything we've done here?" the shaman shouted. "I told you to have them followed, and this is what I get!"

"It's no worse than your botched job with that ambush," Jyang retorted. The two glared at each other. Jyang turned away first.

"Anyway," he said. "We know where they're going. I'm sure our men followed them to the iron mine."

"They will, but so far they haven't managed to locate them yet. At least they hadn't as of yesterday."

Jyang started. "How can you know that? The fastest postal relay takes more than a week."

The shaman smiled. "And yet I do know that. Your men are falling down on the job. I can't have that."

"So what can we do about it?"

"I've ordered those two little twits killed at once. We can't risk having two young pukes who know nothing, but seem to have the luck of quick-fingered gamblers, interfering with our affairs any longer."

"You think that's wise?"

"We don't seem to have much choice. Your people don't seem to be able to find themselves, much less follow those two."

"It will look suspicious," Jyang replied. "Wouldn't it be better to wait."

"The order's already been given. With luck we'll hear of those two young men's deaths in a day or two."

"Hwo Gwang will smell a rat."

"He won't find out for a month or more," smiled the shaman. By then it will be far too late for Hwo Gwang. He won't be able to save his own skin, much less that of his family. Once and for all the Wei clan will be eliminated from the face of the earth."

Though furious, Jyang said nothing. "Soon," he thought. "Soon I'll have the Emperor eating out of my hand, and you will be no more."

The shaman laughed. "Don't count your chickens too soon." Jyang shuddered as the man turned and slipped from the room.

CHAPTER FORTY-THREE

The Mine

The sky began to lighten. One by one the stars blinked out, and then the horizon caught fire. The first light revealed a small village just ahead of the two figures trudging down the road. Li picked up the pace.

"Come on," he said. "If you fall into a ditch now, it's your own fault."

Bao was amused at the change a couple of months on the road had made in his friend's attitudes and abilities. He could not resist tweaking Li just a bit. "Oh," he groaned. "If we don't stop pretty soon, I may just fall right onto my nose without the benefit of a ditch. I don't think I can make it much farther, as I'm just a poor out-of-shape boy from the capital, who seldom sullies his feet with such exercise."

"Oh, for heaven's sake," Li called out as he forged ahead. "Stop whining and get on with…" He stopped suddenly, then turned around, a puzzled look on his face. "You never worried about a simple night's walk before," he began. "What's the big…" Suddenly he realized what was going on, helped by the broad grin on Bao's face.

"Oh, come on," Li said. "I wasn't that bad, was I?"

"Worse."

"Worse?"

"That first night I thought you'd die and I'd end up carrying you the rest of the way just to avoid leaving a corpse littering the road."

"And I was so sore I thought I'd just as soon die." Li smiled ruefully at the memory.

"Now you can see why I always did some strenuous work each day, even back at the capital," Bao commented as the two resumed their walk toward the village.

"And why I shall too, from now on. One never knows when one

will be forced out of a life of ease and into one of exertion. I could have cost us both our lives back there."

"Speaking of our lives, do you suppose there's someplace in this village where we might get something to eat? Last night's dinner lost its magic hours ago."

An old peasant was standing next to the wall of a house rummaging through a bag of what looked like tools. Li called out to him. "Hey, old man!"

The man lifted his head from the bag and looked toward the boys, but said nothing.

"Can you tell us if we're heading towards Old Stone Hill?" Li asked.

The old man spat on the ground and considered for a moment. "Eh," he finally said. "Old Stove Hill? Never heard of the place."

"No, no," Li smiled and spoke more slowly and louder. "Old Stone Hill. There's an iron mine nearby. Do you know the place?"

"Ay," replied the old man. "You're almost there. It's on this same road, just over the next hill."

"Thanks, old sir," Bao called out. The old man nodded, then turned back to his bag of tools.

Bao turned to Li. "Just call me Bao the navigator," he said, feigning modesty.

"Bao the Lucky is more like it," Li grumbled.

"Come, come," Bao said. "I found the way, didn't I?"

"Remarkable," Li said dryly. "The man knows east from west, stumbles in the right direction for a time, then wants a compliment." He bowed low.

"Lead on, Bao the Navigator."

"Just over the next hill," proved to be further than the cousins had expected. The sun was nearly at its zenith, though still low in the sky because it was Winter, by the time they finally crested the "next hill," and had Old Stone Hill in sight. Even then they faced a fair walk. They were well down into the broad valley between the two hills before they could make out the entrance to the iron mine.

"It looks as though there's a proper little village at the entrance to the mine," Li observed. "In fact, that even looks like a temple over there." He pointed to the left of the mine entrance.

"Funny place for a temple," Bao commented.

"The mine is favored by the Emperor. Someone probably put the temple up and dedicated it to him."

"No sign of any explosion. I wonder how true that report was?"

"That's what we're here to find out. Let's go."

They were well into the village before they saw anyone of note. A large, prosperous looking man stepped out of the temple they'd seen earlier, and shuffled toward them.

"Good day, gentlemen," said the man in a booming, but cultured voice, which did not display too much of the peculiar regional accent of the southwest. "I do not believe I have had the pleasure of making your acquaintance. Are you newly arrived?"

Li bowed courteously. "My family name is Soong, and my given name is Li," he said. "This is my cousin, Chiang Bao. We are, indeed newly arrived here. May I ask whom I have the honor of addressing?"

"My surname is Deng," the man replied. "My given name is Liang. I am the third of my family to be sheriff of this township, which lies before the entrance to Old Stone Hill Mine, which my family has likewise owned for three generations—since the time of Emperor Wen, he of sacred memory."

Bao nudged Li and whispered, "Long-winded, isn't he?" Li ignored his cousin.

"Then you, sir, are the gentleman whom we seek," Li responded politely. We are sent from the office of Counsellor Hwo Gwang on behalf of His Majesty himself."

"You amaze me, young sirs," Deng said, bowing low. "I cannot imagine what about me and my affairs could possibly interest the men of the court. It is true that this is a good mine, yielding excellent ore, but I have always paid my taxes in an honest manner. Everything about my family's mine is faithfully recorded by His Majesty's iron tax monopoly inspectors, and all of the fees and taxes are paid in full, and exactly on time! Every catty, every ounce of iron is fully accounted for!"

"I'll bet," Bao said in a stage whisper, and was satisfied to see old Deng turn pale. The government licensed monopolies in salt, iron, and alcohol had proved troublesome ever since the current Emperor had imposed them mid way through his long reign, but in recent years corruption among the tax collectors and inspectors had become rampant. The mere mention of Hwo Gwang's name was sufficient to bring on a fit of nerves in a man like Deng, as Hwo had been campaigning against this corruption (and by implication against the monopoly licensing system itself) for years.

"Oh, there's no problem over the taxes," Li said, allowing a tone of sarcasm to creep into his voice. "We are here on another matter altogether."

"Truly?" The relief sounded so obviously in Deng's voice that it was all too clear that his accounts might be interesting reading indeed. He rubbed his hands together. "I am, of course, completely at your disposal. In what way can I be of help? Perhaps you would like to step into the antechamber of the temple. We can sit facing the inner courtyard—a most pleasant place—and I can have the janitor of the temple bring us some refreshments."

"Thank you sir," Li replied. "We have been some time on the road today, and would be grateful for the opportunity to rest our feet."

"And break our fast in your company," Bao added, avoiding Li's glare of reproach.

"This way, gentlemen," Deng said, eager to please. He led the two cousins up a short flight of stairs and through the shadows cast by the wide eaves of the temple. The antechamber was open to the inner courtyard, but their comfort was assured by the three armchairs the janitor drew up for them around an open charcoal brazier, a necessity when it came to keeping the brisk early Spring air from chilling them once they had seated themselves.

Once everyone was properly seated, the janitor hurried off to fetch the refreshments.

"Now gentlemen," Deng began, once his guests had filled their bellies and so been rendered as amiable as possible, "What is it I can do for you and for your masters in the capital city?"

"We understand you've had some troubles at the mine," Li said.

"Several months ago there seems to have been an explosion…"

"Ah, the explosion." Deng leaned back and smiled. "Let me tell you about that," he said.

CHAPTER FORTY-FOUR

Who Does Hwo Gwang Support?

Hwo Gwang looked around the small reception chamber, wiped the sweat from his brow, and returned the patterned cloth he had used to his capacious sleeve. The hot August weather had penetrated the palace's inner precincts as deeply as any other part of the capital city, though the weather, like everything else, was supposed to serve the convenience of the One Man, Master of all under the Four Corners of the Heavens.

As he had wiped his own face, Hwo had examined the faces of those whom he had gathered. The small room was full, its occupants seated on the narrow wooden chairs which constituted its only furniture. A larger room, or even one of the palace gardens, would have been much more comfortable, but Hwo did not wish to risk eavesdroppers, nor was he interested in the comfort of his guests. Indeed his purpose required him to do everything possible to heighten his guests' discomfort.

"You all know why I've gathered you here?" he began. As he spoke, Hwo looked directly at Liu Jyu, the Heir Apparent.

The latter glared back. Hwo had absolutely no authority over him, but Jyu dared not miss this meeting, so unquestioned was his cousin's moral authority over the family. Tall, heavyset, high colored, his eyes flashing authority, the Heir Apparent reminded the older courtiers of Emperor Wu himself in his younger days. That, Hwo reflected, was a large part of the young man's problem. His youth was a standing reminder to the Emperor of his own age and mortality, and the Emperor had an obsessive fear of growing old and dying. Nor, at a more practical level, could the old Emperor rest easy with ambitious a successor chafing on the sidelines.

"You're referring to the mischief made in my mansion this morning?" the Heir said with a sneer. His voice was surprisingly high pitched for so large a man.

"What mischief?" The voice was that of Lady Jao, the youngest of the consorts. Were something to happen to the Heir, her son—born just three years ago—was the likely replacement.

"What's the matter, dear," purred Lady Li, "hasn't your daddy brought the news into the harem yet for you?" Lady Li's eldest son, Liu Dan, snickered aloud. His brother, Liu Syoo, though smiling broadly himself, dug his elbow into his brother's ribs. Everyone knew that Lady Li was referring to the fact that Lady Jao's father had eluded capital punishment only by plea bargaining and submitting instead to the slightly lesser punishment of castration, and so, presumably, could enter the harem as he pleased. Mr. Jao sat just behind his daughter. His face betrayed no emotion at the cruel words of Lady Li. His daughter, however, did not restrain herself.

"Well," she snapped, with rather more fire than anyone had expected, "at least I know who my father is, and for that matter, who my grandchildren are likely to be."

Liu Dan began to laugh again, but choked it back when he saw his mother, Lady Li, glaring at him. Neither Dan nor his brother had ever been seriously considered as potential heirs, and their promiscuity was the object of delighted gossip outside as well as inside the court.

Hwo Gwang smiled at this exchange. Neither of the brothers were suspects in that morning's mischief for precisely the reasons pointed to by Lady Jao; neither could ever become Heir Apparent, no matter what happened to Liu Jyu or the others.

"Perhaps we should enlighten the Lady Jao." The speaker was Liu Jou-li, a kinsman of Lady Li who had been serving as Chancellor since Goongsun Heh was removed from the office. He was generally considered a member of Empress Wei's faction, and so a backer of the current Heir Apparent. The Empress and her nephew, Hwo Gwang, were less sure of his loyalty.

"This morning," Chancellor Liu continued, "Jyang Choong and that cursed shaman of his dug up the grounds of His Highness, the

Heir Apparent's, mansion." A gasp came from those who had not previously heard this news.

"How dare they?" asked a shocked Lady Jao.

"Indeed," resumed the Chancellor, "before this morning I'd have not believed they'd go so far either, but the prosecutor and the shaman seem to have a powerful hold on the mind and soul of the Emperor. They had his permission."

"Why were they digging?" asked Lady Jao.

"The shaman used incantations and some sort of divining rod to discover one of those disgusting barbarian images, like the one dug up outside the quarters of the Korean whore early in the year."

"Someone tried to bewitch the Heir Apparent?" gasped Lady Jao. "That's an unforgivable crime. Surely they're doing everything possible to discover who would do such a thing."

"That's not our problem," Hwo Gwang interjected.

"The truth is," said the Chancellor with a sidelong glance toward Liu Jyu, "our difficulties involve planning a defense against witchcraft, and something beyond that as well."

"What do you mean?" Lady Jao's voice was now less strident.

"Well... Ahem... The... Uh..."

"He means to say that Jyang's tame shaman is claiming that the image had not yet been activated," Hwo Gwang said softly.

"Not activated? What does that mean?"

"It means," said the Chancellor, "that it hadn't yet been coated with some sort of foul material that would activate its poison."

"And, it was accompanied by a number of charms of various sorts," added Hwo. "The impression given is that a hoard of magical materials had been secreted away by someone in the household of the Heir Apparent. According to the shaman, the Heir Apparent was in no danger at all. Supposedly the Emperor was to be the object of witchcraft on the part of someone with access to our kinsman's household, presumably some member of our clan, or one of our trusted servants."

Consternation showed on the faces of those gathered in the room as the implications of Hwo's words sank in. Punishment for such an offense was likely to involve obliteration of every influential branch of the clan, even unto the fourth and fifth degrees of relationship. They all knew that their lives and fortunes, and even their hope of immortality through possessing descendants to ceremonially feed their spirits were all now at risk.

"The Heir Apparent was not the target?" asked Lady Jao.

"Not directly," replied Hwo.

"I'd call it pretty direct," snapped Liu Jyu. "Someone's out to destroy me—and all of you as well—by planting doctored evidence in my house so as to convince His Majesty I'm involved in some sort of a plot against him. I'd call that direct."

Liu Jyu's glare was at first undirected, striking everyone in the room equally, but gradually it focused onto Lady Jao, who responded with a sharp intake of breath.

"Surely Your Highness cannot suspect me!" she cried.

"Why shouldn't he suspect you?" Liu Syoo's voice was harsh and nasal. "Who will gain the most if His Highness is removed from the succession? Your brat is the only alternative heir."

"Don't be foolish brother." Liu Dan's voice was more pleasant than his brother's, but his words grated equally. "A silly wench and her castrated father would hardly be able to pull something like this off. If we are to suspect someone, we need to look elsewhere, perhaps within our own clan after all." His eyes fixed on Hwo Gwang as he spoke.

"Come now," snapped Liu Jyu. "Why beat about the bush? We all know that Jyang is mortally afraid I will succeed to the throne. He'd make a deal with the King of the Yellow Springs himself to stop that."

"Still," trilled Liu Dan, "some help from within the family would do Jyang immeasurable good. Suppose our great leader, Counsellor Hwo here, had decided that brother Jyu's position had become impossible."

Dan glanced mischievously at his half brother, the Heir Apparent.

Jyu glowered menacingly at him, but Dan rattled on. "If, for whatever reason, it became obvious to Cousin Gwang that brother Jyu could not be kept as heir apparent, what do you think he'd do? Leap into the abyss out of loyalty to his cousin? Hardly. Wouldn't he prefer to see an infant on the throne? Particularly if his only rivals for power behind the throne were a silly little bitch and her eunuch father. Why he might actually prefer that sort of arrangement!"

Hwo Gwang smiled coldly and nodded in Dan's direction. "Am I also supposed to be responsible for the acts of alleged witchcraft Prosecutor Jyang has been uncovering all year?"

"Possibly," Dan replied. "You're quite clever enough to have figured out how to pull off such tricks, though even I must admit I'd never thought you would resort to such things. Perhaps the Prosecutor was responsible for that earlier trumpery, and only just recently, when it seemed expedient to do so, you simply stole his thunder, as it were."

Hwo Gwang stood. During this exchange he had deliberately kept himself in the background, but now he effortlessly dominated the room. He let his eyes travel around the group. Each reacted with a different degree of embarrassment as Hwo's gaze momentarily rested upon him or her. "Are there others who question my loyalty to all members of my family as well as to His Majesty?"

No one spoke, but none could meet Hwo's eyes either. Finally, Hwo looked to the Empress.

Once again Hwo noted how little was left of the beautiful singer and dancer who four decades earlier had so captivated the young Emperor. That youthful Wei Dsefu had long since disappeared inside the protective layer of fat with which she had indulged herself after providing the Emperor with his first-born son. She had not even deigned to resent her many successors for the Emperor's favor. Indeed, she had welcomed them so long as they gave birth to no serious rivals for her son. The old woman retained continued to retain power both over the Emperor and her family, for her attraction had always to do with wit more than with mere physical beauty, though to be sure that lost beauty and an abiding animal magnetism still remained in part despite the overweight.

"Aunt Wei," Hwo Gwang began, "you've said nothing so far. Do you suspect my loyalty too? Have you advice for us?"

"I'm long past giving advice to you, nephew." The voice was surprisingly youthful and energetic. "If you really needed my advice at this point, you would hardly be capable of protecting the interests of our family. You know what must be done, and will do it."

"So," interrupted Liu Jyu. "It is cousin Gwang who leads, and I, the heir to the Empire, am nothing. It has come to that!"

Lady Wei's eyes flashed in anger. "Nonsense, my son. You are to become the head of the Imperial house. You will rule All Under Heaven. Hwo Gwang is merely the overseer of the interests of the house of Wei. It would be improper for you to concern yourself with such matters. You must learn to delegate both authority and trust to trustworthy people, especially to trustworthy kinsmen. You will not be able to do everything all by yourself. When the time comes you will find that Hwo Gwang is as loyal to the ruling house as he is to the house of Wei. You cannot do without a few such men."

"But has he been loyal to me? What of my interests? I represent the future of the Imperial house as well as of the house of Wei. Is Hwo Gwang loyal to me or to the Imperial house? Must I look to my interests for myself?"

"My son, please..."

Liu Jyu, a true son of his father, paid no attention. He stormed out of the room.

The others stayed on a few more minutes gossiping to no great effect, then drifted off. Lady Wei was the last to leave.

"So, nephew, did you learn what you desired?"

"Perhaps, aunt, perhaps."

"You have been stymied since your two protégés seem to have disappeared. Is here any hope they can be of help to us?"

"We shall see," Hwo replied. "We shall see."

CHAPTER FORTY-FIVE

Discovery

I have no thoughts on the matter," said Deng hastily. "I meant no disrespect, sir. If you, or any of the gentlemen at court, want it to be a portent, well then a portent it was. I'll swear to it, if His Majesty wishes." Li shook his head, while Bao grinned.

"We want the truth, and only the truth," Li told the man. "You must not make up some story just to satisfy us. I really mean that."

"I assure you, I will give you no more than the truth of the matter," Deng replied, the relief in his voice obvious. These men from the capital were so hard to figure out.

"What do you think happened down there?" Li asked again. Deng leaned back, and made a temple of his fingers.

"Who can know? Some say the ancestors were angry for some reason or another. One can never know for sure, but I have taken great care to see that the proper sacrifices are made at all the proper times, so I think the ancestors had no reason to be angry. It was my family that founded this Temple to the God of Iron in which you now sit. We have our limitations, but we do not lack piety."

Deng paused for a moment and sipped at his drink.

"Go on," Li prodded.

"Men often die down there," Deng resumed, pointing toward the ground. "One day, all is well. The next..." Deng's shrug indicated that was all there was to say on that subject.

"Why do they die?" Bao asked.

"And how?" Li added.

Again, Deng shrugged. "Who can tell?" he said. "One day the men go down, and little happens, though one or two might faint. The next day they go down and die, unable to breathe. Another time they go down, and the mine explodes."

"Is there no warning?" Li asked.

"Sometimes," Deng replied. "When the mine begins to smell like the salt wells of the next valley, we know that there may be more danger. Fortunately that does not happen very often. Most of the time the smell makes no difference at all."

"What does a salt well smell like?" Bao asked. "For that matter, what on earth is a salt well?"

"You've not heard of the salt wells of Szechwan?" Deng asked.

"Oh, I've heard stories of holes drilled in the earth from which salt is somehow drawn, and even seen their locations specified on maps," Bao said, "but one hardly knows where truth ends and fiction begins in such matters."

"The salt wells of this region are, indeed, holes drilled into the earth," Deng said. "Sometimes they are many hundreds of feet deep. When the ancestors will it, the hole sometimes penetrates to a point where a pool of brine exists—water saltier than the seas. A bamboo tube is lowered into this pool and the brine all gradually brought to the surface, where it is boiled, and salt is obtained. This salt is distributed all through the western half of the Empire. It fetches a pretty price, what with the expense of bringing sea salt all the way from the east coast." Deng paused, decided he could risk a bit more of the truth, winked at his auditors, and added, "Of course the monopoly enforced by the officials also helps keep the price up."

"So, then," Bao interrupted, not much interested in the economics of the situation, "those stories I've heard about wells of salt are true after all."

"I too have heard of such wells," Li broke in. "Tell me, sir, what does a salt well smell like?"

"That's rather more difficult to describe. You'd think they'd smell like the ocean, but people who've been to the shore of the eastern sea tell me it doesn't smell like our salt wells at all. I suppose you would have to smell it for yourselves. If you'd like to go down into the mine..." Deng's voice trailed off.

Li turned to Bao. Bao nodded. "We accept your kind invitation," Li said. "We will go down into the mine immediately."

Deng was astonished. "You will? It's dangerous, you know."

"We were sent to discover the significance of this explosion. It would be a bit difficult to do that job properly without going down into the mine, wouldn't it?"

"Indeed. You must forgive me, sir. Usually the people sent here from the capital are interested only in how much profit they can rake off for themselves before giving the Emperor his fair share. It isn't very often that someone actually comes to do the job they were sent to do."

"Then it is settled," Li resumed. "We will go down into the mine this very hour."

Deng nodded, clapped his hands once to summon the janitor, and sent him off to summon the manager of the mine.

"I don't know how good an idea this was," grumbled Bao as Deng and the mine manager led them toward the mine's opening in the side of the hill. "After walking all night, I could have used a little rest."

"So could I," Li replied. "I'm still not in quite as good condition as you are, but we went to a lot of trouble to steal a day's march on those fellows who were following us, and it would be a pity to give that up just for a few hours rest. If a quick trip down into that mine can settle whether or not that explosion was a genuine portent, maybe we can be out of here before our two friends catch up with us, and perhaps we can lose them permanently before heading back home."

They had now reached the mine entrance, a squat rectangular hole half way up the hill from the village and temple, and braced by heavy, squared off timbers on both sides and on top. A dozen or so workers squatted on the ground on either side of the entrance. A path led around the side of the hill to what must be a smelter judging from the black smoke that arose from behind the hill in that direction. A steady stream of carriers, each bearing baskets full of ore hanging from poles over their shoulders headed out of the mine along the path, and returned toward the mine entrance with empty baskets. The hill was completely devoid of any vegetation larger than a blade of grass. The nearest trees were only visible on the other side of the valley. Everything closer had apparently been sacrificed to the manufacture of charcoal for the smelters.

"I'll… erh… uhm… I'll not be going down," Deng said. "I have a condition. The mine's air is bad for my health."

"It won't be like going to a hot spring for the rest of us either," Bao whispered under his breath.

"We quite understand," Li said politely. "I can see no reason why you would have to accompany us. I'm sure you've seen it all before many times. I'm sure this gentleman can explain the workings of the mine to our satisfaction." Li gestured toward the mine manager.

The complacent look on Deng's face seemed to have been transferred from the face of his mine manager, who now looked as alarmed and embarrassed as his employer had moments before. All the workmen broke into wide grins. Bao's hand went to his mouth as he stifled a sudden spasm. "A cough I've picked up only recently," he explained. One of the workmen guffawed. The manager motioned to one of them, a short, sinewy type with a saturnine look on his face.

"This is Han Chu-yi," the manager said as the man unfolded himself from his squatting position, and sauntered up to them. "He is the shift foreman for the afternoon shift, which is about to go down. He'll take you with him and show you around. The fewer extraneous hands down there the better. Han, you needn't keep these two gentlemen down there for the whole shift. Bring them up yourself whenever they're ready."

"I am honored, sirs," Han replied, pointedly ignoring both of his bosses. "It isn't often that we have visitors in the mine." The mischievous twinkle in his eyes as he threw a quick glance toward old Deng and the manager as he said this disposed both of their excuses and their reputations. Li liked the man instantly.

"When do we start?" Li asked.

Han glanced up at the sun. "It's just about time now to relieve the morning shift. We can start down now. Keep right behind me, gentlemen."

Li and Bao fell in behind the shift foreman. A few steps took them to the opening of the mine. Han Chu-yi stopped, reached into a large box, and pulled out what looked like a headband with a tallow candle fitted into a holder jutting out from its front.

"Put these on," Han asked in a tone that made it apparent no other option existed.

Taking one of the headbands himself, Han showed his young charges how to adjust them then lit the candles for them. Next he reached into another box, and pulled out a lantern, lit it, and led the way into the mine. By this time the rest of the workers had lined up behind them, and one by one they picked up their headbands, lit their candles, and followed their leader into the mine.

Just inside the entrance of the mine Han stopped for a moment to await the rest of the workers. Along the central axis of the shaft a man sat pushing and pulling on a lever that entered a box-shaped device. Bamboo pipes jutted out of both ends of the box, and seemed to lead into the mine. Li was dimly aware of a slight breeze coming from inside the mine. It carried a faint odor.

"What's that?" Bao asked, pointing to the box-shaped contraption.

"A wind-box," Han replied.

"A wind-box? What's that?"

"It's a mechanism that takes in air here," Li explained, pointing to openings on either side of the box, "and pushes it out there." He pointed to the pair of bamboo tubes. The two openings were covered by inward opening flaps. When the workman operating the device pushed in, one of the flaps opened, allowing air to rush into the box; when he pulled his lever out, the flap closed over the first opening, but the second opened and sucked air in.

"Don't street vendors use a small version of something like this to heat up fires for roasting chestnuts?" Bao asked.

Han merely grunted, and led them deeper into the mine, following the route delineated by the bamboo tubes. Every few yards there were joints in the tubes sealed by some sort of mud or clay. "Don't they also use this sort of device to make charcoal burn hotter when they smelt iron?" Li asked when old Han offered no further elaboration.

The shift foreman again only emitted a grunt. At this point the bamboo tubes fed into the openings of another wind-box, the bamboo tubes from which led even further into the mine.

"Why are these devices here?" Bao asked.

"Yes, why?" Li echoed. "I've never heard of such things being used in a mine. Tell us about them."

"Not much to tell," Han said. "You're right that such contraptions were first used to smelt metals. I got the idea of using them to push fresh air into the mine when the brine-well smell appears. These aren't big enough to do the job, though, and old Deng won't spring for bigger ones. He thinks they're just a waste of money and labor. We're going to tear them out tomorrow, so they're of no consequence."

"Nevertheless," Li insisted, "we want to hear about them. Don't forget, we are here as personal representatives of the Emperor. If we wish to know of a thing, you are compelled to discuss it with us." Bao arched his eyebrows at this rather sudden and unilateral expansion of their authority, but merely smiled and trotted along behind. "Besides," Li added more cheerfully, "we really want to know about this."

"Well," the foreman began, "I sometimes visit the works where the ore from this mine is turned into iron. It was last year, that I got this idea. While I was there, I went down to the smelters, and nosed around a bit. Everyone assumed I'd been sent to look around, so I could ask questions as I wished, perhaps a bit like you two gentlemen are doing here." There was no harshness in the shift foreman's jibe as he warmed to his subject.

"I couldn't help noticing how these wind-boxes were used to capture air and push it through the fires of the smelter. I don't know why, but this air makes the fires of the smelter burn hotter than is possible without such a device."

They came to another place where the bamboo pipes led into yet another wind-box. Here the device could only be seen dimly. The mine was in almost total darkness, save for the soft flicker of the tallow candles in their headbands and the steadier beam of the lantern carried by the foreman. Old Han bent down and pointed to the intake holes. "I observed that the air being brought into the device was simply the air nearest the openings." With a twist, he removed one of the tubes from an opening, and held his hand near it. Li and Bao in turn did likewise. Each time the flap opened, they could feel the rush of air into the device. The foreman refitted the bamboo pipe to the intake hole, stood up, and untwisted the pipe from one of the outlets. Here the flap was mounted outside the hole and opened only outwards at each alternate stroke of the workman operating the device. "The air coming out is simply the same air ingested by the device, directed within it by a closed-ended tube moving inside a slightly larger tube, and expelled through this outlet in a more powerful and directed stream." The foreman refitted the outlet tube to the outlet. He was enthusiastic now— the inventor explaining the fruits of his labor.

"At any rate," he continued, once again leading them deeper into the mine, "I had the idea that pure air from the surface could be brought down deep into the mine. So I set up a chain of these devices, and that is what you see here."

"Why is it necessary to bring air down into the mine?" Bao asked.

The foreman's smile was now downright benevolent, as though he had been hoping this question would be asked. "In any mine, the air grows ever more stale as you get further from the mouth. This is a fruitful mine, but an old one. We were approaching a point where there was no longer good enough air to breathe at the working face, even though we were nowhere near the end of the vein of good ore. I hoped the wind-boxes could bring good surface air down to the mine face. More important, I thought they might be a way to avoid the effects of the poison air."

"Poison air?" Li prompted.

"Yes. There was an earthquake here last year, and soon after the stench of poison air could be detected more strongly than before. The men fainted, and many died. finally there was an explosion. After we reopened the mine, I persuaded Master Deng to let me install this chain of wind-boxes. They had been discarded as worn out by the smelters, but I rebuilt them while the mine was shut down. Just one of them didn't make much difference, but setting up a chain of them has allowed us to get enough good air to the working face to continue extending the shaft. I hoped they could ward off the poison air too. But recently the stench has begun to creep back into the mine again. Not as fast as last year, but fast enough to sometimes make some of the men faint."

"Haven't your wind-boxes made a difference?" Li asked.

"Yes, I think they have, but not a big enough difference to keep the poison air out altogether. What we need are larger wind-boxes, each worked by two men. I've also worked out better places to locate the intake and outlet holes, and better ways to open and close them than those flaps I just showed you. But Master Deng doesn't want to stand the expense of making these new kinds of wind-boxes, and he doesn't even want to pay wages for one worker per box, much less for two. He's ordered me to shut them down tomorrow and order the men working them back to the mine face digging ore."

Li shook his head. "People seem never to change. They always resist that which is new. Perhaps, when we return to the capital we can do something to help you. Our master, Hwo Gwang, is always interested in new methods to better accomplish old tasks. He can bring your new idea to the attention of people who count in the administration of the iron monopoly. In any event, I will certainly say something to Master Deng before we leave here. Perhaps I can get him to change his mind."

"Perhaps, perhaps," conceded the foreman, his tone belying his words. "You know, these monopolies don't exactly encourage people to do the intelligent thing. Even though his family has run this mine for three generations, old Deng could lose control of it any time the officials decide to hand it over to another of their favorites. So why should he spend any money on it he doesn't absolutely have to?"

"Don't doubt my friend Soong Li," Bao said. "He isn't like most of the officials you meet. He really will do something to help, if he can."

"Perhaps," the foreman repeated, obviously unconvinced. "I've had such offers of help before on other ideas, but nothing ever came of them."

"Such as?" Bao prompted.

"Years ago, when I worked at the salt wells, I devised a way to store the burnable gas that vented up from some of the wells that would allow it to be conveniently transported some distance instead of just being used right at the well-head to boil the brine down to salt. Several of the salt-monopoly officials said some words of encouragement, but none of them ever bothered to actually do anything, except for that magician. In fact the well manager I worked for got so irked with me for yammering about that stuff instead of just tending to the boiling pots, that he finally fired me. That's why I had to come over here to go down into the mine."

"How did the magician use your invention?" Bao asked.

"Oh, I don't really know. He had some sort of fire trick he did, but I never saw it. By the way, I've been thinking that these wind-boxes could help with that idea too. I've even mentioned it to my nephew who works down at the wells, but why bother thinking about it, if I can't even get old Deng to use them for the mine? I don't want to get fired again. Well, here we are."

The light was now so dim that the shapes of miners moving around them as the shift changed could almost be felt more clearly than seen. There was constant noise as picks and hammers were applied to stone and the loosened ore was loaded into baskets for transport to the surface.

The odd smell noticed before permeated the air. The smell had been faintly detectable since the three had entered the mine but here, at the mine face, the stench was overpowering. Both Li and Bao felt faint.

"Is it always this bad" Li asked holding a cloth to his nose.

"It's only the last few days. It's even worse when the wind boxes aren't being manned," Han replied.

"Where did the explosion take place," Li asked.

Han Chu-yi led them to a wall where no one worked. Jagged stone pieces littered the floor of a short passage abruptly ending in a wall heaped up from the same sort of rubble.

"Twenty men lie buried behind that wall," the foreman said. A sudden shudder ran up and down Li's spine as he peered through the near darkness at the death site.

"Not a pleasant way to die," Bao said softly.

"There are no pleasant ways to die down here," the foreman said, the note of dour sarcasm having returned to his voice.

Li leaned forward and put his nose to the stone. "What is that smell? It seems familiar somehow."

"It's the smell of the salt wells," the foreman replied. "It appeared after the earthquake, along with the poison air."

"Smell this, Bao," Li said. Bao leaned forward and pressed his nose to the crumbling rock of the wall.

"Doesn't that smell seem familiar?" Li asked.

"Some of the dumps we've had to dine in, any smell would seem familiar," Bao replied, grinning for the first time since they'd entered the mine. He pressed his nose to the mine wall again. "I have to admit, though, there's something familiar about it."

"Don't you remember?" Li prompted. Bao shook his head.

"Wait a minute! At the palace!" Bao suddenly said. Li nodded eagerly.

CHAPTER FORTY-SIX

Pursuit

You're as good as dead if the wizard finds out you've lost them again!" The scar on the man's cheek pulsed with color as his anger at this reproach rose to a white heat. "Those two are to die," he interjected. "I want them dead, and I want them dead as soon as it can be done."

The six men whipped their ponies, riding them as hard as could be. By the time they reached Old Stone Hill the animals were broken, and several collapsed as the men leaped off their backs.

A few moments were all that they needed to locate their quarry. Everyone in the village had some connection with the mine, and so the word had spread fast. Visitors from the Emperor had arrived, been entertained by mine owner Deng, and even now were down in the mine inspecting the damage caused when the mine had exploded earlier in the year.

"This time we've got them," the man with the scarred face said. "There's no other way out of the mine. We'll follow them down and see that they never come back up."

"Not me," said the man who had goaded him about losing the trail. "If you think I'm going down that hole, you're growing feeble in the head." The man with the scarred face placed his hand on the hilt of his sword.

"You'll follow me down, and you'll do your duty."

"Or what? You think you can beat me with a sword?"

The man with the scarred face laughed. "I'll do my fighting in a few minutes down in that mine. You don't have to go down into the mine if you don't want to."

"I'm sorry. I'd do almost anything to avoid going down into a black hole like that. I can't stand being closed in that way. I just can't do it."

"Don't worry about it." The jovial smile suddenly disappeared from the scarred face. "It'll be interesting to see what the wizard does to your body as your punishment for disobedience."

"You wouldn't do that? Kill me if you must, but don't put that man—that thing—onto me."

"Obey, or die," replied the scar faced man.

"I can't go down into that hole."

"Then face the wizard."

The man had lost all of his bravado. He looked around the small circle of men with whom he had ridden and fought for the past few months. None of them dared say anything. The man looked around the village square. His gaze settled on the temple. He rushed through the temple gate and disappeared into the outer courtyard. No one followed. Soon a grunt, and then a great, long cry of pain was heard. One man would neither go down into the mine nor face the wizard.

CHAPTER FORTY-SEVEN

Earthquake

It must be a poison of some kind," Li said. "That's exactly the smell we both noticed when the sisters were put to death by Jyang."

"And the Korean girl?" Bao remembered how often in the past months Li had spoken of the odd smell he'd noticed when he first accompanied Hwo Gwang and Jyang Choong into the death room.

"Exactly the same," Li replied.

"But what could it be?" Bao asked.

"It must be some kind of poison made of the ore from this mine."

"But what kind of poison?"

"The immortality drug," Li said matter of factly, though his heart was beating out a pounding rhythm within his chest.

"The immortality drug? Then you think it really exists?"

"Why not?" Li asked. "There've been rumors for tens of years that it was to be found in this region. Didn't the Emperor himself seek it out not far from here just a few years ago? Where there's smoke, there's often fire. We must have found what he sought. Maybe he even had that in the back of his mind when he sent us out here."

"But what makes you think this is the immortality drug and not something else?"

"Jyang killed the two sisters with this stuff."

"That's hardly what you'd call the action of an immortality drug," sniffed the foreman, who had been listening in on these exchanges with growing interest.

"Ah," Li rejoined triumphantly. "He then brought them back to life, even after I'd examined the bodies and satisfied myself that they were completely void of spirit."

"So you really think this could be the stuff the sages themselves sought," said Bao, already half convinced. He rested his hand lightly against the walls of the mine as though afraid of the cool touch of the rock, but even more afraid not touch that which might give immortality.

"It must be!" Li said. "It can only be…"

The head of Han Chu-yi fell from its place atop his body, and rolled down his chest to the ground. The headless body stood for a moment, then began a slow collapse as nerve pathways were suddenly left without signals from the brain.

The three had been so intent on their examination of the mine's walls that they had failed to notice the approach of the shaman's men. Now the dim light of the lantern Han Chu-yi had carried gleamed dully up from the floor, reflecting from unsheathed swords. Li stared at the intruders, his mind as yet not comprehending what it saw. Bao was faster. His sword was out and ready.

"Now we have you," snarled the scar faced man. He stepped forward, his sword raised to strike. Bao steeled himself for the blow. It never came.

In that split second between thought and act, the earthquake hit. Suddenly the ground swayed, throwing everyone down. The shaft filled with a suffocating fog of fine dust. All light vanished, and the world became one in which eyes were useless. Li had just begun to react to the intrusion of the attackers when this new, still more incomprehensible phenomenon thrust itself over his consciousness. He found himself lying on the ground, blind, choking and quite devoid of any idea as to what had hit him, or even whether he was still alive at all. It was only when he felt a tug at his cloak that he could be sure he indeed still lived.

"Li?"

It was Bao's voice. "Is that you, Li?"

"Yes!" Li cursed the tinge of panic in his voice. He quickly groped toward the hand that had touched him, and grasped it tightly.

"Quiet!" Bao commanded in a harsh whisper. Moans and cries of pain could be heard nearby.

"Get me out of here!" The shout came from no more than two

paces away. An answering shout came: "Shut up and look for those two. They must not escape!"

Bao tugged at Li's cloak. "Grab hold of my sash," he whispered. "We've got to get out of here." When he felt Li's hand take hold, Bao began to crawl towards what he hoped was the wall of the mine they'd been examining before the universe exploded. Behind they could hear shouts and curses as men stumbled about in the utter darkness.

"Come to me." It was the voice of the leader of the assassins. From the direction of the sound Bao could tell he had begun to crawl in the wrong direction, across toward the center of the shaft. He also realized he had been lucky in making the wrong choice. The leader was assembling his men near the far wall.

"Link hands." Again it was the voice of the leader. "They were somewhere near here. If you find a body, check the middle finger of the right hand for the seal ring the elder of the two was carrying. If they live, kill them."

Bao sensed the presence of the opposite rock wall. He reached out a hand and touched it.

"How are we going to get out of here?" Li whispered.

"The entrance," Bao gasped. "If we keep to the right , we should come to the entrance sooner or later."

"They're not here." It was the voice of one of the attackers.

"They must be here," replied the leader. "We've got to get out of here ourselves!" There was panic in the voice.

"Not until we find them," came the reply, calmer than ever.

"I'm getting out of here now!" a third voice shouted in what was very nearly a scream.

"You'll stay until we've found those two," said the leader, his voice now closer to the other two.

"I'm going now," came the reply, interrupted by a cry of agony, followed by a gurgle.

"Anyone else plan to leave?" asked the leader. There was no answer.

Li and Bao were gradually making their way up the right side of the shaft. There was much debris on the floor, making the going slow, but they finally came to a place where the wall seemed to disappear.

"Do you really think this is the way to the surface?" Li whispered.

"I think so. I think I feel a difference in the air, and I think the slope continues up this way. Besides, it's our only chance. I can hardly breathe."

"Same here. I don't think I can go much further." The air seemed to have become more stagnant. It was not just the dirt suspended in it. There was something else that made the air literally unbreathable.

Bao led the way into the new passage. In a moment he stumbled hard against something jutting out from the middle of the passage. "Damn!" he exclaimed.

"What is it?" Li hissed.

"I stumbled into something."

Li reached out and felt the thing. It was made of wood. "We're in the main passage, all right," he whispered excitedly. "This is one of the wind-boxes."

"Good. Now there's only one other problem."

"What's that?"

"Which way is up?"

"Why…" Li suddenly realized that he did not know which way was up any more than Bao did. There was absolutely no suggestion of east or west, up or down, in this black hole. Even the wind-boxes were set directly in the middle of the passage, with bamboo tubes coming out of them symmetrically at both ends.

"Well," Bao said after a long silence. "I guess we'll just have to take our chances and pick one direction." As he finished speaking both were thrown to the ground again. They could still see nothing, but they could feel the air in the shaft boil around them as it was shaken by the agitation of the earth all around. The tremor seemed to last for hours. Finally the eerie movement ceased.

"We've got to get out of here now!" Bao insisted grimly. "We'll just have to pick a direction, and hope it's the right one."

"Wait," Li said. He bent once more and felt for the bamboo tube inserted into the wind-box. He tugged at it until it came loose from the box, then felt into the orifice. He tugged at Bao. "This way," he commanded.

"How do you know?"

"The wind box. The flaps on the orifices. They open out on the side toward the mine, and in on the side toward the surface."

"Hmmm. I see why it's sometimes wise to travel with a man of learning."

Li chuckled. "A strong arm and a sharp sword seem to have been of more use to us lately."

"Except in case of earthquake."

They were on their feet again now, trudging up along the line of bamboo tubes, Bao in front, Li behind, his hand firmly gripping Bao's sash. Beneath them the earth rumbled.

The air seemed to grow more and more foul as they progressed up the passage. This worried Li, who understood from poor Han's explanation that the air should grow purer as they approached the surface. Unless... That would not bear thinking about. They tried to hurry, but their path was strewn with huge stones and broken wooden beams. The air continued to grow more and more fetid. Again the earth rumbled. A great beam swung down behind them. They could not see it, but they heard it crash into the spot they had traversed a moment before.

"Look!" Bao pointed. The exciting thing to Li was his ability to see Bao point, even if only dimly. Ahead, through the hell that the mine had become, there was a flicker of light. They broke into what passed for a trot compared to their stumbling progress before. The light was a torch, the first they had passed that had not been extinguished by the quake.

"Let's go," Bao shouted as he tore the torch from the wall.

"No," Li shouted back.

"What?" Bao was astounded.

"There may be more trapped men coming out behind us. They'll need light too."

"Including the shaman's gang! What do you suggest? We've got to get out of here now or die." In answer, Li took off his headband, and lit the candle which had somehow remained fixed to its holder. Bao reached up for his headband, found, without surprise, that it had disappeared, replaced the torch in its niche on the wall, and stepped behind Li, who had replaced the headband on his brow. "Never thought of that," mumbled Bao, as they hurried forward again, with Li now taking the lead.

The light from the headband candle was minimal, but sufficient. At least the major obstacles could now be seen. Deep below them, the earth continued to rumble.

Finally, after what seemed an eternity, the dim blue hint of daylight began to filter through the thick air of the main shaft.

"The entrance!" Bao gasped. In a few more moments they stumbled out of the mouth of the mine. There was no one there to greet them.

"Let's get away from here," Li gasped as he and Bao gulped great lungsful of air. There seemed to be a consensus behind that last sentiment. The hillside below them was dotted with running figures. People were pouring out of the village like ants from an anthill that had been kicked open. Without another word Li and Bao joined that mad rush away from Old Stone Hill.

When they were half way down the hill from the mine, a huge tremor again threw them to the ground. They picked themselves up, and sensing something dark looming up behind them, looked back at the mine.

The sight was awe inspiring. Great columns of dust and smoke boiled from the mouth of the mine, and rose to the sky, blocking out the sun. Once more the earth shook, and then, with a savage roar, the column of smoke turned into a column of fire as the earth literally exploded. It began as a rising of the earth over the area of the mine, almost as though a great bubble was rising just below the earth's surface. Then the column of fire roared out of the mouth of the mine, carrying up huge blocks of stone which soon began landing all over the side of the hill, and bounced down to flatten what little remained upright in the village at its foot. It was all over in a few seconds. The maelstrom subsided as the earth collapsed in on itself. The entrance to the mine remained invisible behind a cloud of smoke. Slowly, an eerie silence settled on the land.

Miraculously, Li and Bao had remained untouched and upright

amidst this rain of destruction. Neither said anything for a long time. Finally, Bao broke the silence.

"You know, if somebody told me that was a portent, I think I'd believe them."

"Yes, but of what?" Li whispered. "We'll have to think on it."

"While we're thinking, let's be running away from here!" The earth was still rumbling beneath their feet. Li nodded and followed as Bao began to pick his way along the remains of the trail down toward the village.

Behind them, there was a feeble stirring in the rubble behind which the outlines of the mouth of the mine were only just barely discernible. A man with a scar on the side of his face painfully pulled himself out from under the heavy wooden beam that had protected him from the falling boulders. He rolled over and slowly opened his eyes. As he focused, he saw two figures pause in front of the ruined village below, and then turn to the left to circle around it. The man with the scarred face grinned, and began to brush the dirt off his torn gown. He would wait until the two figures had disappeared behind the ruined village before painfully pulling himself to his feet and staggering down the hill after them. Every now and then he fingered the hilt of his sword. This was becoming personal.

CHAPTER FORTY-EIGHT

New Ideas

The devastation was widespread. Time after time the two young survivors passed dull-eyed men staring at the ruins of what had been, just hours earlier, family homes. Even the children could barely bring themselves to play in the rubble as sad eyed women sifted through the dust in an effort to retrieve salvageable belongings. Li and Bao had walked several miles down the valley before they encountered a structure that had managed to withstand the force of the quake.

"That's the last time you'll ever see me going down into a hole in the ground," Bao growled.

"Next to the last," Li grinned. For a moment Bao did not understand. He gave a gesture of disgust when he finally figured out Li's meaning.

"Maybe my body won't protest," he conceded, "but only because my lower spirit will be kicking and screaming as the priests send it off to the Yellow Springs."

"It was pretty bad, wasn't it," Li said, shuddering at the memory of their blind struggle to reach the surface. Bao nodded.

"Someone must truly have angered the spirits of Earth to bring that on."

"Who knows," Li replied, grinning at the look on Bao's face. "Don't worry," he laughed. "I'm not quite ready to challenge the gods yet. It's just that this sort of thing is fairly common in this region. It sometimes makes more sense to assume that the spirits of Earth have nothing in particular in mind for us, so we mortals must just go our own way."

"Go which way? Can we go back to the capital after failing here? Any chance we might have found the immortality medicine is lost down at the bottom of that mine shaft."

"Maybe not." Li reached into his robe and pulled out a handful of rocks. He nodded in response to Bao's look of inquiry. "From the bottom of the mine," he confirmed. "If this is the source of the poison Jyang used to kill the Korean girl and the others, we should have him."

Bao reached out and took one of the stones. "It's hard to believe one small pebble could have such power," he said, holding the stone up to his nose.

As soon as he saw Bao sniff at the stone, Li knew something was wrong. Bao silently handed the stone to Li who sniffed, looked surprised, then sniffed again.

"It's gone," he said. Bao nodded.

"Where?" As he asked the pointless question, Bao sniffed at another stone, then another, and then yet another. The peculiar smell they had noticed in the mine was gone.

"Are you sure you picked up the right stones?" Bao asked. "Perhaps there was a vein of the stuff, and you picked up the wrong stones."

"No. I checked them as I picked them up. They all reeked of that odor at the time."

"Then what's happened?"

"I don't know. I just don't know. Wait a minute. Maybe it isn't the stone, maybe its…"

"What are you talking about?"

"Look. You're the one who memorized the maps. You got us to Old Stone Hill. Now, can you get us to the salt wells?"

"What salt wells do you want? The map had salt wells all over this area?"

"The closest salt wells, dear cousin. Preferably the ones poor Han Chu-yi used to work at."

"Well, he never actually said which ones, you know, but if they were within this county, my guess is that all we have to do is cross that ridge and head back in the general direction of Old Stone Hill, just one ridge further west of it. Assuming, of course, that this quake didn't wreck those wells as badly as it did the iron mine. Funny about those salt wells."

"What's that?" Li asked as they turned toward what looked like a path across the ridge to their west, an extension of the same hill on which the iron mine was located.

"When I saw them labeled on those maps back at the capital, I just thought they were some fantasy of the mapmakers, something to fill in the blank spaces on the maps. But I guess they're real enough after all."

"They're real enough, all right. Maybe real enough to provide the answers we're looking for once and for all."

Well behind them, the scar faced man limped along in the shadow of the trees by the side of the road. So, he thought, they're turning back to the west. That can only mean the fire well country, and that means they've finally gotten onto the right track. Just as well I made it out of that mine alive after all.

CHAPTER FORTY-NINE

An Open Secret

The narrow valley to their west was already deeply shadowed by the setting sun by the time Li and Bao reached the crest of the ridge, but a cluster of blue-rooted flames back lit a strange set of shapes at the center of the valley.

"Oh, hell," said Bao. "It looks like the salt wells got hit too. Everything's on fire down there."

"Maybe not. Remember what old Han said, about how they used the foul smelling air from the wells as fuel to boil down the brine into salt. Maybe that's what we're seeing. Those odd looking frameworks don't actually seem to be on fire themselves. Come on, let's check it out."

And so they trudged wearily down into the valley, their scar faced shadow moving in closer as darkness fell.

"Why, those things look like oversized well-digger's rigs," exclaimed Bao as they came up to the first of what appeared to be a dozen odd elongated, pyramid-shaped frameworks scattered over a flat field several hundred yards on a side.

A tangle of bamboo pipes and sluices crisscrossed the spaces between the frameworks, running between them and several dozen enormous cast iron kettles. Beneath these kettles burned the blue-rooted flames that they had seen from the top of the crest. What was burning was not at all clear, as nothing but the flames themselves was visible beneath the kettles. Whatever it was, however, was burning with a dull roar, as of distant thunder, which very nearly masked the considerable noise of boiling water coming from inside the kettles themselves. Enormous clouds of steam rose from the kettles, high and fast enough to be swept away by the wind heading down the valley. Li swept his eyes across this scene, then focused on one particular well near the edge of the field. He strode toward that well. Bao followed. Finally Li stopped before a large, oblong box set next to the frame-work. Two pairs of bamboo pipes led out of the two ends of the box. One pair converged to enter the boarded up well which lay beneath the well digger's rig. The others, plugged at their outer ends, lay on the ground before them.

"Old Han's nephew?" Bao said more than asked.

"Could be. This is the only rig that seems to have a wind-box fitted to it. Where do you suppose the fellow could be?"

At that moment the door opened of an earthen, thatch roofed shack leaning up against the framework opposite the wind-box, and a young man stepped out. He looked like a younger, and at this moment a more worried version of Han Chu-yi.

"What can I do for you? Judging by the state of your clothing, you haven't by any chance come from Old Stone Hill, have you?" For the first time Li and Bao became aware of how tattered and dusty their garments were.

"Yes, we have," Li began. "Are you by some chance the nephew of Han Chu-yi, the afternoon shift foreman at Old Stone Hill iron mine?"

"I am. You have news of my uncle and his family? We hear the quake was much worse on that side of the hill, but I've no one with whom to leave the well and pots so that I could go and check. Mother and Dad are visiting in the county seat, and won't be back until tomor-row. You have some news for me?"

"Not about your uncle's family. But if they lived in the village below the entrance to the mine, there is a good chance they escaped. We saw many people running away. But your uncle, I'm afraid, is dead."

"In the mine? He would have been in the mine at that hour."

"In the mine, but not from the earthquake. Or even from the explosion that followed. There were some men… This will take some time to explain. Can we…?"

"You had better come in and sit down." Han's nephew gestured toward the door of the shack, but Bao noticed that he carefully scanned the area behind them as he did so, setting the hair on the back of Bao's neck crawling. It did not, however, seem a good idea to look back, and so Bao merely followed his cousin into the shack.

The shack looked much better inside than out. The usual waist-height compressed earth stove occupied half its floor area. The stove, walls and floor were carefully smoothed and whitewashed, maximizing the effect of the one small vegetable oil and wick lamp resting on a low table atop the mud stove. Several clean if tattered mats were arranged around this table. The glow of charcoal was visible through the cooking hole atop the stove. Chopped greens and the inevitable Szechwan peppers lay, already cooked, in a wok sitting next to the cooking hole. The small window on the same wall as the door was closed, and the heat from the stove had taken the edge off the early Spring evening's cold. It was a welcome, if homely sight for the two earthquake refugees.

"Please, take your places next to the stove table." Han's nephew took one last look out into the night, then closed and bolted his door. By then Li and Bao had kicked off their shoes and scrambled up atop the mud stove and squatted down on the mats furthest from the stove opening. The gentle heat radiated through the mats and almost instantly began to warm their bottoms and feet.

"You can not have eaten."

Without waiting for an answer, Han's nephew took down two small bowls and two pairs of chopsticks from a shelf above the stove, filled the bowls with rice from a pot next to the wok and set them down next to his two visitors. His own filled bowl was already at his place. He next scooped the vegetables and peppers into a larger serving bowl which he placed in the center of the table.

"Eat first. Talk later."

His two guests took him at his word. Young Han confined himself mostly to his rice, leaving the vegetables for his guests to drape atop their rice and eat. Both quickly finished their bowls and Han silently filled them again with the last of the rice from the pot. In a few more minutes both rice and vegetables were gone.

"I'm afraid we've done you out of most of your supper," Li said, looking too content for his face to match the regret expressed by his words.

"I'll eat again tomorrow. Perhaps we should introduce ourselves. My name is Han Ming-li."

"I am Soong Li. And this is Chiang Bao."

"Underneath that grime are fancy capital gangster's clothes, but you don't talk like gangsters. You don't talk like people from around here either. Those people who killed uncle. Were they after you?"

"Yes. They were after us. They followed us all the way from the capital. By chance he was between us and them. He was killed instantly. They would have gotten us too, except that the earthquake struck at just that moment."

"These men. They are still alive?"

"No. They all died in the explosion after the earthquake."

"They didn't all die," Bao interrupted. "You saw something out there behind us, didn't you, Ming-li?"

"There was someone, several dozen yards out, holding to the shadows."

"Only one?" Li could not keep the consternation out of his voice.

"Only one that I could see." Young Han rolled off the stove and jiggled the bolts on the door and window. "It won't take siege machinery to get through these things. Perhaps we'd better join some of the other salt-boilers nearer the center of the well patch."

"Are they any better equipped to stand a siege?" asked Bao.

"No, but there might be safety in numbers. I see you are armed well enough." Young Han nodded toward the sword and knife each still had in his sash. "If you're not actually gangsters, do you still know how to use those things?"

"Gangsters aren't the only ones who can handle this sort of cutlery." Bao was getting annoyed.

"Well, the only ones we see around here who are expert at that sort of thing are the occasional gangster and the county soldiers, who aren't too far from being gangsters themselves. What shall it be, gentlemen? Shall I deliver you to my friends? Or will you stick it out here 'til morning?"

"What do you mean, 'deliver us'? Won't you stay there with us?"

"Can't. Have to come back here to see to the pots. I'll be up off and on all night anyway, and most of the morning, 'til Mom and Dad get back."

"Well," muttered Bao in his best gangster manner, "I guess we'll stay here and give you a hand."

"There's a good deal we have to learn about salt boiling," Li added, "and this peculiar 'poison air' you cook it with."

"Fair enough," young Han said. He rose, casually took down a sword from the other end of the wall and slipped it into his sash. "We'll rinse the bowls out in the morning."

"Can you use that thing?" asked Bao, smiling.

"Maybe as well as you, even though I don't have the gangster costume to go with it. We can talk while I check the equipment."

With that, young Han unlatched the door and led the way out. Though darkness had now fully descended, the whole salt well area was as well lit as most interiors of those times, so that the cousins were reasonably confident that no attacker could slip up on them unnoticed. Their host first strode up to the salt well itself. He pointed toward the heavy wooden framework towering several dozen feet up above their heads.

"We set up this thing when we start digging the well. In principle, it's just a scaled up version of the same sort of rig people use to dig ordinary water wells: We drop a pointed weight hooked to a rope looped over the top of the framework. The pointed weight falls through a hollow tube that keeps it from wobbling off course until it hits the earth. After every few drops, we substitute a scoop for the pointed weight, and dig out the loosened earth and pieces of rock the weight has broken."

"How far down do you have to go?" asked Li.

"It varies. Sometimes just a hundred feet or so. Sometimes as much as eight or nine hundred feet. This one's a five hundred footer. That's why the rigs have to be so big. Even with all that weight and height of drop allowing the point to penetrate a half a foot or so at each drop, it might take months until we hit brine."

"How do you know where to dig?"

"How does any well digger know where do dig? There are signs, though they're different for brine than for ordinary wells. Sometimes the salt water even bubbles up to the surface. Or people occasionally smell the poison air. Sometimes the geomancers can help, just as they can for ordinary wells, or for deciding where to place your ancestors' graves. There's one thing, though."

"What's that?"

"Once one well comes in, you're bound to be able to bring a few dozen more in the same area."

"Like here."

"Like here."

"How do you get the brine to the surface? Particularly from one of those really deep wells?" asked Li. "You don't just drop a bucket at the end of a rope for eight hundred feet, do you?"

"Oh no. That would be a lot of labor for one bucket of brine. What you do is hang a bamboo bucket every three feet or so on an endless loop of heavy rope that you hang from the same framework that you ran the well-digging rig from. And you use the same set of pulleys you used to dig the well to multiply the effort of the laborer who keeps the endless loop scooping brine up out of the well. As each bucket reaches the level of that sluiceway over there, a big wooden tooth pushes out from that train of gears under the sluiceway, and tips that bucket into emptying its brine into the sluiceway."

"And those gears are turned by the same crank that keeps the endless loop moving. Very ingenious," said Li, fascinated by the logic with which the enterprise's many parts fit together.

"What about the poison air?" Bao broke in. "Have they always used it to boil down the brine?"

"Oh no. For a long time people thought of it as just a nuisance: Something smelly that occasionally caught fire. They tried to get rid of it by dropping a torch down a particularly smelly well. There would be a sound like thunder, and then a flame would shoot out. It might burn for days or even months, and be visible at night several dozen miles away. People called those kinds of wells 'fire wells,' and wouldn't pay as much for them as for the other kind."

"When did they start using the stuff as fuel?"

"Who knows? People have been digging salt wells around here for hundreds of years. Long before Han unified All Under Heaven. The poison air was already being used as fuel at least by Granddad's time, and maybe for a few generations before that."

"Do all the wells have poison air mixed in with the brine?"

"Not necessarily. It just so happens that all the wells on this patch of land do. About half the well patches in this county don't, though. And that makes it tough to boil down the brine to dry salt. Sometimes you have to take the trees off all the hills for miles around. The transport of the wood alone eats up all your profit. That's where Uncle's idea came in."

"His idea of transporting the stuff?" asked Li.

"Yes. It would allow us to nearly double salt production in this county alone. Lots of the wells without poison air have had to close down for lack of fuel. And when they open up a new well, and it has no poison air, they abandon it on the spot. Of course the officials don't give a damn about increasing production. It might only serve to threaten their monopoly, and drive down the official price of the stuff, unless they wanted to lose part of the market to smugglers who would sell the stuff in smaller quantities and more cheaply. And all that would do would be to make life a little easier for all the poor dirt-kickers in the countryside. I hope I'm not stepping on anyone's toes around here?"

"If you are," said Li ruefully, "They deserve to be stepped on. Your uncle had much the same attitude, and I'm ashamed to say that almost the last words we exchanged with him were to reproach him for his cynicism. I'm afraid, though, he was much more nearly right than we were. But to return to his idea for transporting the poison air, how did he propose to do that?"

"He had several ideas, actually. The first was just to use sections of bamboo tubing—the same things we've long used to pipe the stuff from a fire well to a nearby brine pot. You'll notice that this well head is sealed off, with a bamboo tube leading out of one side of the cap. When we're ready to pull up some more brine, we break the seal around the endless loop, and open up that half of the well head."

"Doesn't that allow the poison air to escape?"

"Sure, but there's plenty of it down there. Sometimes too much. So much that we can't pipe it off to the boiling pots fast enough, and we have to open up a safety hole. See that bung-stopper on the tube side of the well cap?"

"Oh yes," said Bao. "How do you know when to pull it out?"

"The well itself decides. We fit the bung-stopper just tight enough so that it pops before the whole well cap gives way."

"Interesting," said Li. "So your uncle's idea was to let the poison air force itself into a section of bamboo."

"Yes. A big, foot around section, with the joints still intact, and a bung-stopper placed in the filling hole in one end. That was his first idea."

"What was the second?" prompted Li.

"A large bamboo tube is pretty heavy. And when it's empty, it's still quite a load to transport back to the fire well. So he thought of substituting a tanned pig's bladder or even some larger container tightly sewn from pieces of tanned animal hide. He actually made it work with pigs' bladders. His best idea, though, was to use these wind-boxes to force the poison air into the bladders. That way you could maybe get quite a bit more poison air into each bladder. And you could make use of the poison air from wells that didn't produce very much of it."

"Are there very many like that?"

"Quite a few. More like that than like this one. As I say, though, you've got to handle the wind-box carefully. I've been experimenting with this one that uncle fixed up for me, and a couple of times I've actually managed to make a pig's bladder explode."

"Like the mine this afternoon!" exclaimed Bao. "The earth around it bulged out just like an enormous pig's bladder. And then the whole thing just exploded!"

"Hmm. Just so," mused Li. "Could poison air have gotten into the iron mine?"

"Sure, the same way it gets into the brine wells. The iron mine isn't that far from here. I don't see why the poison air couldn't have diffused through the cracks and fissures of the earth into the deeper shafts of the iron mine."

"Just so," admitted Li. He seemed impatient to get off this subject. "Does it take very long to boil down the brine?"

"Only a couple of days. The stuff is pretty concentrated. It's already nearly half salt. We have to be careful, though, as we get to the point where most of the water has boiled off. If we keep the heat coming after all the water is gone, we're liable to crack the pot. In fact we'd better go over and check pot number two right now."

Like its twin, pot number two was set in an iron framework which also served to distribute the poison air more or less evenly across its underside. Blue flames rose from a dozen or more iron jets beneath the pot. A wooden catwalk reached by a vertical ladder was set just below the lip of the pot on one side. Young Han leaped onto it with a single motion. Prudently, Li and Bao remained on the ground. The salt manufacturer peered through the veil of steam rising from the surface of the pot.

"Yup, I'd better cut the heat in half." With that he leaped down from the catwalk with a single bound, and loped over to where a large, oar-shaped piece of wood rose at right angles from the bamboo pipe. He rotated this oar about forty-five degrees, then pushed back into place the clump of blackened hemp which formed the seal between it and the bamboo pipe. The blue flames beneath the great pot immediately dropped to half their former height. "In another hour, we'll be able to turn it off altogether."

Suddenly, a loud hiss arose from the pipe two joints back from the valve, and the strange, sour smell became almost overwhelming. "Oh, hell," exclaimed young Han. "That joint's given way. Stay away from it. I'll be right back." He dashed toward the shack. Li and Bao backed apprehensively away from the leaking joint. The air shimmered above the leak, and the stench of the poison air reached as far back as the two cousins had moved.

Then they were aware of a squeaking sound high above. A fluttering black object dropped out of the darkness to the ground between them and the leaking pipe. Bao leaned forward. Li put a restraining arm across his chest.

"It's a bat," said Bao. "Now why would that…"

Young Han ran back out of the shack, a long strip of heavy cloth in one hand and a pot of what seemed to be pine pitch in the other, with which materials he quickly and expertly restored the seal in the joint of the pipe.

"That poison air seems to have done in a bat," observed Li.

"Oh yes. Maybe not, though." Young Han bent over and picked up the creature. He held it out toward Li.

"It looks dead enough," said Li.

Han smiled. "Let me try this." He brought the limp creature up to his lips and began to blow gently into its mouth, slightly squeezing its small body after each breath. Li and Bao exchanged looks. The bat's wings stiffened, then began to quiver, and finally to beat wildly as young Han hastily moved the creature well away from his mouth. Frantic squeaking noises proceeded from what was obviously a very much alive bat. The salt manufacturer, smiling benignly, held the creature at arm's length, hesitated for a moment, then released it from his hand. Instantly the bat shot up and disappeared into the darkness, its call fading only well after it had blended into the night sky.

"So," said Bao quietly, "that's how he did it."

"Yes," agreed Li. "That's what I suspected ever since we realized it couldn't have been the ore from the mine that did the trick. He gave the sisters just enough of the poison air that first time to all but kill them, and then revived them by breathing into their mouths. For the Korean girl, he must have piped the stuff in through some unobtrusive hole in the ondol heating system. That's why he couldn't push it in fast enough to kill her right off, and so she had time to scratch out that message. Tell me," he asked, turning to young Han, "when people are overcome by the poison air, does their skin turn blue?"

"Why yes. May I ask, who are you talking about? And what two sisters did he give doses of this stuff to? And, for that matter, who is this he you speak of?"

"I suspect you know the man. Or at least your uncle did. He mentioned a magician who was interested in transportable poison air."

"I knew the fellow too. Big, heavyset man, with a fierce air about him. Around the eyes, particularly. Used to give people the willies. He started using the stuff for tricks with fire. Then, when uncle showed him how, he added the trick I just showed you. He did it with doves, though, not bats. From what you say, apparently he's moved up to people. I'm not surprised. He was an ambitious fellow, and not overly honest. Took off a year or so ago. Dad sold him quite a few bladders' worth of poison air just before he left. Haven't heard a thing by or from him since, though. I take it you've had some sort of a run in with him."

"Have we ever!" Bao interjected.

"I'm not surprised he's turned out trouble. There's one thing I liked about him, though."

"What's that?"

"He's the only customer we've ever had for that poison air."

"If we have any luck at all," said Bao, "I'm afraid you'll never have a chance to sell him any again." He turned to Li. "That settles things, doesn't it? Now we know how he killed the Korean girl, killed and revived, and then permanently killed the Emperor's daughters, and blew up Jyu Anshih's place of detention. That last was just a small scale version of what happened to the iron mine this afternoon. All we have to do now is live through the night, dodge whoever it is out there waiting for us, and hotfoot it back to the capital."

"And tell Hwo Gwang what?" asked Li, staring thoughtfully out into space.

"You'll not be telling anyone anything," roared the scar faced man as he literally leaped out of the darkness. Young Han, who by chance was between him and his two intended victims, was simply pushed aside. This, though, gave Bao, who was furthest away, time to draw his sword. As usual, Li was slower to react. The scar faced man saw Li was still unarmed, and with a stiff arm merely flung him aside. Li's head struck heavily against the side of the evaporation pot, and he crumpled to the ground next to it.

Bao defended himself manfully against the scar faced man's passionate attack, but it was quickly evident that he was no match either in weight of blow or accumulated skill for his opponent. In a matter of seconds the scar faced man had set him up for the kill: A missed thrust by Bao left his whole left side open, and the scar faced man was bringing his sword down two-handed toward the junction of Bao's neck and left shoulder.

He had not, however, reckoned with the young salt manufacturer. Han Ming-li had quickly recovered his feet, and drawn his sword. His blow landed from behind at the juncture of the neck and right shoulder of the scar faced man just as his sword was descending. The latter's blow was deflected down and to the right, but not so far to the right as to miss Bao altogether, and so great was the scar faced man's strength that his sword's pommel snapped against Bao's thigh, ricocheted further down, and cut deeply into his calf, even as young Han's blade was killing the young cousin's nemesis.

The blood of both men spurted and mingled as they crumpled together to the ground at young Han's feet.

CHAPTER FIFTY

Home

Li opened his eyes. The lush aroma of Summer flowers had awakened him. Without raising his head he sighted down his nose out past the opened shutters of the window. Summer flowers, some of which he did not recognize were indeed blooming just outside the window. He sighed and stretched. There seemed to be a bit of a crick in his neck.

Summer flowers! This was only the third month! He sat bolt upright. The world spun around him, and he fell limply back onto mat atop the compressed stove.

"Oh, don't sit up so abruptly." A gentle contralto voice sounded softly behind him, and then its possessor shimmered into view by his left side to press a cool wet cloth on his brow.

There was a thumping noise to his right. Li turned his eyes in that direction. There stood Bao, looking rather lean, but tanned, a large crutch tucked under his left armpit.

"So, our sleeping beauty has finally arisen," said Bao, his voice catching a bit.

"Just how long have I been out?"

"Long enough. You can sit up in a bit. Ming-li's doctor said that if you woke up at all, there should be no problem. He just wasn't sure you would wake up at all."

Li closed his eyes, sighed again, opened them, and slowly rose to a sitting position. He gazed ruefully out the window. "This does not look like the salt well patch. And this does not feel like the end of the third month."

"Very good. In fact this is not the salt well patch. This is a little place up in the hills west of the patch that one of Ming-li's cousins has.

And this is not the end of the third month." Bao paused. "As a matter of fact this is the beginning of the sixth month."

"I thought so! I've been asleep for more than two months! Good grief! Have you gotten word to the capital? What's happened to the shaman, and to the prosecutor? What is Hwo Gwang saying?"

"Look." Bao allowed some annoyance to show in his voice. "I was kind of out of things myself for more than a month. That scar faced dog broke this leg in two places. They could have folded it up like a map! Most of my blood was on the ground too. It was a long time before I knew what was going on either."

"You've been up and around for over a month now. Why haven't you gotten in touch with Hwo Gwang?"

"Because I wouldn't let him." Han Ming-li, looking much as before, though without the grime of the salt well patch, stepped in out of the garden. "I recognized that scar faced fellow. He used to work for the magician. So I suspected there might be more like him on the way. That's why I had you two moved up here the very next morning. I dug three graves, though, in the village graveyard back home. Only that scar faced bastard's was filled, but the other two seemed to satisfy some people who came by nearly a month later to ask some questions about a pair of young fellows who might have passed this way. I guess everyone in the capital thinks you are both dead. At least nobody's come by asking about you since then."

"All right, then. We'd better be heading for the capital ourselves. At least nobody will be dogging our footsteps now. Bao, have you heard nothing from court?"

"Look at you," expostulated Bao. "Or rather, don't look at you! It might make you pass out again. You are as thin as a rail. And no wonder. All you could do for nearly three months was suck in a little rice gruel a couple of times a day. Even then, half the time you choked on the stuff."

"That's right," interrupted Ming-li, "It will take at least a month to feed you up to strength, and at least that long for Bao to even think of being able to sit a horse. As for your last point, none of us hear anything from court. I, for one, like it that way. That's why I can smile so much. With a little luck, that mess Bao has been good enough to describe for me will clear itself up, one way or another, before you ever get back there. Maybe it already has. Maybe you two ought not to go back. Maybe you should consider a new line of work. Ever consider the salt business? I do hear things about that."

Li glared quite uncivilly at their host. Suddenly he stiffened and reached inside his robe. Ming-li laughed. "Dad's got your money belt. Your cash will be ready for you when you leave. What do you take us for, officials?"

Li blushed. "Who is the girl?" he asked, mostly to change the subject, even though she was a comely young thing.

"You remember Aunty Chen's niece?" Bao said. "The one from Jiangywan, who was so highly recommended to us by our caravan guard mate? Well, she's earned her dowry in the big city of Chengdu, and she's come home to buy herself a husband." He blushed too.

The late afternoon August sun was doing his leg good, Bao reflected, though perhaps not quite enough good to make up for the constant motion his mule imparted to that damaged limb. No doubt they should have taken the doctor's advice, and delayed their departure for a few more weeks. He looked up at his cousin. Li slumped heavily in the saddle of the mule just in front of Bao's. He looked almost as frail as when he had first awoken from his three months' sleep. The month they had spent on the road up to the capital seemed to have taken off nearly all the flesh he had put on during the weeks after his awakening.

Bao glanced back at the rest of their little caravan. The girl, riding just behind him, looked up, and smiled. So far she was the only unambiguously good thing to have come out of this strange adventure, at least for him. She had insisted on accompanying them on this long trip. The two of them needed nursing more than ever, she had said, though Bao was certain she really wished never again to have to leave Jyangywan. Come to think of it, Bao reflected, he would have been more than content to remain there too. Then again he would have been happy to stay anywhere she was.

Behind the girl were four more mules, each fitted with five large skins pumped full of poison air by Han Ming-li's wind-box. Li had spent just about all their remaining money on that awful stuff, leaving just enough to rent the mules and pay for their own expenses while on the road.

Han Ming-li, bringing up the rear on an exceptionally large white mule, was not being paid. He had said he wanted to see just what Li proposed to do with all that poison air, and perhaps at long last hunt out a market for the stuff. He had reacted with considerable interest to Li's description of the denuding of the hills for tens of miles around the capital to provide firewood and charcoal for its million odd inhabitants. Perhaps his transportable poison air might find a market cooking the meals of the people of the capital. After a few days on the road calculating the cost of feeding the mules, though, Ming-li had shaken his head and ruefully conceded that the only profitable thing to do with the stuff was what the shaman had used it for: poisoning ladies and blowing up gangsters. Bao suspected that Ming-li had known this all along, and had merely sought an excuse to leave home on an adventure for the first time in his life.

Ahead rose the high city wall of the capital city. Li showed no sign of stopping for a break. Clearly he intended to be within the walls before they closed for the night. Bao winced as he kicked his mule into moving up parallel to his cousin.

"Are you sure we want to head straight for Hwo Gwang's headquarters?" Bao asked.

"Where else could we go? There's not enough money left even for one more night in an inn."

"We could borrow some money from Ming-li."

"What difference could it make? This way, at least we'll arrive at headquarters just after dark. I doubt if anyone will recognize either of us in these clothes." More for lack of any alternative than for reasons of disguise, they were dressed in the simple garb of petty manufacturers provided them by Ming-li's father. Bao would not have admitted the fact to his worldly cousin, but he actually preferred what they were wearing now to the high style gangster's robes they had been fitted out with by the Gaos near the beginning of this journey.

"I doubt if anyone would recognize us even if we were still dressed as we were when we left this place."

"I'm sure you're right," Li grimaced. "We're both quite a bit leaner. Anyway, they all think we've been dead for over four months. That should make it easier for us to keep under cover for as long as we have to."

"It may also make it tougher to talk our way into Hwo's presence."

"Maybe not. Remember how many odd people he used to see."

"Yeah. Claimed he could keep up with what was going on in the country better."

They did indeed manage to reach the main south gate well before sundown, and remained in the sunlight for a time after that as they made their way up the broad main south to north avenue toward the official quarters just south of the Forbidden City.

"The place looks different somehow," said Bao, still astride his mule. Li, leading his animal on foot next to his cousin, frowned.

"It's more the atmosphere than the physical arrangements of the place. They, at least, don't seem any different. There aren't as many people on the streets as I remember at this time of day, and they seem to be hurrying more than usual."

"Maybe it's because His Majesty isn't in town." Bao had picked up that bit of gossip at the inn the previous evening. The Emperor, feeling poorly again, had once more gone, just as he had six months ago on the occasion of their departure, to take the waters at Gan Springs, some fifty miles northwest of the capital. "I hope that doesn't mean Hwo Gwang has gone with him!"

"That's possible," Li conceded. "If he has, we'll just have to follow after him first thing in the morning."

Now they had come up to their turnoff from the main avenue to the narrow street leading up to Hwo's headquarters. Li dismounted and took the lead. Bao got painfully off his mule and followed. His limp was noticeable. Han Ming-li also got off his mule at the end of the line. Only the girl remained mounted, leading the four pack mules behind her.

Li was rehearsing what he would say to the gateman as they came up to Hwo's headquarters, and so for the moment did not notice the tall, pale skinned, bushy browed man who was approaching the gate from the other direction. The man saw him, however, and strode quickly past the gate to intercept him.

"Soong Li! Can it be you?" Hwo's resonant baritone was diminished to a whispered croak. Startled, Li brought his eyes to focus on his employer.

"Sir! I..."

"This is not the place for long explanations. Follow me into the courtyard, quickly."

In a matter of seconds the small caravan had been mustered into the courtyard, and left there under the girl's supervision. Hwo recognized Bao too, with a silent nod, and when Li motioned Han Ming-li to accompany them, Hwo merely looked a question at his erstwhile assistant, then turned and led the way into the rear office.

CHAPTER FIFTY-ONE

Rebellion

Hwo leaned back against the wall, and placed his empty still-beer cup on the table next to him. He let his eyes travel around the table from Li to Bao to Ming-li, and then back to Li.

"It is a remarkable story you tell," Hwo began. "You have indeed accomplished the mission upon which you were sent by His Majesty, though you have both paid an enormous personal price for so doing. I can only apologize for having abandoned you in that far outpost of empire. I had Mr. Gao's agents make inquiries, but Mr. Han here had covered your tracks too well. I am afraid too that Merchant Gao's loyalties were not entirely undivided. So it may have been just as well he was never able to track you down. Nevertheless, thanks to you two we now know precisely how the shaman accomplished his murderous tricks, and tricks they were, just as you always insisted, my boy." Hwo smiled at Li. "The question now is, however, what are we to do with this information?"

"We ride post haste to His Majesty, and expose the shaman, don't we? And when we've exposed him, we've exposed the prosecutor, his buddy." Bao blurted these words out passionately.

"Remember, though," Li interrupted, "that we figured out that the shaman might well be playing a double game, working for someone else in addition to the prosecutor. Maybe we had better pin that down before we show our hand." Hwo Gwang raised one of his heavy eyebrows. He seemed to look amused.

"Things may have gone too far for that extended an exercise," Hwo explained. "You won't have had a chance to hear this yet, though I'm sure that by tonight it will be all over the city. Another one of those filthy images was found this morning, only this time right on the grounds of my cousin's mansion."

"Why that should let him off the blame, if he is the victim." Li seemed to be puzzled.

"I'm afraid the thing was not activated yet," Hwo said. It was apparently buried to be kept in reserve. The assumption is that someone in my cousin's household was getting ready to use it against His Majesty. And that is the interpretation which has been sent off to His Majesty at Gan Springs. I only just left a meeting with my cousin and others. He stormed out of the room in what I can only characterize as a desperate state."

"Perhaps we had best go to him first," Li suggested.

"I think that would be a good idea. And I think it would also be a good idea to take one of those skins of poison air along with us so that you can show him how the stuff was used. Yes, that might be a very useful thing to do." Hwo's voice turned cold, and he stroked his whiskers as he uttered these words.

"In that case, sir, we had better take Ming-li with us. He's the one who really knows how to use that stuff."

"Does he now? An interesting young man. He and I will have to have a long talk some time before this night is done."

Hwo Gwang led the way back out into the courtyard. One of the pack mules was broken out of the string, and Han Ming-li led it off behind the three officials as they made their way out of the courtyard in the direction of the Heir Apparent's mansion.

"Your office seemed unusually quiet this evening," Li commented as they reached the end of the long walk to the Heir Apparent's place.

"Much of my household has left for the country," Hwo explained, breaking off a whispered conversation he had been having with Ming-li most of the way. "As a matter of fact, I am myself scheduled to join His Majesty at Gan Springs tomorrow morning.

"Looks like a lot of activity at the mansion, though," Bao observed as they approached the palace of the Heir Apparent. Men, most of them soldiers in the red livery of the Heir Apparent, were coming and going in a steady stream.

Hwo's eyes narrowed, but he exhibited no other reaction. The gateman saluted Hwo.

"Where is your master?" Hwo asked the man.

"In the rear courtyard, your honor."

"Very well. Come."

Hwo led the way toward the back courtyard, the hubbub only increasing as they approached their goal.

Liu Jyu, the Heir Apparent, stood head and shoulders above his subordinates as the latter took turns coming up to him, each receiving a few whispered words and a clap on the back or squeeze of the shoulder before turning and striding off on their master's business.

"Cousin Gwang!" Liu Jyu's unlikely sounding tenor carried across the courtyard. The Heir Apparent, seemed genuinely pleased to see his cousin. "What brings you here, sir? No hard feelings about this afternoon, I trust?"

"None at all, I assure you."

It was, as always, hard for Li to avoid thinking that Hwo Gwang's booming baritone would have been more appropriate coming from the young man's mouth. "I believe I am the bearer of good news for you on this occasion."

"A welcome change from this afternoon. And what might that news be?"

"The prosecutor and his tame magician. I now know how they do their tricks, and can demonstrate them to you, and then to His Majesty."

"Can you indeed? I assume these are the young men you sent out to the southwest earlier this year, and that it is they who have brought back this information?"

"They have indeed, Your Highness."

"I am glad to see that they are alive, despite the reports of their deaths."

"Once you have seen the following demonstration, you will be even more happy about their survival," said Hwo, motioning Han Ming-li to step forward leading the mule.

Ming-li had already picked the object for his experiment, a small, pale serving maid standing by a table laden with food at the edge of the courtyard. With an abrupt gesture he called her over. He then unfurled what looked like a short length of tanned pig's intestine, one end of which proved to enter one of the stiffly distended pig's bladders carried by the mule. With one hand he jammed the open end of the tube under the nose of the girl. With the other he removed a clamp which had been pinching closed the end of the tube closest to the bladder.

In an instant the tube went stiff, and a faint hissing noise could be heard coming from it. The girl started to jerk her head back, but Ming-li quickly moved his other hand from the loosened clamp to the back of her head to keep her nose pressed against the open end of the tube. She struggled for only a moment, then went entirely limp. It was clear that only Ming-li's hands were keeping her erect. Already pale to begin with, the girl turned still paler, and gradually her skin took on a faintly bluish caste. Finally, Ming-li lowered her gently to the floor, stood up again, and refixed the clamp to the inboard end of the tube. Finally he bent down again, gathered the serving maid into his arms, and carried her over to Liu Jyu.

"Please examine the girl carefully," Hwo Gwang said. "She is not breathing, nor does she exhibit any other signs of life. Note also the faintly blue color of her skin."

"Exactly like my sisters."

"And the Korean," Hwo Gwang prompted.

"And the Korean," the Heir Apparent conceded. "Too bad you had to kill a perfectly good serving girl to make your point."

"Wait and see." Hwo nodded to Ming-li. The latter knelt, resting the girl's limp body upon his raised knee, then bent over her face. At first he seemed to be planting an impassioned kiss upon her opened mouth, while fondling her breast. It was soon obvious, however, that he was doing something more puzzling, if far less lascivious: He was alternately blowing into the girl's mouth and pushing in on her chest. After a few moments of this, faint color returned to the girl's skin. Then she stirred, coughed, began to cry aloud, and finally to retch quietly as Ming-li turned her over onto her face. Two other maids rushed over and dragged away the miserable, but clearly very much alive young woman.

Li and Bao exchanged looks which indicated that while it was all very well to pull this sort of trick on a bat, it was something else again to inflict it on an innocent human being. Ming-li caught Bao's eye, and flashed a look of supreme arrogance, which shocked Bao even more.

"Very well done," conceded the Heir Apparent. "You have exactly duplicated the shaman's trick."

"There is one more trick," said Hwo, and nodded again to Ming-li. The latter turned back to the mule, took from a saddlebag a long, slightly funnel-shaped tube of iron, and fitted it to the open end of the flexible tube protruding from the skin of poison air. He next took a tripod shaped piece of iron from the saddlebag and fitted it to the iron funnel, allowing the latter to form a kind of open platform. He then set this arrangement on the ground, strode to the food table and returned with several pieces of raw meat which had been made ready for the cook pot next to which they lay. He draped these upon the iron framework, unloosed the clamp from the tube, then used a pair of tongs to retrieve a hot coal from under the cook pot on the table. He waited. The hiss of poison air sounded faintly from this peculiar apparatus. The air above it began to shimmer. Finally, Ming-li flipped the hot coal onto the apparatus from a distance of a foot. The results were immediate, and alarming: A thunderous whoosh, accompanied by a cone of blue flame arose well above the apparatus, quite enveloping the meat temporarily. In a few moments the meat was again visible. Its smell, however, had anticipated what they now saw: The meat was charred black. After another couple of minutes, Ming-li reclamped the tube and the fire quickly went out.

"Very interesting cook pot," observed the Heir Apparent with a grin. "It's quick, but it cooks the meat much too thoroughly. I will concede, though," he hastened to add, "it seems a perfect miniature of what happened to Jyu Anshih. I will not require you to explode a whole building to establish your point."

Hwo Gwang bowed. "I think you will agree that His Majesty will find it equally persuasive. I can be at Gan Springs with this gentleman and his apparatus by tomorrow evening, and be back here with His Majesty's warrant for the arrest of the prosecutor and shaman by the evening following that. Your danger will then be over, and harmony restored to the imperial family."

"I have anticipated you, cousin."

"In what way, sir?"

"I have already arrested the prosecutor and his pet magician."

"Without an imperial warrant? Are you mad? You will be beheaded for treason! How far have you gone in this lunacy?"

"Far enough so that it cannot be undone. My men and mother's chariot archers and the Treasury and Palace Guards under her influence have occupied all gates to the Forbidden and Official cities, and are even now taking over command of the city militia."

"Apparently not without some resistance." Faint sounds of combat were now audible even in this rear courtyard. "Still, if word has not yet spread beyond the city gates, something may yet be done to save the situation."

"I am afraid I have anticipated you there too, cousin. I have issued orders to my kinsman, Chancellor Liu, to rally to the new sovereign, and have sent similar messages to the commanders of the northern army."

"You are indeed far gone in folly, sir! Chancellor Liu should never be put in a position where he must make a risky decision himself. If rebel you must, then confront him with a fait accompli. Now you've put him in a position where it is morally easier for him to resist than to obey you. And if he resists, the people of the city are bound not to accept you either. As for the northern army, time enough to consult them when you have the city unambiguously in your hands."

The Heir Apparent's face had turned bright scarlet, but he was obviously trying to control his temper.

"I much appreciate your advice, cousin. But what is done, is done. I daresay it will turn out all right."

"My aunt—the Empress—does she know what you've done?"

"How should I not know. It is my soldiers who are doing his bidding." Empress Wei stood in a doorway. Hwo Gwang strode over to her side.

"Have you advised this, madam?"

"I have acquiesced in it. It was fated. Do not trouble yourself so much about it, nephew."

"Mother, cousin Gwang has discovered how the shaman does those tricks the prosecutor put him up to. You know, cousin, I think it would be best after all if you repaired to Gan Springs. You can not only tell His Majesty about the shaman's tricks, you can reconcile him to the inevitability of Our accession to the throne. His retirement can be an easy and honorable one."

"If that is your wish, sir, I can but…"

The tumult suddenly grew louder. A disorderly crowd of soldiers burst into the courtyard, driving a bound Jyang Choong before them. The shaman, also bound, swaggered into the courtyard in the wake of the crowd. One of the soldiers stepped forward. "Jyang Choong, public prosecutor of the imperial court, arrested as per orders."

"By what authority and with what charge am I arrested?"

"By Our authority, as Ruler of All Under Heaven, are you arrested. And you are charged with high treason, damn you!"

"Treason to whom?"

"To the entire imperial family! You have been betraying members of our family from the time you first weaseled your way into a public job back in Jao. You rose further by betraying our cousin, the heir to Jao. You used that bit of treason to wangle an audience here at court, and once here you found it easy to usurp a place in the northern army. There, instead of killing the Hunnish dogs, you tamed one of them and brought him home with you." The Heir motioned toward the shaman. "But first you sent him down to Szechwan, where he could learn some new tricks with their 'poison air,' and come back up here seeming to be independent of you." The shaman remained impassive, only shifting his gaze momentarily until he picked up the presence of Han Ming-fu, and then Li and Bao. "Here he could be your tame wolf, helping you malign the innocent."

"Your sisters? Innocent? Your servant, the one you had deliberately ride in the imperial lane? You yourself with this act of treason? And as for my 'magician,' as you choose to call him…"

"Enough of this treasonous bantering. We will hear no more of it!" Liu Jyu drew his long sword, and with one sweeping stroke, cut off the prosecutor's head. Instinctively, all drew back from the body as it crumpled to the ground, all but the shaman, who gazed steadily at the Heir Apparent. "As for this one, lock him up in the rear chamber of this house. But keep him under careful guard. We will wish to interrogate him later."

The Heir Apparent watched as the shaman was escorted out of the courtyard. He then turned back to Hwo Gwang. "Truly, cousin, I think it would be best if you went to my father to prepare him for the inevitable."

"I too think that would be best," said Empress Wei.

"I must defer to both your judgments," said Hwo Gwang. "In addition to my two assistants, I should also take Han Ming-li here to give His Majesty the same demonstration he gave you this evening."

"I do not think that will be necessary, Counsellor Hwo."

Hwo Gwang registered surprise at Han Ming-li's contradiction of him. "Besides," Ming-li added, "as long as I am going to be involved in this sort of business, I might as well remain on the winning side."

The Heir Apparent laughed aloud. "I like this fellow. By all means stay with me, young man. There may be some military use for that 'poison air,' and you are the only one competent and trustworthy enough to give advice on it." He turned to Hwo. "Don't worry about demonstrations at this point, cousin. There's time enough for them later. Just talk to father. That will be enough. Now be off with you."

"Before you leave, nephew, come with me for a few moments," said Empress Wei. "There are several things I can tell you which may be of use in persuading His Majesty."

"Yes," urged the Heir, "by all means take Mother's advice. I must be off now myself, and be seeing to the good order of the city. You, young fellow, come on along. And take that mule with you. Let's see what we can do with that stuff." The Heir Apparent strode off toward the front of the mansion, Han Ming-li and the mule at his heels.

"Come with me, nephew, and these two as well." The old lady gestured toward Li and Bao as she glanced quizzically in the direction of her departing son. The three men followed her into what proved to be a large sitting room. She gestured again at some thick mats arranged around a low table, and seated herself on one of them. The others followed her example.

"This is impossible," Hwo began. "It was folly to even make the attempt, and what little chance there was for success has been lost in the execution. Aunt, do you believe he can succeed?"

"Of course not. He did not consult with me before he sent his messages off to Chancellor Liu and the northern army. He merely came to demand my household garrison. What good would it have been to have refused him at that point? But that doesn't matter anymore. Of course you are right. He and I are doomed. He's inveigled his three sons into this folly too. They cannot live through this either."

"So then our family is finished. The succession can only go to the Jao woman's baby."

"Don't lose hope. If you lose hope, we are indeed finished. It may be, however, that only two generations must pay the price for my son's folly: His and his sons."

"The grandson, of course. Shih and Madame Wang's boy. But where is he? Is he in some safe place?"

"Alas he is right here in this house. My unfortunate son is incapable even of thinking so far ahead as to assure the safety of his own posterity. You must take him out of the city with you tonight. Keep him hidden as long as possible. And never let it be known that you were the one who protected him. Make yourself indispensable to both the Jao girl and His Majesty. Neither of them has anyone else but you to depend upon. That is your chief advantage in coming years. Now, however, you must be at Gan Springs as soon as possible. Attempt to do nothing for my unfortunate son or for me. Preserve yourself at all costs, and my great grandson."

CHAPTER FIFTY-TWO

Escape And A Family's Future Preserved

The old lady sighed, paused, then snapped her fingers as she rose heavily from the mat. The others hastened to rise as well. A maid hurried in carrying a three year old boy. Another maid followed, with a large bundle of what appeared to be the child's clothing. The old lady took the child into her own arms, kissed him, scanned the three men before her, and without hesitation passed the child into the arms of Bao. Li accepted the bundle of clothing from the other maid.

"Delay no longer. Follow me to the back entrance," she said, and turned to lead the way.

Outside the mansion, they paused for consultation. "Once we have left the city, the child must go its own way, separate from ours. Can you handle it alone?" Hwo Gwang addressed Bao.

"Alone? Good God no! With this leg? The girl who was with us, if she could…"

"You think she can be trusted?"

"Yes. No question."

Hwo grimaced. "I have no choice in the matter. Very well. Back to my office."

That proved more easily said than done. Bao's rapidly weakening left leg was the least of their problems. The city was now teeming with soldiers, and not all of them wearing the red livery of the Heir Apparent by any means. Chancellor Liu had hurriedly arranged to have the forces loyal to the Emperor pin yellow banners atop their livery, and the further they moved from the Heir Apparent's palace, the more yellow and the less red did they see. They were stopped a half dozen times by patrols from one side or the other. Fortunately, for reasons that Li, at least, could not quite fathom, not only was Hwo

Gwang recognized each time, but he was also taken for a member of whichever faction they had run into.

Everyone, including the gateman had fled Hwo's compound, but the girl and all seven remaining mules still awaited them. The girl, with the baby in her arms, was placed atop one mule, and the baby's clothing lashed behind. An exhausted Bao was hoisted atop another mule. Hwo and Li led the rest of the mules ahead of these two.

As usual, Hwo seemed to know exactly where he was going. He led them on a zigzag path northwest across the official city and then around the palace district. Li thought they must be heading for the Lwo City Gate, which was roughly equidistant from the two main palace precincts, and he was wondering how Hwo proposed to get through what was one of the main entrances of the city, but as they came up to within sight of that gate, Hwo turned sharply to the left and led them parallel to the wall for some distance.

Finally they came abreast of what appeared to be a stable built right up against the city wall. Hwo led their little caravan straight into its open door. The door closed behind them, and lanterns were uncovered by a number of men who had waited within, revealing an interior spacious enough to contain their seven mules with enough room left over on its periphery to hold more than a dozen horse stalls, at least half of which contained horses.

Li noticed that these horses were of the kind recently imported from Fergana, far to the west and just north of the fabled land of India. These large, slim legged and exceptionally fast horses were called "horses of Heaven", or sometimes "blood-sweating horses." Riding a pair of these through the night, they had every chance of making it to the Gan Springs Palace well before noon the next day.

Hwo took Bao and Li aside. He quickly drew a map specifying the location of the country estate of a friend who could take in Bao, the girl and the baby, and all the mules with their deadly cargo. Li wondered to himself how long it might be before Hwo finally ran out of conveniently located friends.

He was also wondering how they were going to get through the thirty odd foot thick city wall, when he suddenly noticed that the walls of this stable were made of rammed earth, the stuff which formed the core of the city wall, and that the far wall seemed to be made of the same sort of stones as the facade of the city wall itself. They were actually inside the wall! Of course he, like everyone else, had heard the tales about the elaborately disguised secret exits from both the Forbidden City and the city proper which were designed for situations like the current one. No doubt there were several more such exits, including tunnels leading directly from the palace, under the city wall and moat to some innocuous seeming building in the nearby suburbs.

While two of the stable hands saddled a pair of the blood-sweating horses for them, a number of other men were performing some obscure operation on the far wall of the stable to make a portion of it swing out like a door. They then set to work sliding out and launching into the moat a rather substantial raft, one capable, as it turned out a few moments later, of holding all nine of their animals as well as themselves and half a dozen men to punt the structure across the moat.

As they crossed the moat, bright but flickering lights shone and tumultuous noises sounded from the direction of both the Lwo City Gate and the Heh City Gate on either side of them. It was clear the Heir Apparent's forces were by no means in full control of the outer city. The suburbs through which Hwo led them were, however, quiet, which was also a bad sign. This meant that the Heir Apparent's forces were being bottled up inside the city, setting the stage for a siege which would surely very quickly seal their fate. Soon, however, Li had to put all such thoughts behind him. Once Bao had been set off on the right track, Hwo had moved his horse out at a gallop faster than anything Li had ever seen, or as his own steed had immediately matched that impossible pace, than he had ever experienced. At this rate they would reach Gan Springs Palace by dawn, if they did not kill their mounts and themselves before then.

CHAPTER FIFTY-THREE

Vindication

When Li retraced the ride along that road on another blood-sweating horse, it was at the conclusion of the most eventful and confused five days of his life. He was sure that those days had extended him physically even further than he had been on the long trip back up to the capital.

By contrast, Bao looked relaxed, plumper even, as he cantered along beside him. No wonder. He had spent this time resting at Hwo Gwang's friend's estate, the baby and the mules the responsibilities of others. Now, however, the mules and their ominous cargo were once again their joint responsibility as they and their handlers cantered along behind them.

Li had already been as exhausted as he thought possible by the time they had galloped up to the Gan Springs Palace just after dawn. He and Hwo had changed horses at a postal relay station at the half way point. As in the city, the postal staff assumed Hwo's loyalty without question.

Nor did the Emperor seem to have any doubts on that score when they hurried in, the dust of the road still upon them, for their first audience. Though much was still unclear, the Emperor's information was more detailed than their own, and in the course of even the first day had become ever more detailed. The Emperor kept them by his side all during that grim first day, and turned them loose only for meals and occasional naps during the days after that.

Chancellor Liu had not only not surrendered, he was stubbornly holding on to several strong points, including even parts of the official city, within the walls of the capital. At first the people of the city had been happy to hear of the beheading of Jyang Choong, whose witchcraft raids within the outer city had not endeared him to its denizens. They were puzzled, however, that Chancellor Liu had not approved of this move. Indeed this clash between the officials was enough to keep the markets closed and most people holed up in their houses during that critical first day. By the morning of the second day the people of the capital had made up their minds: The yellow banners of Chancellor Liu's forces were being called the "loyalist flags," and the bearers of the Heir Apparent's red flags were being sneered at as the "crimson bandits." More important, refugees seemed to be slipping out the gates controlled by the Chancellor, but not in through the smaller number controlled by the Heir Apparent.

By the beginning of the third day word was received back from the northern army: The Heir's emissaries had been repulsed, executed on the spot, and units of the army were moving down to place themselves between Gan Springs and the capital. The rebellion was being contained. The Emperor's morale improved, but his temper grew worse. Just before evening, he finally consented to listen to Li's report on his and Bao's mission to the southwest. At its end, the Emperor was silent for a moment.

"So," he finally began, "it would appear that the prosecutor did not after all deserve of Our confidence." He then lapsed back into silence and did not return to the subject for the balance of that day.

At the dawn audience on the fourth day, the chief eunuch brought forward an anonymous petition addressed to the throne. No one could recognize the handwriting. Nevertheless the Emperor ordered that the chief eunuch read it aloud. The petitioner asserted that the greatest share of the blame for the crisis rested on the Emperor himself. He had brought on this trouble by favoring an obscure commoner, Jyang Choong, over his own son, whose affections he had thereby alienated. Unpleasant though it was to have to do so, it was the duty of a loyal official to point all this out, just as Beegan had done to the last, bad King of the Shang dynasty, even if, like Beegan, the official had to pay with his life for his forthrightness. Unlike Beegan, Li noted to himself, this particular official was being prudent enough to remain anonymous. The Emperor should, the petition concluded, give his son and heir a chance to be forgiven.

Li was surprised to see that the Emperor was moved. Tears glistening in his eyes, he turned to Hwo Gwang for his opinion.

The latter, Li was relieved to note, remained true to his aunt's advice. He alluded to the risk-free version of Beegan's act of self-abnegation practiced by the petitioner. He conceded the truth of the petitioner's main point. The prosecutor had indeed abused the Emperor's confidence. But so too had the Heir, who would not wait for Hwo to come to Gan Springs to reveal the evidence convicting the prosecutor and his shaman of their conspiracy against the imperial family. It was his impatience even more than Jyang Choong's deceptions which had tripped off the current crisis. Sound administration (Hwo forbore to mention whose sound administration had done the job) had already laid bare these deceptions. It was for the Heir to cease his rebellion and voluntarily place his head at the disposal of his father. Should His Majesty wish, he, Hwo Gwang, would send his young assistant back to the capital to make such an offer to the Heir, but he could not advise such a move at this time. It would be best to await some first move of repentance from the man himself.

The Emperor remained silent, looking as somber as Li had ever seen him. It was at this point that the news arrived that Chancellor Liu's forces, reinforced from the northern army, had taken full control of the capital. The prosecutor's shaman was said to have been buried alive in the Imperial Park on the north side of the Forbidden City. The Emperor's mood lightened at this news, and his mood remained good until he was informed somewhat later that Empress Wei had committed suicide, and that all three of the Heir's sons were also dead.

"And my grandson?"

"No word yet, Your Majesty."

"And my... Jyu, what of him?"

"He has fled, Your Majesty. Through the southeastern gate. There was supposed to have been a guard there, but the fellow claims some sort of spell was cast over him, put him to sleep. Chancellor Liu is furious. He wanted to execute the fellow on the spot for conspiracy, or at least for neglect of duty in the face of the enemy, but the judicial officer accompanying him pointed out that an Imperial Warrant is necessary for capital punishment, except when some great emergency, like a state of rebellion, has been proclaimed." The chief eunuch paused for a moment. "Your Majesty has not yet issued such a proclamation."

"No, We have not." The Emperor's eyes glinted dangerously. "Nor does it appear now that such a proclamation will be necessary. Please so notify the Chancellor. Where has my son gone?"

"Chancellor Liu is not yet certain. Somewhere to the east."

The Emperor had then turned to Hwo and suggested that while his son had not met all Hwo's preconditions, he had in a sense ended his rebellion, and it might not be out of order for his father to make the first move toward a possible reconciliation. Hwo had conceded the logic of this, and said he would send Li off first thing in the morning, as soon as more definite word had been received as to the location and intentions of the Heir.

"It is precisely his intentions that we are sending your man there to discover," said the Emperor in an ominous tone. Hwo bowed in silent acquiescence.

By the next morning, the Heir Apparent was reported heading for Hu County, not far to the east of the capital, but his purpose there was not yet certain. The Emperor urged Li to emphasize to the Heir his father's willingness to consider a return to filial obedience by his son.

Hwo Gwang's advice as they walked toward the stables was more specific, and yet more cryptic. Li was to detour by way of Hwo's friend's estate, where he would pick up Bao and the three remaining mules, with their cargo of poison air, and then proceed forthwith to Hu County, avoiding if at all possible all contact with loyalist forces. Once he had reached Hu he was to be guided by the logic of the situation, and by his own understanding of the teachings of the Confucian sages.

Li was still pondering that advice the next day as their little caravan rode up to the Hu County seat. Though he carried imperial orders, Li had obeyed Hwo's injunction to have nothing to do with the loyalist forces or anyone else in government until his mission had been completed. He well understood that it would not do for anyone to know that the Emperor was seeking reconciliation with his son. That might be interpreted as weakness. Fortunately, though several regiments of the northern army were already converging on the place, the Hu County seat was by no means as yet under siege, and depending upon how favorably the eastern garrisons reacted to the Heir's cause during the next few days, this small place might well serve as the nucleus for a renewed rebellion. So, though they were able to ride up to the town wall without escort, Li thought it best to hoist a formal flag of truce, and even so could not be sure of their reception.

CHAPTER FIFTY-FOUR

Justice

A man who looked like Han Ming-li glanced down at them momentarily from atop the gate. Quickly thereafter the gate opened to admit them. It was Ming-li. He now stood before them, not at all abashed.

"It looks like you didn't pick the winning side after all," snapped Bao.

"What brings you here?" said Ming-li, blandly ignoring Bao's remark.

"We seek to meet your master," said Li. "We bring a message from His Majesty."

"Then meet him you shall. Follow me. You had better bring your mules with you."

Li and Bao dismounted, handed over their horses, and led the three mules behind them. Ming-li took them into the courtyard of the county magistrate's office, just down the street, then led the mules away. The Heir Apparent was seated on the magistrate's throne on the north side of the otherwise empty courtyard. This little county town was now the only corner of All Under Heaven which he ruled. Li felt a twinge of sympathy for the Heir Apparent.

The shaman stepped out of the shadows and up to the right hand of the Heir Apparent. Li's last doubts disappeared.

"You have come some distance," began the Heir, obviously para-phrasing the opening sentence of Mencius's book. "Surely you have brought something to profit my kingdom."

"Why talk of profit?" replied Li, capping the quotation. "I have come here to speak of righteousness, and nothing more."

The Heir smiled, but Li kept his features bland.

"I take it that you and Hwo Gwang did not succeed in persuading my father to step aside in my favor."

"My master did not even try to make such an argument."

"Then why have you come here to me?"

"To advise you that your game is up. That you have been found out. And that the only thing that remains is for you to put an end to your rebellion, to yourself and to your tame magician here."

"Strong advice. I am afraid, though, that I cannot take it. I find that after all this fellow can be of some use to me. That is why I have kept him alive."

"No sir. That won't do. He's been your man for some time. Perhaps he always was. He was your man inside the prosecutor's camp. Even when he did his worst, he was only helping to create a situation which finally provided you with an excuse for rebellion His atrocities provided you with a kind of test of His Majesty's love for and trust in you. Finally it became evident that His Majesty had irrevocably failed that test. He was willing to trot off to Gan Springs, leaving you dangling in the hands of the prosecutor.

"As for the shaman, so-called, he joined with you because he coveted the same position the prosecutor hoped to enjoy: the power directly behind the throne. And he had pegged you for what you were: Behind all the bluster, a weakling, and an inefficient weakling at that. You were a good deal for him, a much better one than the prosecutor, who after all knew what he was doing and was intelligent enough to do it right."

"That will be enough of that," snapped the Heir. He glanced to his right at the shaman, then up at the canopy of state extending over his chair from the inner wall of the magistrate's office behind him.

Li thought he knew what was coming, but he could not be certain, and so it took all his self control not to flinch. Then it came. Two great thundering tongues of flame shot down from the canopy, one angling to the right engulfed the shaman, one straight down embraced the Heir Apparent within a glowing corona of light. Neither man had a chance. The very intensity of the flames froze them in place until they were so far engulfed that survival was impossible.

Han Ming-li stepped out into the courtyard, seemingly to admire his handiwork. "You're a trusting soul," he told Li. "Either that or I'm less of an actor than I fancied myself."

"I'm not so trusting as you might think. You're not so bad as an actor either. You still have some way to go to equal my master in that respect, though."

"Old Hwo must have done a quick job recruiting you during that short walk to the Heir's mansion. I thought he was just filling you in on what kind of demonstration of the poison air he wanted you to give once we got there." Bao grinned in admiration.

"I didn't figure that out myself for some time," admitted Li. "In some ways it was easier to figure out the Heir Apparent's involvement. If you recall, Bao, we had almost worked that out on the way into Szechwan. Our friend Ming-li here was another matter. In fact," Li turned back to Ming-li, "I didn't realize you must still be on our side until Hwo Gwang told me to be sure to bring all the remaining poison air with us. He must have been counting on you to use the stuff, since neither Bao nor I could really be trusted with it. Even so, I still had a few lingering doubts about you until the moment you led the animals out of the courtyard. You obviously had some task to carry out that involved them, and once I saw that the shaman was alive after all, I knew it could only be to finish him off. From everything you said back in Szechwan, I knew you could not abide the man. Besides, you sounded too sincere whenever you sneered at officials."

Ming-li laughed. "Now that's reasoning like an official! I don't believe you thought it through at all. You just jumped to the conclusion and then thought up some cockeyed reasons to support your prejudice. Come on, there's no time to waste in here. The rest of that poison air will go off in another minute, and we had better be out the back door by then. We can honestly report that the Heir committed suicide, and then his aides burned down the building where the deed was done. I'm afraid, though, His Majesty will have to find himself another heir apparent."

"Nothing to worry about there," yelled Bao as they sprinted toward the rear door. "We officials have got that all worked out."

www.ingramcontent.com/pod-product-compliance
Lightning Source LLC
Chambersburg PA
CBHW030105260626
47156CB00008B/2535